D1542096

SCORE HER HEART

A PHILADELPHIA BULLDOGS NOVEL

DANICA FLYNN

Score Her Heart

Copyright © 2021 Danica Flynn

ISBN: 978-1-7342012-4-6

Cover Photography: Wolfgang Zwanzger /Shutterstock

Cover Designer: Emily's World of Design

Editor: Charlie Knight

For my Soul Sisters, thanks for letting me annoy you on the daily in the group chat!

CHAPTER ONE

FIONA

I bit my nails nervously, and this time my maid of honor, Katie, didn't slap my hand away. For the fifteenth time, I fixed the veil on my head, but I still thought it was crooked. Deep in my bones, I knew something was off. As soon as I woke up this morning, I knew something was going to go wrong. That's not exactly the feeling you want on your wedding day. Especially when the groom was missing.

What the fuckety fuck!

"Did he answer?" Katie asked and studied the bouquet of flowers that I was gripping a little too tightly. Her white face was tinted red with frustration, and her brown hair was starting to come undone while she raked her fingers through it in agony.

I looked down at my phone still in my hand. When I

unlocked it, I saw a text from my best and oldest friend, Riley.

RILEY: *Girlllll!!! I can't believe you're getting married today. Can't wait to see you tonight!*

A smile curled up on my lips. I was afraid he wasn't going to make it. I knew that my fiancé was hoping he couldn't, which was why he insisted on a wedding during hockey season. Let's just say Eric didn't exactly love my best friend or want the two of us to see each other all that much.

"Well?" Ellen, my bridesmaid and one of my other childhood friends, asked. With her tanned skin and perfect blond hair, I was kind of annoyed that she wasn't as frazzled looking as I knew I was right now.

I shook my head and put my phone down. My fiancé was late for our wedding, and I couldn't help but have a bad feeling about this. Like Han Solo flying into the Death Star bad feeling.

I only had two people in my bridal party. Well, three if you counted my mom, who was the matron of honor. Eric didn't even want to get married, and I never pushed it because I had been happy with him, but his mom kept pushing the topic. After his dad died, he had finally asked. He hadn't even done it very romantically. He turned to me one night, sighed, and asked, "Hey, should we just get married already?"

So charming.

I wanted a courthouse wedding, but neither of our moms' would go for that. Somehow, by the grace of the hockey gods, we had managed to keep this wedding small, but Eric had insisted we do it in Vegas. I had never been a Vegas person or interested in gambling, so we fought a lot about it. Since he was the one who asked me to marry him, I eventually gave in.

Honestly, I would have had a better time if we had just eloped in Vegas, but we were basically told we would have been shunned if we did that. I didn't really care for weddings; they were fine for other people, but not for me. I felt like it was a pageant for my parents, and I was honestly pissed about it. Especially since they complained about how expensive it was. Even though I told them we would rather pay for it ourselves, but Dad insisted. Irish men were so stubborn; I guess that's where I got it from.

I chewed on my bottom lip and turned at the sound of the door opening. My mom stood there in her wine-colored dress, her dirty blond hair pulled smartly into a chignon at the nape of her neck. I was hoping for good news, but her mouth was a thin line.

FUCK.

"Anything?" I asked but couldn't help hearing the slight hitch in my voice.

She shook her head sadly, her brow furrowing in a worried expression.

"FUCK!" I screamed out loud this time and tore the veil off my head, taking some of my copper-colored strands with it.

Mom narrowed her eyes at me. "Fiona Marie Gallagher! Language!"

I rolled my eyes but wanted to yell, "Fuck you, Mom, this is my wedding!" Yeah, that would have gone over well.

This was turning into a fucking disaster. Where the hell was Eric?

Katie tapped away on her phone. Katie was Eric's older sister, but we had grown close over the five years I had been with her brother. I was bad at making friends. Ellen was one of the only people besides Riley who still put up with me. Scratch that; I was good at making friends but bad at keeping relationships intact. I assumed everyone would eventually abandon me, so what was the point? Why put in the work when everyone would disappoint you in the end?

"The guys brought him back to the hotel early last night. So it's not like he's passed out drunk somewhere," Katie commented, but worry was still etched across her pale face.

A stone dropped down into the pit of my stomach. This was really bad.

Ellen put a hand on my shoulder. "Hey, it's going to be okay. Maybe he slept through his alarm," she tried to reassure me, but she didn't sound convinced.

Somehow, I knew that we both knew that line was complete and utter bullshit. Eric *never* slept through anything.

I pulled out my phone and texted him again while Katie tried to call him for the tenth time.

ME: *WTF!!!*

ME: *Where are you?*

ME: *Mother fucker, I know you aren't passed out drunk somewhere.*

ME: *Answer me!*

I saw Katie repeatedly saying the word "okay" into her phone, but she wasn't looking at me. Almost like she was too embarrassed to look me in the eyes right now.

I looked back at my phone and saw the three dots indicating typing, then they disappeared and immediately came back up. Finally, I was getting an answer on what the actual fuck was going on.

ERIC: *I'm sorry.*

ERIC: *I can't do this. I don't want to get married. Can't we go back to the way things were?*

ME: *Are you FUCKING kidding me?*

ERIC: *I don't want to marry you.*

ME: *Go fuck yourself. Get your shit, and get out of my apartment.*

ERIC: *It's our apartment.*

ME: *And everything's in my name. Kindly go fuck yourself gently with a chainsaw.*

I wanted to hurl my phone at the wall, but instead, I hurled myself out of the room.

"Fiona, where are you going?" Mom shrieked after me.

"The fucking bar!" I yelled back and hitched up the skirt of my ridiculous dress. I couldn't even think of the fiasco this would cause for my parents. I didn't care; I needed a drink.

I parked myself in front of the hotel bar in a huff. The bartender blinked at me in surprise. He glanced over my shoulder and then back at me. "I think you're early?" he asked in confusion.

"It's off," I seethed. "Give me a whiskey."

His face fell, and he nodded before getting to work behind the bar. He put a glass of whiskey down in front of me. "On the house, Miss."

I shook my head. "Oh, no, don't pity me."

He pushed the glass closer to me. "I insist."

I cocked my head at him. He was kind of cute with his spiky blond hair and five o'clock shadow. *Maybe I should fuck him just to get back at Eric.* Maybe it was the fact that my sex life had been lacking in the past couple months that I was entertaining the idea of sleeping with a stranger. I took the drink and downed it in one fell swoop. I looked at my phone and saw more texts from Eric.

ERIC: *I was happy before, but I don't see why we had to get married.*

ERIC: *Marriage is stupid. We don't want kids.*

ERIC: *Fi, don't be this way. I know you don't want this wedding either.*

I frowned but noticed my drink had been refilled. The cute bartender winked at me, and I nodded my head at him in thanks.

The truth was we hadn't decided that we didn't want kids; Eric had decided that and never gave me the chance to really think about it. I had been fine with that because I had loved him, but the fact that he didn't want to go through with the wedding either meant he didn't love me. How could I expect him to be committed to me if he didn't show up on our wedding day? PLUS! Canceling all of this shit was going to cost a shit ton of money. I didn't even want to think about it. My dad was going to be livid if he wasn't already. I might need to get him a whole bottle of whiskey to apologize. Maybe even a freaking case.

I maddeningly typed out my response into my phone.

ME: *AGAIN, how about you go fuck yourself, you fucking asshat? I can't believe you did this to me. We are DONE. Have a good life, Eric!*

My phone was blowing up with texts from guests wondering what was going on, but the only one I looked at was Riley's.

ME: *Don't come.*

RILEY: *What's going on?*

ME: *Wedding's off. Don't come. I'm sorry, I know it was hard for you to get here with your hockey schedule.*

RILEY: *Where are you?*

ME: *Bar.*

I put my head in my hands and finished off my second glass of whiskey. I put my phone down and decided answering all those texts was not what I was going to do right now. When I pulled my hands away, my eyeliner was smudged on my hand, along with some wetness. Great, I was the crying bride left at the altar drinking alone at the bar.

Way to be a cliche, Fiona!

A glass of water and another whiskey was placed in front of me. "You want to start a tab?" the bartender asked me.

Before I could answer, a deep voice from behind me said, "Yeah, put it on my card."

I turned to take in Riley in all his glory. He looked great in a suit, his broad shoulders and thick biceps filling it out nicely. His blond hair was tousled in that 'I couldn't care less' style that meant he spent a long time on it. I'd only seen him a few times this year; with his professional hockey career and my writing career, we were both traveling a lot and rarely in the same city. But damn, he looked good today, filling out that suit tailored specifically for him. I felt heat pool in my lower belly, but maybe it was just from all the whiskey. I definitely wasn't remembering all those times in high school when Riley's mouth had been on mine. Definitely not.

Riley slid onto the stool next to me and ordered a beer. When the bartender handed him the bottle, that's when he turned to me and pulled me into a big bear hug. Maybe that's all I needed because I relaxed into his strong arms, leaning my face against his hard chest. But then I started crying again. To his credit, Riley was a good sport who let me cry on his shoulder as he rubbed my back soothingly.

It felt like an eternity had passed before I pulled away. "I'm sorry," I offered.

He placed his hands gently on my cheeks and wiped my face with the pads of his calloused thumbs. "Don't apologize. That dickweed should be the one apologizing. Fi, I'm so sorry. You want me to fight him?"

I slunk out of his arms and took a sip of my drink. "It's not your fault. And on that last part...maybe."

He eyed me cautiously and took a sip of his beer. The way he was looking at me sent shivers down my spine. Here's the thing. Riley was kind of a player, which was fine; he could do what he wanted. But we also lost our virginity to each other in high school. Then proceeded to experiment with each other.

Okay, we were fuck buddies. So sue me, Riley was hot back then and even more so now. Seeing him here looking sexy AF in that suit had me thinking a little too much about all those times in my parents' basement. Fuck. I shouldn't have drunk so much whiskey in such a short time. Whiskey makes me horny.

And it was no secret that my best friend was the hottest man I had ever seen. EVER. Which might have explained why Eric didn't exactly like him.

"So what happened?" he asked.

I sighed and took a huge gulp of my drink. "He said he couldn't do it but wanted to go back to the way things were."

Riley narrowed his blue eyes at me. They flashed in anger, but I knew it wasn't aimed at me. "What the fuck?"

I raised my arms in triumph. "Thank you!"

"What a fucking asshole," he spat out. "This douche can't show up to your wedding but expects everything to go back to normal?"

I hung my head. "I can't even imagine all the cancellations we have to do now. My poor parents."

He ran a hand down his clean-shaven jaw as if he was thinking really hard about something. He had this weird look in his eye, and it made me feel uncomfortable. "Well...do you still want to get married?" he asked.

I nearly spat out my drink. "To who?"

He smirked that signature crooked grin that I'm sure melted all the girls' panties. Mine included, but that might have been the whiskey talking.

He pointed a finger at me and then to him. "It's Vegas, right? So let's get married."

"What?!?"

CHAPTER TWO

RILEY

*H*er green eyes were saucers staring me down. "Are you fucking serious?" she asked incredulously.

I shrugged, but my eyes roamed down her body.

Fi was one of my oldest and best friends, but I would be lying if I said I wasn't attracted to her. Fiona Gallagher was fucking FIIINNE. With her slender frame, nice ass, and long, bright red hair, she was my dream girl. Always had been, always would be. Probably until the day I died, if I were being honest. She still made my dick stand at attention, which wasn't something that was supposed to happen when you thought about your best friend. Even if you lost your virginity to that best friend and had already been inside her multiple times.

We were both so different now, but clearly not older

and wiser if I was asking her to marry me on the spot right now. Who does that? Me, apparently.

I watched her, kind of impressed as she downed the rest of her whiskey. "Riley..." she trailed off.

I looked her dead in the eye. "Fiona."

She glared daggers at me, and I couldn't help but think about how cute she was when she was mad. I think my thing for fiery redheads started with the woman sitting next to me.

"You're not serious!" she shrieked.

I shrugged. "What? You were supposed to get married today anyway! What's the difference if it's to a different groom?"

"A very big difference. I mean, we need to get a license and figure out—"

I cut her off, "Are you saying yes?"

Her eyes softened, and the hungry way she was looking at me made me think she was also remembering all those times sneaking around in high school. "You would seriously do this? You would marry me right on the spot?" she asked.

"Is that a yes?" I repeated.

She stared at me bemused but then nodded. "Okay."

"Okay?"

"Okay. Yes, fine, let's get married. What the fuck, YOLO, I guess? Is that what the kids are saying these days?"

She was babbling, and it was so cute. We were still the best of friends after all these years, but we rarely got to see each other. Partly because I traveled a lot due to my hockey career, but also because her douchebag ex never liked me. She'd deny it, but I think he actively tried to keep us apart. The day I met him five years ago, I knew he was a little weasel, but she had seemed happy. She deserved happiness, and I guess that's also why I suggested this foolish plan to marry me instead. I think in the back of my mind, I was hoping if we went through with this, maybe she would fall in love with me in the process. It wasn't a very good plan or a smart one, but if she really wanted to go through with this, I was going to try my hardest to make her happy.

I stood up off the barstool and bent down to kiss her cheek. "I'll be back."

I brushed past a bridesmaid who was heading towards Fi and found her parents with solemn faces talking to the hotel staff. Fi's dad saw me coming towards them. He was a tall man with fading red hair that was seventy-five percent grey and had been thinning for a long time. My hands started to sweat at the question I was about to ask him. Maybe this was a bad idea. Who proposes to their best friend moments after she got left at the altar? I wiped my hands on my dress pants as I approached Mr. Gallagher.

He shook my hand firmly and clapped his other one on my shoulder. "Riley!" he greeted.

"Mr. Gallagher."

"It's good to see you. Wish it was under better circumstances," he told me with a grimace.

"Yeah, I heard about that. Listen, I have a solution. It may sound a little reckless, but she agreed so..."

Fi's mom stopped mid-sentence when she saw me and stepped away from the hotel staff to see what was going on. "Riley?" she asked cautiously.

"So I want to ask for your blessing..." I continued.

"My blessing?" Mr. Gallagher asked with a confused look on his face.

"Riley, what are you saying?" Mrs. Gallagher asked, but she had this sparkle in her eyes. Of course she did. My mom and Fi's mom had practically been planning our wedding since before we were even born.

I ran a hand down my jaw. "What if I married your daughter instead?"

"Like right now?" Mrs. Gallagher asked, but she was beaming like I had told her she won the lottery. Katherine Gallagher had been praying to the hockey gods for me to marry her daughter our entire lives. No wonder she was on board about this. She wasn't even questioning my motives here.

Cillian Gallagher was a different story. The middle-aged man scowled at me and crossed his arms over his chest. "Why?"

"Why?" I echoed.

"Yes, Riley, why do you want to marry my daughter?" he elaborated and gave me a stern look. "You aren't exactly the type of guy who wants to be tied down."

I cringed. That might have been true if you were looking from the outside. I did have a good time with a lot of women who I never saw again. Sometimes my teammates teased me about being the 'King of Hookups,' but lately, I'd been thinking about finding someone to share my life with. Someone who didn't mind my grueling hockey schedule. And maybe sometimes I pictured that woman being tall and having red hair.

I straightened up and squared my shoulders. "Cillian, I could make your daughter very happy."

He scoffed. "I know she would live comfortably with you, but money's not everything."

"I don't mean because of money. It's not just about providing for her."

He arched an eyebrow. "Then explain it to me. Explain it like I'm five."

"Because she deserves someone who will love her. Not

some ass-wipe who can't even bother to tell her to her face that he didn't want to go through with this."

Cillian studied me for a tick, and I started to get nervous. "She agreed to this?"

I nodded. "I know it's really unconventional, but—"

Katherine cut me off, "Cillian! Give him our blessing! We've always wanted Riley to be our son-in-law."

"Kat," Cillian began.

"Cillian! It's finally happening; they finally realized they're meant to be."

Cillian gave me a bemused look, but he still didn't seem like he was exactly on board with this whole thing. He rubbed a hand down his tired face. "Fuck it, whatever. I'm already paying for this wedding."

"I can—"

He held up his hand. "No! I'll pay for my daughter's wedding, and you make sure you make her happy for the rest of your lives. You got me, Riley?"

I nodded. "Yes, sir."

He sighed but shook his head. "Good thing we flew all the way out here to Vegas where you can get a wedding license right away. Go on, get out of here before I try to convince the both of you that this is a bad idea."

Katherine beamed at me and hugged me tightly. Then she fixed my tie for me and smoothed down my suit jacket. "It's not a tux, but Fiona won't care. You look handsome. Welcome to the family, Riley."

I let her fuss over me for a few minutes, but I eyed my mother, sitting in the ballroom and staring at me in question. I shrugged at her; I was probably going to get an earful about it later, but I didn't have time for that right now. I said my goodbyes to my future in-laws and walked over to Fi, who was still sitting at the bar. She handed a big diamond engagement ring to a familiar-looking bridesmaid who looked really sorry. Fuck, I didn't think about rings. We could always do that later.

"Come on, girl, we need to go get a license," I told her. Luckily, it was Vegas, and there was no waiting period in this city, so I was sure we could get this done quickly. I hoped.

The dark-haired bridesmaid widened her eyes, and that's when it clicked in my head that she was Eric's sister, Katie. "You can't be serious. You're going to marry Riley?"

Fi rolled her eyes. "Yeah, well, tell your brother to fuck off. Also, please stay. I need you," she urged the other woman, gripping her hand tightly.

Katie looked me up and down and shook her head in disbelief. I didn't blame her; this was impulsive, but we were doing this. "What's your ring size?" Katie asked me.

"My what?"

"You're not getting married with the rings my brother chose. I'll get the rings since I know Fi's style, and you get the license," she explained.

Oh, I liked this girl. "Ten," I told her with a crooked grin.

I held up my hand for the bartender. He came over quickly. "Another round?" he asked.

"Nah, can I close out my tab?"

He nodded. While I sorted that out, the two women beside me talked about ring types. I really hadn't thought about that at all. When I saw Fi in her wedding dress in tears, it broke my heart, and asking her to marry me instead was the first thing that popped in my head to solve it. I was honestly surprised she had agreed to this.

I held out my hand to Fi, which she took, and I helped get her off the barstool without getting caught up in her skirts. She let go of my hand and bunched the bottom of the dress up around her. I put my hand on the small of her back and guided her to the exit, where we ran into Ellen Forrester.

Ellen was wearing the same wine colored dress as Mrs. Gallagher and Katie. Her blond hair was pulled back into a bun, but her eyebrow raised up in amusement at seeing the two of us. Ellen was another old friend from back home who one hundred percent had a crush on me in the third grade, and I would never let her live it down. We liked to give each other shit. I think Ellen thrived on it.

"Um, what are you doing?" she asked and eyed the two of us suspiciously.

"Going to get a new marriage license," Fi deadpanned.

Ellen did a double-take and looked back and forth between the two of us. Then she tipped back her head and laughed. "You two? Fi, you're not going to marry Riley instead!"

I glared at her. "What's wrong with me?"

Ellen sighed. "Did you agree to this? I can't believe you would agree to this."

"Hey! It was my idea," I protested.

Ellen shook her head at me. "I don't think I have enough words to explain why this is a bad idea."

Fi bit her lip and looked up at me. "She has a point. This is impulsive, right?" she asked.

I smirked at her. "Yes, but we're gonna do this. I triple dog dare ya."

She smiled back at me. "Well, in that case, we better get that paperwork done!"

There was my girl.

Ellen threw up her hands in exasperation and walked away. She would get over it. She had a point that this was not my best idea, but I wasn't about to back down now. Fi was supposed to get married today, and she would, just maybe not to the guy she thought.

I walked Fi outside to my rental car and opened the passenger side door for her. "Ugh, you don't need to do that," she sighed at me, but I think she was thankful because I had to help her in and make sure her dress didn't get caught in the door.

I started the car and drove out of the parking lot.

"Are we really doing this?" she finally asked.

"Yeah, we are. Why not?"

"Why would you want to marry me?"

"Because you're my best friend, and I want you to be happy, and maybe I can make you happy," I explained.

She looked down at her manicured hands and didn't say anything else.

I pulled into the Clark County Marriage License Bureau and parked the car. "Fi, if you don't want to do this, tell me now."

She shook her head. "No, it's good. Let's do this."

"There's my girl," I told her with a smile.

I got out of the car and helped her out of the passenger side, so she didn't mess up her dress. She held the skirt with both her hands and I put my hand on the small of her back. It was late afternoon, but luckily, there wasn't a long wait before we could apply for the license. The woman at the counter walked us through all the paperwork, and we showed her our IDs. We had the license in no time, and we were on our way back to the hotel pretty quickly. Driving toward my wedding - and especially my wedding to Fi - felt good. Not just good; it felt right. I was tired of the single life, and if I did this for Fi, I was doing this for real. She might wake up tomorrow and want a divorce, but today, I was going to marry her.

When we got back to the hotel, her bridesmaids ushered her away, and the wedding planner took me to the ballroom to stand at the altar. Only her brother Finnegan was a groomsman; I guess the rest were all Eric's friends, and they left when he didn't show up. He mouthed to me, "What the fuck?" but I shrugged.

Before I knew it, the bridesmaids were walking down the aisle, and then Fi herself was standing in front of me. We clasped hands, and even though I had already seen her in her dress, she looked as beautiful as ever. I didn't understand how anyone could have up and left this woman high and dry on her wedding day.

When the official asked about vows, we looked at each other in horror. We had forgotten about that.

"We have our own," Fi said. "Improvise," she mouthed to me.

My lips quirked up into a smirk, and I nodded to her so she could start first.

"This is really weird," she started. "Today, I was supposed to marry someone else, but he left me. Then you came in like a knight in shining armor and offered to marry me instead. The years have been hard with us being apart, but you have always been my best friend. I'm not sure if I'll be a good hockey wife, so don't get mad when I tell you that you played like hot garbage. Let's do this thing."

I laughed at that, and Katie handed her the ring. Fi took my hand in hers and slipped the simple wedding band onto my left hand. I looked at her and started my own vows. "Fiona, I know this is weird, and I'm honestly surprised you agreed to this in the first place. Although, I know our moms have been praying for us to get married pretty much our whole lives, so they're probably stoked. I promise you that I will always support your writing, even though I don't think there is enough sex in sci-fi books. Come on, girl, let's get married."

Katie handed me the ring, and I slipped the matching ring on Fi's slender left hand. The smile she gave me filled my chest with warmth. No woman ever made me feel like Fiona Gallagher did.

The official smiled at us and said, "I now pronounce you husband and wife. You may kiss the bride."

I leaned down, wrapped my hands around her neck, and kissed her with all the passion I could muster. I felt familiar sparks flying between us, and I couldn't wait until I could get her alone later tonight.

"Come on, Wifey, let's go party," I whispered into her ear. That earned me a glare, but she couldn't hide the smile behind her emerald eyes.

CHAPTER THREE

FIONA

I woke to what felt like a sledgehammer against my skull, and my mouth was as dry as the Sahara. The room was spinning, and I was sure I needed to go throw up all the whiskey I drank last night. Why did I decide to drink so much damn whiskey?

I shifted in the bed, fighting off the spins, and realized I couldn't move. I was pinned down by a large forearm wrapped around my waist. I looked down at the familiar red and gold phoenix tattoo and then realized I was naked under the covers.

SHIT.

I laid there for a minute, blinking up at the ceiling in confusion. When I saw my wedding gown hanging up in the open closet, all the memories of last night came back to me in a drunken flash. The reception had been a drunken good time, and Riley hadn't been able to keep his hands off me. Not like groping my tits in front of everyone, but when we danced together, he held me close, his big hands dangerously close to my ass. During dinner, his hand had stayed clasped onto my thigh in a possessive yet protective manner that made me feel safe. Then we kept on drinking and drinking until we were kissing hungrily, and we finally left the party to fulfill our duties of consummating our marriage.

Which we did. Multiple times.

He had been careful to help me out of my dress and even hung it up for me before he worshipped my body for hours. That wasn't an exaggeration; he spent a good deal of the night with his head between my legs, giving me pleasure like I had never felt before. I had returned the favor, very eagerly, and when it came time for the final act, he was kind and gentle and let me be in charge. And then we did it again with him on top, and then a third time before he finally got aggressive with me and bent me over the bed until we were both spent. Still drunk, I vaguely remembered us passing out on the bed naked but clutching each other.

Holy fuck, I was married to Riley, and we had so much sex last night. Like more than I'd had with my fiancé in the last three months. Which was, unfortunately, the last time I had sex with the man I had been with for half a decade and was supposed to get married to. This was so fucked.

The need to vomit brought me back to reality. Luckily, Riley had moved to his back, so I was able to slink out of the bed and rush to the bathroom, where I emptied pretty much all the contents of my stomach. A shadow came across the wall, and I felt a warm hand at my back, rubbing it in comforting circles. Another hand pulled back my long red hair so I didn't get sick all over it. It was sweet, but a little too late for that. I wiped my mouth with the back of my hand, the silver band of my wedding ring gleaming in the light as if taunting me.

I stood up to turn to Riley. We were both still naked, and my eyes couldn't stop staring at the hard lines of his chest. I dipped my gaze down past his pectorals to the insanely ripped six-pack he had going on. I knew hockey players were pretty fit, but fuck, my best friend was all hard muscle and strength. He was such a man now, and last night he had treated me like he was mine and I was his. In the light of the day and with my head pounding, I wasn't sure if that was what I wanted.

"Sweetheart," he whispered to me quietly, and I felt something soft and warm come over my body at his tender voice calling me that. One finger lifted my chin up to look at him. "You okay?"

I nodded but looked down, which was actually a bad idea because I was looking right at the thing that I had begged to have inside me last night. I shook my head, went over to the sink, and gargled some mouthwash.

Riley stood in the doorway of the bathroom, leaning against the frame, watching me.

"What?" I snapped.

"You sure you're okay?" he asked.

"I'm very hungover. Can you please fuck off?"

He smirked. "Come back to bed, feisty."

I shook my head and waved him away. "I want to take a shower."

He nodded, but instead of leaving like a normal fucking person, Riley shut the bathroom door behind him. I watched him get into the shower stall and turn the faucet on. I stared at him through the glass door, watching the water droplets running down his muscular back. I continued to stare, unable to believe what my life had turned into.

I married my best friend.

My fiancé left me at the altar, and I married my best friend instead.

And had really hot married sex with him. Like so good, I can't remember the last time a man made me feel that fucking good during sex. A man who was patient and let me have multiple orgasms before coming himself. A man who ate me out with so much vigor and who made little noises of enjoyment while he did it. As if he actually liked to be down there doing that!

"You coming in?" he asked over the running water.

Oh, right. I wanted to take a shower because I was majorly hungover and felt like death.

But showering with Riley right now? I mean, sure, we had fucked all over this suite last night, but taking a shower together felt so intimate. Still, he technically was my husband, so it shouldn't have been that weird. With a sigh, I stepped into the shower next to the big man, who was all soaped up and looking yummy.

Fuck, am I still drunk?

Possibly. My vision did seem a bit cloudy.

Riley smiled and switched spots with me so I could be under the showerhead. I stood under the hot water for a few minutes. My skin felt like it was on fire, but the water felt good despite the temperature.

My thoughts assaulted me while I stood under the showerhead. Riley was a decent guy, which was why he had offered to marry me, but I think this was a mistake. I loved my best friend, but it was no secret that he was kind of anti-relationship and the king of casual hookups. There was no way he seriously wanted to be married to me. It was an impulsive decision to correct a terrible problem, but I could fix this. We had to get an annulment, and then everything would be fine.

I bit my lip to prevent the moan from escaping my lips when I felt his hands begin to massage my scalp. It took a bit for my drunken, foggy brain to realize he was washing my hair for me. Oh my God, this man was something else. His fingers massaged tenderly, but I kept my eyes closed. There was no way I could look at him. He was being so gentle and caring. Fuck, was he going to be a good husband or what? But not for me.

His hands moved from out of my hair, sliding through the suds and across the top of my shoulders. He slid the bar of soap across my body until I finally opened my eyes and muttered, "Thanks."

I looked up at him. I was a tall woman, but at six-feet, Riley still had a few inches on me. Like three inches, but still. The water poured down his face, and he looked as tired as I felt. Maybe he was as hungover as I was, and he was just better at hiding it. His hand was still on me, slowly sliding across my skin until it rested on my hip. That's when I felt his erection pressing up against my leg.

"Riley!" I yelled at him.

He laughed. "I'm sorry; it has a mind of its own. Can you blame me, though? In the shower with a hot naked woman? Of course I'm gonna get hard."

I rolled my eyes. "You mean I didn't break it last night?"

He laughed. "You sure did try."

I shook my wet hair at him, and he laughed. He pulled his hand away from me, and we switched spots so he could wash his hair while I put conditioner in my hair and washed my face. The water had started to cool, so Riley cranked the handle closer to red, and we switched again so I could wash the conditioner out of my long hair. Riley stepped out of the shower by then, but I spied him rubbing a towel over his head behind the glass door. I shut the faucet off and wrung my hair out as best I could in the shower.

Stepping out of the stall, my eyes traced again over Riley's ridiculously fit body. He was at the sink gargling mouthwash, so maybe he was suffering from a hangover too. I grabbed a towel from off the rack and dried myself off as best I could before wrapping it around my head and walking back into the bedroom.

I didn't feel quite like death warmed over anymore, just death slightly cooled, but it was better than nothing. I went into my suitcase and pulled on a fresh pair of underwear and a t-shirt. I unraveled the towel from my head and began to brush my hair out, then checked the clock on the bedside table and saw that it was seven am. Why the fuck was I awake so early? I didn't even want to think about looking at my phone yet.

Big arms wrapped around my waist from behind, and kisses were peppered down the slope of my neck.

Why is he being so sweet to me right now?

"How do you feel?" he asked against my ear, and I had to pretend not to shudder. Maybe I was still drunk because I wanted him to keep on kissing me and never stop.

"Like hot garbage," I muttered.

He laughed and hugged my back closer against his chest. "Come on, sweetheart, come back to bed. Sleep will help you."

I finished brushing out my hair, but it was still damp. Fuck it. I turned in his arms and saw he was still in his towel. Something inside me snapped to attention, and I leaned up to kiss his mouth tenderly. He kissed me back, and then the towel dropped to the floor, and he led me by the hand back into the bed. But we didn't have sex again, and I was partly disappointed but partly thankful because I still felt sore from the previous night even though we used a lot of lube. He stretched out on the bed beside me and tugged me closer to him, so my head was tucked onto his chest. While I drifted off to sleep, still a little drunk, I felt his arms around me, making me feel safe and secure.

When I awoke again, it was to a cold bed, and I half wondered if I had dreamt of having sex with my best friend all around my hotel room. But then I looked down and saw the silver ring on my left hand, and I knew it had happened.

I ran a shaky hand through my hair with a sigh. Riley was nowhere to be found, which was bad because we really needed to talk about this marriage of convenience thing we had going on. It was nice for him to step in and marry me last night, but it would be best if we got it annulled and went back to just being friends.

The honeymoon suite had an adjoining living room with a kitchen, so I wondered if Riley was already up and ready for the day. I had to drag myself out of bed, still very hungover and feeling like death. I went into the other room, but there was no sign of him. I walked back into the bedroom and opted for putting on clothes that weren't pajamas, and went to check the fallout of last night on my phone. There were a bunch of text messages and two missed calls. The calls were from my mother, as were half of the texts.

MOM: *Are you two going to come to the brunch we're supposed to have?*

MOM: *Fiona?*

MOM: *Call me when you wake up!*

I rolled my eyes. I really didn't want to have to deal with all the people that were at my weird-ass wedding. It was almost like a fake relationship, like in those romance novels I read. Because there was no way Riley and I could stay married. I mean, if he wanted to bone, I was good with that. Like more than good with that. I could go back to being friends with benefits with Riley again, especially now that I knew how much his technique had changed since we were teenagers. That would have been great for me. But actually being married to each other? He would quickly learn it was a big mistake.

I scrolled down to the other texts on my phone.

KATIE: *So...how was the sex?*

KATIE: *Tell me!!!*

I snorted at that. You would think that since I was supposed to have married Katie's brother, she would have been completely against me marrying someone else. Not Katie; she had been so cool about everything. I glanced at the plain silver band around my finger. Katie had sprung into action, going out to get rings for us while we got the license done. I was kind of glad she got something really simple because I was never one for flashy anyway.

I saw that Riley had texted too.

RILEY: *Hey, I didn't want to wake you, so I'm gonna go work out.*

RILEY: *I can see you making fun of me.*

I laughed at that; he was right. He drank as much as me, but he was going to go work out. Ugh, I guess I shouldn't have been surprised. Those muscles did not create themselves.

I glanced at the time on my phone and was surprised that it was already noon. I must have been feeling really shitty when I woke up earlier and we showered together. Or rather, I stood there under the water while Riley washed me because I was too tired. That had been rather loving and intimate, and I was too hungover to even think about the implications.

I debated crawling back into the bed and going back to sleep for the rest of the day, but I didn't think that was going to help any. I didn't want to answer anyone either until I talked to Riley and discussed what we were going to do next. I slid my phone in my back pocket and walked out of the bedroom into the adjoining living area and kitchen. Before I did anything else, I really needed a coffee. I smiled when I saw a pot was already made. That was kind of sweet of him.

I was settling down with a cup and my writing journal when I heard the door click open. Riley must have swiped my room card from off the bedside table this morning. He came into the kitchen in workout gear and carrying his suitcase. I eyed it suspiciously but said nothing. His face was red, and his blond hair was dripping with sweat.

"Morning," he greeted when he crossed the living room floor. He planted a long kiss on my lips, which surprised me so much that I froze. He pulled away with a cautious look when I didn't return the kiss. "Here," he said and handed me a coconut water. "For your hangover."

I took it in thanks and started sipping it down.

"Are you okay?" he asked and cocked an eyebrow at me.

I shook my head. "No. I think we should talk."

His brow furrowed. "Okay…"

I took a sip of my coffee and sighed deeply. How do you tell the husband you just married, who was also your best friend in the entire world, that you thought marrying him was a mistake?

"Um, listen..." I stared into my coffee cup. "I think maybe we should get an annulment."

"What?" he asked, but it wasn't really a question. I glanced up at him, and I wish I hadn't. He had gone slack-jawed, and his face had this look of hurt on it. It made me feel awful.

I turned away and put a hand on my face. "I think maybe getting married was a rash decision. For both of us. I mean, you're the king of hookups; you don't want to be tied down."

He settled into the chair beside me and took my hands in his. I couldn't help but notice that we were both still wearing our wedding rings. "Fiona, when I married you, it wasn't for show. I think this could really work between us. Why don't we stick it out and see how it goes?"

"See how it goes? Look, it was very sweet of you to do this for me, but you'll get bored of me," I urged.

His eyes softened, and his big hands cupped my face. "How can you say that? You're my best friend. We know everything about each other, we get along great, and we definitely have great sex. So why not try this?"

"You really want to stick this out with me? You want to try being married to me, for real?" I asked, but I wasn't really believing what he was saying. Why would he want that? To be tethered to his best friend and the girl he lost his virginity to? What man wanted that?

"Look," he started and rubbed his hand on the back of his neck, "my life is complicated. I'm on and off the road for hockey half the year. It's hard to maintain a relationship, but I think we could be good together. I mean, last night was good for you too, right?"

I bit my lip but nodded. I don't think he even knew the half of it.

Sex with Eric hadn't been the best lately. Honestly, it felt more like a chore, if anything, and on more than a few occasions, I didn't get any pleasure out of it. Nor did he ever give in to any of my desires, which really weren't that weird! It's not like I was asking to tie him up or for him to tie me up. I liked sex a little bit rough, and I could only come from behind, but he never was a fan of the doggy-style position. He claimed he hated not being able to see my face, which I thought was sweet at the time, but now I felt like it was bullshit. It should have been a sign to me that something was off, especially when I realized we hadn't had sex in three months and neither of us had noticed.

Last night with Riley...he had been so considerate and generous. I mean, he even ate me out! I can't remember the last time that happened. I was wracking my brain to remember if Eric ever had done it in the five years we had been together.

Riley's eyes searched my face. "When was the last time you had sex?"

I balked. "That's kind of personal."

He glared at me. "Fiona, I'm your husband now. Nothing's too personal."

I groaned. "Three months."

"Three months! Oh, Fi, I had no idea."

"I should have seen this coming. God, I'm such a fool."

"No, you're not," Riley reassured me. "I promise as long as we're married, that won't happen."

I was still uneasy about this whole being married to Riley thing, though. He never seemed like a one-woman guy. Would this be enough for him? Could I be enough for him? "You sure about this? About being married to me?" I asked again.

"We both took vows...a little unorthodox, sure, but give

me a couple of months to prove to you that this is gonna work."

I don't know why, but something about the way he said it convinced me that he wanted this to work. "Okay."

"Okay?"

"Yeah."

He leaned over and kissed me. "I promise you, Fi. I'm gonna make you happy."

I pulled away, but when I looked into his eyes, I could tell he meant every single word. Riley always had been a man of his word, and even though I had my reservations about this marriage, a part of me really wanted to believe what he was saying.

"We good? Because I need to take a shower," he mused.

"Yeah, you smell," I joked.

He gave me the finger and walked back into the bedroom. I heard the shower kick on, and then I sat there in silence, thinking. How the hell did he convince me that we should stay married? I picked up my phone and decided to finally call my mother back.

CHAPTER FOUR

RILEY

—

Fi ambushing me about wanting to get a divorce threw me for a loop. I guess I shouldn't have been surprised. She had been with someone else for five years, and then I waltzed in and married her. I mean, who does that and then expects the person to fall in love with them? Apparently, I did.

I wasn't lying to her when I said I wanted to make this work. I knew my job would make things difficult, but I was ready to settle down, to have someone to come home to, but it never seemed to work out. In the back of my mind, I knew it was because none of those other girls had been Fiona Gallagher, the girl who stole my heart years ago.

I quickly showered and dressed. She was on the phone when I walked back into the room, and by the sound of her voice and the way she rolled her eyes, I knew she was talking to her mom. Fi never really got on with her mom.

They had fundamental differences, but they loved each other. Fi's mom and my mom had grown up together, and when my dad left, her mom had been the second mom I needed, especially when I got busy with hockey. I would always be grateful to her, but it was kind of weird that now she was my mother-in-law.

Fi's voice got louder. "Mom, it's not any of your business!" She was silent for a moment, but she looked pissed. Finally, in a small voice and through gritted teeth, she said, "Yes."

She clicked end on her phone and then turned to me.

"Um...so there's this brunch my mom organized that she wanted us to be at like an hour ago."

I nodded. "Okay, I'm ready when you are. Is everything okay?"

She shook her head. "It's fine."

"What's going on?" I asked.

She sighed. "My mother wanted to know if we consummated our marriage last night."

I couldn't stop the laughter from escaping my lips. "She really asked that? Damn, Katherine, didn't know you had it in you."

"Oh, yes, because now that I'm married, my mother's expecting me to have babies."

I stared at her. We hadn't talked about the whole kids thing, and I was honestly still surprised she was willing to try this marriage with me. A part of me was sure she would change her mind and still want a divorce. I wanted to take these next couple months and use them to convince her to fall in love with me, but I couldn't force her to stay.

"Do you want kids?" I asked her.

She shrugged. "Eric didn't, and I was okay with that."

"That's not what I asked you," I told her.

"I don't know! But I'm only twenty-seven; I could turn thirty and change my mind. Do you?"

I shrugged. "If that's what you want."

"Riley! You can't do whatever I want. If that's important to you, we should talk about that."

I gave her a funny look. "You literally asked me for a divorce, and now you're worried about whether or not I want children?"

"Ugh! You're so annoying!" she fumed. "If we don't see eye-to-eye on this, I don't think we can stay married."

I chuckled. She was so cute when she was mad. When she got all riled up, I wanted to knock all the things off the counter and fuck her on top of it. If only to shut her up and hear her moan my name again like she did last night.

"Stop looking at me like that!" she screeched and threw a pillow at my head.

I ducked, and it fell to the floor. I crossed the room to her and gripped her waist with my hands. Fi was tall, and I only had a couple inches on her, so we were usually at eye-level. "How am I looking at you?" I asked huskily.

She wrapped her slender hands around the back of my neck. I was only slightly worried she would try to choke me. What did it say about me that I would have been okay with it if she did?

"Like you want to throw me down on this counter and fuck me," she huffed out.

I couldn't keep it together and laughed. I pulled her closer to me, so she was flush against my chest, and kissed her roughly. She kissed me back in such an angry fashion, I should have been concerned at how hard my dick got. Unfortunately, we couldn't act out my fantasies because we were interrupted by someone knocking on the door.

Fi hung her head against my chest and groaned. "I guarantee that's my mother."

"Yeah, don't we have to be somewhere?" I asked.

She nodded, then walked away to the door and opened it to reveal her mother. Her mom looked flustered, but she smiled when she saw me peek out from the kitchen. "Oh, good, you're awake. Are you coming downstairs?" she asked.

"Riley?" Fi called me. "You ready?"

I adjusted myself in my jeans and tried to think of something to make my boner go away. Hockey stats. How bad my team was doing. Granny panties. Pittsburgh winning the cup. *Ah, there we go.* I grabbed the room card off the counter. "Coming."

"Riley!" her mom smiled at me. "I was afraid she would have scared you off, too."

Fi frowned. Her mom was the queen of passive aggressiveness, but I had to admit that comment was plain rude. I ignored it and hugged her mom. "Mrs. Gallagher, it's good to see you again. We were just on our way down."

Her mom softened. "None of that Mrs. Gallagher stuff. Katherine or Mom now."

"Sure, Katherine..." I trailed off and looked to Fi. She looked pissed. I held out my hand to her, and I was surprised she actually took it. "Come on, sweetheart," I urged and laced my fingers through hers. I was surprised that she didn't bite my head off for the pet name, but this morning, in the shower, something in her had softened when I said it. It fit her.

She rolled her eyes but let me lead her out the door. Her mom smiled at our joined hands and started talking about more stuff that I knew Fi did not want to hear about at all. "So, we should probably talk about your honeymoon..."

"I'm gonna cancel it," Fi deadpanned as we waited for the elevator.

"What? Why?" her mom asked and looked questioningly at me.

"Mom, Riley can't come. He has hockey."

"When were you gonna go? And where?" I asked.

It was true, I did have hockey and couldn't go, but maybe we could reschedule until after I made this stubborn woman fall in love with me. Maybe we could move it to the off-season. The only reason I was able to make her wedding was because it was during an unusual break in our schedule. Which she admitted to me she had done on purpose because she really wanted me to come. I knew her ex had insisted on a wedding during hockey season because he didn't want me to attend. That guy hated me, but the joke was on him because now she was wearing *my* ring on her finger, not his.

"Tomorrow. We were gonna go to Iceland. It's fine; I'll see if I can cancel and eat the cancellation fees. I mean, I'm on a deadline, so I'd probably spend more time in the hotel room anyway." She dipped her head down. I didn't like that sad look on her face.

"I'll take care of it," I offered.

The elevator dinged, and the three of us walked into it. Fi glared at me. "Don't you dare. It's fine."

Katherine waved her hand at her daughter. "Oh, honey, let him help. He's your husband; let him provide for you."

"Mom, I didn't marry him for his money. It's fine," she seethed through gritted teeth. I felt her grip my hand harder, her fingernails digging into the back of my hand, so I dropped it. She was stubborn, so I would let her handle it her way.

Her mom changed the subject and asked me about the

team's season, and I dived into it, so Fi had a chance to cool down. I could tell she was still seriously hungover. I was a little bit too, and my workout this morning had been a nightmare, but I had to do it.

We walked off the elevator and into the ballroom. Fi wandered away from me to get a coffee and talk to Katie and Ellen. Finnegan and their dad showed up in front of me, and Finnegan pulled me away from his parents.

"What the fuck?" he asked.

"What?"

He glared at me, a look mimicking the one his sister had been giving me all morning. "So you married my sister?"

I shrugged. "People have gotten married for dumber reasons."

"She's still my sister." He punched me in the arm. "Did she ask for a divorce yet?"

I grimaced. "I convinced her to give it a shot. Was that stupid?"

He had a shocked look on his face. "Oh my God. How long have you been in love with her?"

I ran a hand down my face. I really didn't want to be having this conversation with him.

Fi eyed me from across the room, and I knew she was reading my discomfort. She walked over to us with two plates in her hands and shoved one at me.

"Oy! Stop harassing my husband, you dick," she said to her brother.

Finnegan laughed and shook his head. "I don't understand you two."

She ignored him and looked at me. "Come on, let's go sit and eat."

Finnegan shook his head and walked away while I followed Fi to a table in confusion. Ellen stared me down with an amused look, but I nodded my head at her. I knew this was such a weird situation, but Fi was taking it like a champ, snapping at anyone who questioned why we got married and defending me to anyone that said something even slightly rude. I gripped her thigh underneath the table whenever she needed to be told to calm down.

"How's the team looking?" Ellen asked me.

"Fucking awful," Fi answered for me.

I shot her an amused look. She shrugged and held her hands up. I rubbed my jaw, feeling the raw stubble of my facial hair starting to grow out. "Well...she's not wrong," I admitted.

"But you have that new coach and that hot new goalie, right?" Ellen asked.

I nodded. "Yeah, Metzy's hot right now. We'll have to take it game by game."

Ellen made a face at me. "Are you just gonna give me media answers or real answers?"

I laughed and took a sip of my coffee. "You know the answer to that."

She scoffed. "You two are the worst. I can't believe you actually went through with this sham of a marriage."

"Thank you oh so much, Ellen," Fi snarled.

I hid my smile behind my hand, but I put my arm around her shoulder. "Play nice, Fi," I whispered into her ear and gave her a gentle kiss on the neck.

Ellen and Fi had a weird relationship. They fought a lot, and it was almost like they were more sisters than friends. I guess I understood Ellen's concerns, but I didn't want this to be a sham of a marriage. I wanted something real.

Little by little, the guests started filtering out and saying goodbye to Fi, and soon we were free from all the hassles of wedding stuff. When we got back to the suite, she kicked off her shoes and dropped herself onto the couch in the living room.

"I am so hungover. I think I'm gonna take a nap," she told me.

I sat on the couch next to her, pulled her head into my lap, and stroked her hair. "Okay, so when are you going back to Philly?"

She groaned and sat up. "Right, I forgot. I have to deal with all the cancellation shit. When were you planning to go back?"

"My flight's tonight, but I can reschedule it."

"Oh, Riley, no. When do you need to be at the airport?"

I waved her off. "It's fine; I'll reschedule. I can go back tomorrow; I have a practice that I need to be at."

She bit her lip but got up to pull her computer out of her bag on the floor. She spent the next couple of hours dealing with canceling everything while I looked up flights for us to go back to Philly tomorrow. I changed my flight and then ordered a seat next to mine going home so she could come along with me.

"Oh my God, finally!" she said after hanging up the phone. "Now, I need to book a flight back to Philly." She looked down at her phone, and I knew by the scowl that she saw the email I sent her. "Did you...ugh, you did not buy me a flight home!"

"Yes..." I trailed off. "You were busy. Isn't that what husbands are supposed to do?"

She leaned against me. "Thank you. This has been a nightmare."

I pulled her into my side and kissed the top of her head. "I know. At least we have the rest of the day to ourselves. You should take that nap."

"So...you never answered my question," she said, giving me a sly look.

"Huh?"

"This morning, I said you looked like you wanted to throw me on the counter and fuck my brains out. Did you?"

Uhh...yes. Yes, I very much wanted to do that. Now I very much wanted to fuck her again here on the couch, on the kitchen table, in the shower, and then finally in the bed.

"Riley?"

I gulped. "Yes."

She laughed. "Knew it!"

"Tease."

She smirked at me but stood up from the couch and walked over in front of the kitchen table. She stood with her hands on her hips and cocked an eyebrow.

"Then fucking do it," she dared.

I stared at her for what felt like an entire minute. "What?"

She crooked her finger at me. "What, you don't want to fuck me? You don't want to shove me up on this table and fuck me like a wild animal?"

I curled my hand into fists at her crass words and exhaled. I stood up from the couch and walked across the room to where she stood. She was egging me on, but I was going to call her bluff. I wrapped one hand around the back of her neck, and the other went to her hand and placed it right on the straining zipper of my jeans. Then I kissed her hard. I smiled against her skin, traveling down her jaw and onto the side of her neck while she massaged me over my jeans.

"Is this what you want?" I whispered against her ear.

"Riley," she whispered.

"I think the question is, do *you* want me to fuck you?"

"You know you didn't have to marry me if you just wanted to fuck," she huffed.

"Um, you kind of had a long term boyfriend."

"True, who I should have broken up with sooner. But let's not talk about him right now."

"Answer the question, Fiona," I urged.

She ground herself against me, teasing me because I was already as hard as a rock. "Yes," she breathed. "I want your cock inside me again. Give it to me hard."

I growled, placed both my hands on her waist, and lifted her up, so she was sitting on top of the kitchen table. Her hands hurriedly unbuckled my belt and unzipped my pants while I slid her shirt over her head and threw it across the room. I stepped back to shed my t-shirt and smirked at her drinking in my chest. She bit her lip and dug her nails into the wood of the table. God, it was fucking sexy. It was nice to be desired by her, and it turned me on even more when her fingers splayed across my chest and ran all the way down to the waistband of my boxers.

"Hm..." I started while batting her hand away from diving in to grab my throbbing cock. "I still think you have too many clothes on."

She unclasped her bra and threw it at me, then shimmed out of her jeans and underwear. I stood back and looked at her, sitting on top of the table, all naked and waiting for me to give it to her. I kissed her again to distract her and slid two fingers inside her, my thumb brushing against her clit.

"Aaron," she moaned and shamelessly thrust herself into my hand like she was offering her sex up as a gift to me. One that I couldn't wait to unwrap again.

I kissed her neck and traveled down to her left breast, leaving kisses in my wake, and then swirled my tongue around the bud of her nipple. "I love when you say my name," I mused against her breast. I smiled when she arched into me while I rotated kissing and sucking on her.

"Riley?" she asked, confused. She started making the sexiest panting noise while my fingers worked her up. It was hotter than any fantasy I had ever dreamed up.

I slipped a third finger inside her and moved to her other breast, pulling it into my mouth and sucking on it hard. Her breathing was ragged, so I knew she was about to come. I loved that I was able to give her such pleasure, and it was clear that she hadn't been getting this before, which I guess stroked my ego a little bit. It also made me mad that the man who was supposed to have married her clearly never appreciated this amazing woman.

"No, Aaron. No one calls me by my first name," I explained in-between kisses down her chest.

"Oh, you just like when I moan your name," she teased, and I felt her hand try to reach down so she could stroke me.

I batted her hand away again and ceased what I was doing. I smirked when she whimpered at the loss of my fingers. I looked her dead in the eyes and licked her off of my fingers one by one.

"Oh, fuck. Aaron, please take me now," she begged and grabbed my hips.

"No," I growled.

"No?" she huffed.

I dropped to my knees in front of her and pulled her slightly off the table. I pushed her knees further apart so I could see her in all her glory. She was shiny and wet, glistening with her need to be pleasured, and I was the man for the job. I licked my lips and grinned up at her.

"No, I want you inside me," she argued, but the protest died on her lips after my first lick.

I remembered last night, how responsive she had been when I had eaten her out. It kind of got me off too. Although, that might be because this was one of my favorite things to do for a woman. I loved worshipping a woman's body with my tongue and feeling the power of being the one to make her legs shake. If Fi wanted it all hot and rough right now, I wanted her to be begging for it. She whimpered above me while I explored the deepest parts of her with my tongue. Her legs shook, which only encouraged me to lick and suck her in a deliberate and slow manner. I lapped at her center and moaned quietly on her skin, enjoying the way she was thrashing around above me.

"Please, baby," she moaned while she shuddered through her pleasure.

I had never been with a woman who called me baby, but I kind of liked it coming from Fi's lips. Especially as she begged for my dick to be inside her.

I gave her a couple final slow licks across her sensitive nub and smiled into her skin as she shuddered above me. I kissed the inside of her thigh and traveled back up her body. "Hold on, sweetheart. I need a condom."

"Aaron, it's okay; I'm on the pill. Please give me your fucking cock," she demanded.

Hearing her beg for me was such a turn on, but remembering our conversation from this morning, I wasn't trying to have an oops baby. Even if she was on the pill, I was okay with gloving up. I slid my boxers off and fisted my cock to make sure I was hard enough. Her eyes darted down to it, and she licked her lips like she wanted to put it in her mouth again. Oh, she wanted it, that was for sure, and I would have loved to shove my dick down her throat and have her swallow my come, but right now was about what she needed.

Last night I didn't want to hurt her, but she seemed to like it when I took charge. I was getting the distinct feeling that she enjoyed rough, passionate sex as much as I did. If she liked doggy-style as much as I did, maybe this marriage would work.

I reached into my jeans and pulled out a condom from my wallet. I slowly rolled it on and watched her eyes get heavy with desire. I positioned myself between her legs and kissed her hard, my tongue darting into her mouth. She clawed at the back of my neck, gripping the short blond hair there while I thrust hard inside her in one quick motion. She wrapped her legs around the small of my back, and my hands went to her ass, digging into her soft skin. She moaned with each thrust, and holy fuck, I was fucking my best friend *hard* on top of a table in her honeymoon suite. And she was one hundred percent into it.

"Fuck, Aaron, fuck me harder," she begged between moans, digging her nails down my back so hard it kind of stung. I smiled at the sensation; I loved that shit.

"Oh my God," I muttered into her neck. "Love when you say my name and tell me what to do."

She gripped my bicep and moaned some more, which definitely encouraged me to keep going. I slammed into her harder and harder until she was moaning her orgasm into my chest. I loved feeling her slender hand wrap around my arm while she did. I loved that I made her feel that way. I felt her shudder against me, and she clutched my shoulders while she moaned right into my ear. I squeezed my eyes shut to focus on not coming right then and there.

I pulled out of her, and she looked at me, surprised. "Hey, you didn't—"

Her words were cut off when I spun her around and leaned her over the table. She leaned up against the surface on her elbows and looked over her shoulder back at me, her eyes wild with desire. Oh, fuck yeah, she was so into this.

I kissed up her spine until my lips were on her ear. "I'm not done with you yet," I whispered.

"Oh, fuck. Baby, yes," she moaned, and I was pretty sure she didn't know that she said that aloud.

I ran my hand down her back and lightly swatted her ass, gauging if she would be okay with it. "Is that okay?" I asked.

"Uh huh," she mumbled.

"Fiona..."

"Aaron, you can spank me again. I..."

A smile curled across my lips. "You what?"

She looked back at me with a sheepish look, like she was embarrassed by it, which pissed me off. Why be embarrassed by what you liked in the bedroom? Fuck that noise. If my wife liked to take it from behind and have her ass spanked, I was going to give her exactly what she wanted. If she wanted to tie me up, I would do that too. And if she wanted to spank me? Well, shit, I would probably let her do that too. I would let this woman do whatever she wanted to do to me.

"I like that," she admitted.

I grinned and slapped her ass again, this time a little harder. "Oh, yeah?"

"Uh huh. You can do it harder...if you want. I like it...a lot."

I might have come just by hearing those words, but I didn't slap her ass again. Instead, I gripped her hips and took her, the table shaking hard as I thrust into her with all my might. She moaned her encouragement for me to keep the hard and fast pace, and I pulled her further down the table so her lower half was more accessible. I dipped a hand around her to rub her clit at the same time as I pumped in and out of her as hard as I could. I held onto her hips as she came undone on top of the table, and soon I joined her in ecstasy. The last thought as my brain was coming back into focus was that I wished she loved me like I loved her.

CHAPTER FIVE

FIONA

*W*hen my brain came back online, I blinked and noticed that my chest was completely folded over the top of the table, and my cheek was pressed up against the wood. I felt Riley pull out of me, but his big hand lingered on my ass, rubbing one of the cheeks soothingly. I had to admit, it did sting a little when he had been slapping my ass, but at the same time, it was exhilarating. Eric never was interested in ways to spice up our sex life; it was rare if he wanted to do doggy-style, which pissed me off because the angle always made me come immediately. Actually, it was like the only way I could come. Okay, that wasn't necessarily true, but it was my favorite position.

"Sorry," Riley offered in a quiet voice.

I removed myself from the table and turned around to face him. "For what?" I asked, confused by the apology.

What was he apologizing for? Giving me the best sex of my life?

"You have a handprint on your ass," he explained with a sly grin. "Was I too rough?"

I shook my head slowly and started gathering up my clothes. He walked away to get rid of the condom, which was great because then I didn't have to look him in the eye. The sex had been rough, but I fucking loved it. I liked a man who could take charge like that. Eric had always treated me like glass, like if he wasn't gentle enough, I would break. I loved an aggressive alpha-male that liked to be in charge in bed. And I may have goaded Riley into that sex session because I wanted to know if last night was a drunken fluke. It certainly was not, and there was this thing digging its way inside my heart when he had apologized for being too rough. I still didn't understand why he wanted this marriage to be real, but if sex with him was always going to be that passionate, maybe I could be persuaded to stick around.

He walked back into the living room, still naked, his chest glistening with sweat. I couldn't get over how sexy my best friend was or how he just fucked my brains out. He smiled as he crossed the room to me and placed a gentle kiss on my lips. "You okay?" he asked, running his hand across my face in a gentle caress.

"Uh huh," I breathed out.

"That good, huh?" he teased.

I shook out of it and pulled away from him. "Don't be a dick."

"You should still take that nap," he insisted.

"Can't," I started to explain, but then yelped when he picked me up into his arms and walked into the bedroom. I glared when he deposited me onto the bed. I still hadn't pulled on all my clothes. I only got so far as my underwear, and now I laid annoyed and topless in the bed.

He joined me in the bed, still naked and sweaty. I couldn't get over how weird this whole situation was. Like, was I really married to him? And had he really convinced me to give it a couple months before asking for a divorce again? It would have been one thing if we had boned after Eric left me at the altar, but nope, Riley had to be extra AF and married me instead. I mean, Riley was my best friend, but I couldn't force him to be married to me when I didn't love him. Well, I did love him, but not like that. At least I didn't think so. This was so fucked, but right now, I couldn't think about it. I hadn't written in two days, and I really needed to meet this deadline.

"I want to," I admitted, "but I can't."

He slung his arm around my waist and pulled me into his chest, my exposed breasts crushing up against the hard lines there. "Why not?" he asked.

I tried not to be so distracted by how good it felt to be held in his arms like this. It would be so nice to fall asleep with him post-coitus, but I couldn't. "I need to meet a deadline. This stupid-ass wedding put me behind my writing goals. I need a little time to bang out a couple chapters," I explained.

"Wait, isn't your book already out?" he asked, clearly confused.

"Book two came out last week; this is book three," I explained.

"Your job's weird."

"Books take a long time. This is the first draft to my publisher, and it will go through a million revisions before it gets published. I'm afraid of turning in the final book in this trilogy and they realize they made a mistake and I have to beg for my day job back."

He kissed the top of my head. "I'm sure it's fine. Can't you write on the plane tomorrow?"

"I probably will, but I need to put in the time right now."

He loosened his grip on me, and I got out of the bed before he changed his mind and tried to keep me there. It was super tempting to snuggle into his strong chest and go back to sleep. I was super hungover, so writing was going to be hell today, but I had to put the words onto the page. Even if they were bad.

I stopped in the bathroom first and ended up fixing my hair, now tangled from our sexcapades. I pulled it into a messy top knot, and when I came out, Riley had fallen asleep. Good; that meant I wouldn't have any distractions.

I put on a pair of comfy leggings and a t-shirt, grabbed my computer and headphones, and tip-toed into the adjoining room. I shut the door to the bedroom quietly behind me and set myself up at the counter in the kitchen. I couldn't look at the kitchen table without thinking about what we had just done. I put on another pot of coffee, put my headphones on, and started writing garbage.

Every line, every piece of dialogue I wrote wasn't working. I had to push through and get something on the page, but I was unhappy with what I was writing. There was a gaping plot hole in the ending, but I couldn't figure out how to solve it. I flipped back to the novel outline to figure it out, but I couldn't figure out how to solve it without completely rewriting this book. I was screwed.

I tried to just write to get it all out, but I got distracted by my phone buzzing across the counter. I had been ignoring it, but the buzzing pulled me away from my thoughts.

Three missed calls from Eric. Four text messages.

What the fuck?

ERIC: *My sister told me you got married anyway. What the fuck?*

ERIC: *To Aaron fucking Riley???*

ERIC: *Tell me this is a joke.*

ERIC: *Have you been fucking him this whole time?*

Anger swelled up into my chest. How dare he? He left me at the altar, and now he was accusing me of cheating on him. My fingers flew in a rage across my phone screen.

ME: *How about...go fuck yourself?*

I sent him a picture of my left hand with my ring finger sticking out as if I was giving him the finger to show him the wedding ring.

ME: *Yeah, I got married to someone else instead. Not that it's any of your business.*

ME: *I'm coming home tomorrow. Let me know when you get your shit out of my apartment.*

Immediately my phone started ringing, and I didn't even need to see the caller ID to know it was Eric. I didn't know why I bothered to answer it; maybe I wanted closure.

"What could you possibly want?" I seethed.

"Are you serious? You seriously up and married someone else?" my ex asked on the other line.

"You LEFT me. LEFT ME! You made it pretty clear you didn't want to continue a relationship with me."

"I didn't want to get married!"

"Do you know how much money you have cost me? I had to cancel our honeymoon!"

He was silent for a moment.

"Yeah, I guess you didn't think of all the repercussions of what you did to me."

"I never said I didn't want to continue a relat—"

"You really think we would continue on after you left me, completely embarrassed me in front of everyone? You really thought I would come back to you?"

Again, silence.

"Did you ever even love me? I mean, fuck, Eric, we haven't had sex in three months!"

"Wait...really?" he asked, with a hint of confusion in his voice. That sealed the deal; he hadn't noticed either. How did I ever think I could have had a happy life with this man?

"Oh my God, if you didn't notice, clearly something was wrong. You know what? I'm glad this happened. I'm glad to know that this never would have worked out between us anyway. Have a nice life!"

"Answer me this first. Did you sleep with him?"

"Who?"

"Riley!"

"Yeah...I married him. That's kind of what people do on their wedding night."

He sighed on the other line. "No, I mean before."

"Are you asking me if I cheated on you? No. What do you take me for?"

"You didn't?" he asked. He sounded surprised, like he didn't believe me. I think that hurt more than him leaving me at the altar.

"Not while we were together. And it's not any of your business who I fucked before we got together, like it's not your business now."

"So you did have sex with him? I knew it."

"It was in high school!" I argued. "We lost our virginity to each other. What, am I supposed to be jealous of every girl you slept with before you met me? I don't know why I'm still talking to you."

He was silent on the other line for a moment, and I contemplated hanging up on him. I was steaming mad. I wanted to cry. Who the fuck did he think he was? Accusing me of cheating on him when he left me on what was supposed to be the happiest day of our lives. Now, I was married to my best friend, who I really shouldn't have married, but he was kind and gentle, and he wanted to see if we could make something real out of this marriage. My life had spiraled out of control in the span of twenty-four hours.

"Do you hate me?" he finally asked.

I had to be honest with him. "A little bit," I admitted. "Can you blame me?"

He sighed again. "No, I guess I can't. Katie gave me hell for what I did. I shouldn't have asked you to marry me if I was gonna back out."

"If you didn't want that, you should have never asked," I snapped.

"Yeah, maybe you're right," he finally admitted.

"Good. Have a nice life!"

"I'll be out of the apartment in a couple days, earlier if I can," he told me and then promptly hung up. What a dick.

I wanted to chuck my phone across the room. I had gotten closure, sure, but that didn't mean that it didn't hurt. Being left on your wedding day like that sucked, and now I was even more confused because I immediately rebounded with Riley!

Maybe that was the real reason I had asked him for the divorce. Not that I couldn't be happy with him, because maybe in time we could find happiness in each other. I think the real reason I wanted to get a divorce was because it felt like a rebound, and I knew it would only end in heartbreak. Most of all, I was afraid of losing my best friend if this trial marriage of ours didn't work out.

I heard footsteps in the bedroom, and the door creaked open. Riley stood in the doorway, clad in a pair of jeans now, but no shirt. His eyebrow was raised, and his face was scrunched up in confusion. I set my phone down on the counter and ran a shaky hand over my face. Riley crossed the room towards me and put his hands on my shoulders.

"Hey, what's wrong?" he asked.

I shook my head and waved him off. "I'm sorry, did I wake you? Just got into a fight with my ex, but it's fine."

"Yeah...I heard you yelling a lot. Everything okay?"

I shook my head, and he pulled me towards his naked chest. I don't know what it was about that move of his, but it seemed to relax me. I sighed into him and rested my head there. I was comforted by the thump-thump-thump of his heartbeat underneath me.

"What happened?" he asked while he stroked my hair.

I sighed and pulled back so I could look up at him. "We fought, he thinks you and I have been fucking the whole time anyway, but he said he'd get out of my apartment in a couple days."

Riley frowned at that. "Yeah, I wanted to talk to you about that..."

"My apartment?"

He nodded but looked down at the floor. "Yeah. I mean...should you come move in with me now?"

I crossed my arms over my chest. "I like my place in Fishtown."

He closed his eyes and shook his head. "I know, but I have a big condo in Old City."

I looked at him sternly. "I would like to keep my own place." I left off the part where I said, "In case we decide to get divorced anyway" but from the look on his face, I think he knew that was what I was thinking about.

"Did you get any work done?" he asked, changing the subject.

I sighed again. "Not really. I'm stuck on this book. I think I need to completely rewrite it."

He checked his watch. "Why don't you let me take you to dinner tonight? We have an early flight tomorrow, so write for another hour, and we'll go at seven, okay?" I opened my mouth to protest, but he put a finger on my lips. "For once in your life, Fi, don't argue with me."

Normally I would have argued some more, but something inside of me let it go. "Okay, sure."

CHAPTER SIX

RILEY

I was honestly surprised she agreed to dinner, so I wasn't going to try to push the whole living arrangement thing. I was hoping that maybe I was worming my way into her heart since she had initiated having sex today, but maybe she just needed something physical. I was not complaining, but I didn't know how I was supposed to go about showing her that I really wanted this to work.

It had been rash of me to offer to marry her, but I had been in love with this woman since we were teenagers. She always thought I was another dumb jock who had hoes in different area codes, though. My life was complicated, and sure I had some one-night stands...okay, more than some. There had been a couple girls in the past couple years that I thought could be something, but they couldn't take my schedule.

I watched her return to her laptop, pulling the headset

over her head, and the room filled with the tip-tapping of her fingers flying across the keyboard. I walked back into the bedroom and threw a t-shirt over my head. I took out my phone to see if I could get a reservation somewhere nice. It was kinda iffy, but someone must have recognized my name because I was able to get something at one of the nicer sushi bars. I knew she loved her sushi.

After hanging up, I saw a text from my teammate and probably my best friend on the team, Benny. Benny was a massive, brown-skinned, six-foot-four left-winger from Boston, and we had bonded over being two of the few Americans on the team.

BENNY: *When you coming back from that Vegas wedding?*

I scratched the back of my neck. I wasn't sure how I was going to break it to my teammates that I had randomly gotten married. I sighed but figured I had to come out and say it.

ME: *Uhh....her fiancé flaked on her...so I kind of married her instead???*

BENNY: *What in the actual fuck? Are you serious?*

I ran a hand over my face and groaned. Benny was my best bud, so I knew he would give me shit for this, but I had no idea how I was going to break this to my other teammates. I texted him back immediately.

ME: *Yes.*

BENNY: *Wait...this is the girl from home that you're legit in love with?*

ME: *Yup.*

BENNY: *What the actual fuck?!?*

What the fuck indeed. Not like Benny had any room to talk; he was in love with our teammate TJ's twin sister. Too bad the curvy Canadian hated his guts. Women didn't like it when a guy stared at their tits and asked if they were real. Poor Benny.

I flicked over to the sports news and looked at a few articles that talked about me and whether if Philly was getting the right value in me. One article was calling for me to be traded because I was taking too many penalties. As if I didn't know that! As if it was news to me that you could take a bad penalty and cost your team everything?

I threw my phone down on the bed in anger and sank onto it in defeat. Like I didn't know that this was a bad season for the team. With Metzy in the net, we had a good chance; we just had to work really hard. I shouldn't have missed my flight home today. I could have used an extra day on the ice for conditioning to get my head in the game. We had been on a hot streak, but it came to an end, and it was like we lost our mojo.

I shook off the emotions and picked up my phone again to try to watch some video to see what I had been doing wrong in the last couple games. I wanted to work hard to stay in Philly and stay with the Bulldogs. My contract expired in July, but since I was an older player, I had a feeling they would let me become an unrestricted free agent and let another team waste their money on me. I really wouldn't have blamed them if they did. But I loved Philly, and I needed to stay there if I wanted to make my wife fall in love with me.

I set my phone on the bedside table and got up off the bed. I went over to my suitcase and pulled out the extra suit I had brought. I hadn't been sure which one to bring for Fi's wedding, so I brought two. It was good to have a spare sometimes. I took the iron out of the closet and ironed out the wrinkles, then hung it up in the closet. I checked my watch; we still had plenty of time, and I heard Fi tapping away at her keyboard, so I didn't want to disturb her. I rubbed a hand across my face and felt the annoying scratchiness of my beard coming in, so I went into the bathroom to shave and fix my hair.

By the time she padded into the bedroom, I was suited up and adjusting my tie in the mirror.

"Oh, should I dress nice?" she asked.

"I guess so. It's Vegas, sweetheart."

She put a finger on her chin, as if in thought, but then went into the closet and rifled through some clothes she had hanging up in there. She pulled out a black dress with thin straps and looked over at what I was wearing before changing into it. The dress hugged her in all the right places and showed more cleavage than was normal for her. My mouth watered, and I knew if I didn't unclench my jaw, we would never even leave the suite tonight. I watched her slip on a pair of heels before shaking her bright red hair out of the messy bun.

"I think I need to straighten my hair and do my make-up. Can you give me like twenty minutes?" she asked.

I straightened my tie again. "Sure."

She eyed me from across the room. "Are we even going to make it to dinner?"

"What?"

She smirked. "You're looking at me like you want to throw me down on the bed."

I coughed into my hand, and she laughed again before coming into the bathroom to plug in her straighter. She wasn't wrong, so I got out of the way before I did anything too bold. I shuffled into my suit jacket and offered her my hand when she finally came out of the bathroom. Surprising me, she took it, and I guided her out of the suite.

"So, where are you taking me?" she asked when we stepped onto the elevator.

"Sushi."

Her eyes lit up. "I love sushi."

"I know."

"You actually listen to me?" she asked with a surprised look on her face.

I rubbed my thumb on the back of her palm. "Of course I do."

"Oh," she said and looked down at her shoes.

My gut told me she was thinking again about whether we should call this thing off. The idea of her leaving and not giving me a chance to show her that I could be the right man for her gutted me. She didn't try to wrench her hand out of mine, though, so I thought that was at least a good sign.

The silence filled me with dread, but once we got into my rental car, the music from the stereo made it not as noticeable. I focused on driving, even though I could tell that her mind was on something else.

I knew something was up when she was still quiet after we were seated at the restaurant. She sipped slowly on a glass of red wine, staring off at something behind my right shoulder. I reached across the table and put my hand on top of hers. She jerked suddenly and looked at me with a sheepish look.

"Sorry," she offered.

"Where did you go?" I asked.

She shook her head. "I get in my own head sometimes. I'm trying to figure my way out of this plot hole."

The waiter brought our dinner, and I smiled at how happy she looked once she started eating. Huh, maybe she was just hangry. I took a sip of my wine and speared a California roll with my chopsticks.

"Oh my God, I was pretty hungry," I admitted.

"Oh, me too," she agreed and took a huge gulp of her wine. I poured her some more from the bottle on the table. We clinked glasses, and I loved seeing the sweet smile across her face. "This is really nice, Aaron. Maybe too nice; this place is fancy."

I couldn't help the grin spreading across my face, especially at her using my first name. "I'm kind of surprised you're gonna let me pay for dinner."

She stuck her tongue out at me. "Usually I would fight you, but you know I can't afford this place."

"You know you don't have to worry about that. I'm—"

"Don't start with that."

I held up my hands in surrender. "Fine, fine. So tell me about the book."

She looked taken aback. "You want to hear about my work?"

I furrowed my brow in confusion. "Yeah. Why wouldn't I?"

She avoided the question by shoving another piece of sushi in her mouth and then taking a long sip of her wine. I cocked my head at her, waiting for her answer.

"Sorry. Eric never wanted to hear it. He was actually pretty pissed when I quit my job last year. But, I mean, the sales on the first book allowed me to."

I narrowed my eyes. The more she revealed about her relationship, the more I thought it was a good thing that Eric didn't show up yesterday. There was no way she would have been happy with him. I curled and uncurled my fist under the table. Man, did I want to throttle that guy.

"I liked the first book, but I haven't read the second one," I admitted.

I watched her bring her hands to her chest. "You bought

my book? Really? I mean, I know you read the very bad first draft I wrote, but..."

"Of course! I'm so proud of you. You always wanted to write, and you're finally doing it."

She clenched her hands to her heart and gave me a look of adoration. "You have no idea how much that means to me to hear you say that. My family hasn't been that supportive about this career change."

I nodded. I vaguely remembered my mom saying something about how Katherine thought this was just a passion project. That really rubbed me the wrong way. It was clear that this was what made Fi happy, and when she talked about her writing, her eyes sparkled with delight, and her hands waved about excitedly. I definitely had to remind myself to pick up book two in her trilogy for my upcoming road trip.

"Tell me how it's going," I encouraged.

"No spoilers!" she exclaimed and then launched into vaguely telling me about trying to fix the problem she found in her draft today. She had a deadline that she really needed to meet, and she was super close, but having discovered this plot hole today, she was afraid she wasn't going to meet it. I nodded while she told me all of this, feeling like she really needed someone to listen to her rather than have a solution to her problem.

She paused after a long breath to take a sip of her wine, and then her eyes widened.

"What?" I asked.

She downed the rest of the wine. "Holy shit, I think I figured it out!"

I laughed. "Just like that?"

She nodded, then pulled out her phone and typed away at it. I tried to say something, but she held a finger up to shush me and continued whatever she was doing. A few minutes later, she put the phone down again and looked at me with an apologetic look on her face. "Sorry, sometimes I have to write out some notes, or I will lose it," she explained. "Enough about my stuff. Are you going to truthfully tell me how you think the Bulldogs are doing this season?"

I groaned, and this time, I shoved sushi into my mouth, so I didn't have to answer.

She laughed heartily at my reaction. "Am I not allowed to ask you that question? I thought since I'm your wife, you'd actually tell me the truth."

I ran a hand down my face and gave her an exasperated look. "You know how the team's doing."

"Yeah, like shit. Are you afraid you're gonna get traded?" she asked cautiously.

I shrugged. "No clue. We're past the trade deadline now, but yeah, I'm worried. If they don't re-sign me by July, I'll become an unrestricted free agent."

"You want to stay in Philly?" she asked while spearing another sushi roll. I had to smile at how happy she looked when she ate.

"I do," I admitted.

"Why?"

"I want to stay near you."

Her face flushed at my admittance. "Oh."

"Philly's home for both of us, Fi. I want to make sure we stay in the same city."

"But what if you got traded? Or signed somewhere else? Where would you want to go if they gave you a choice?"

"Minnesota," we said in unison and then laughed together.

I shrugged. "I can't really think about it right now. Have to focus on this season first."

She nodded. "It's hard to know when I read so many articles ripping you to shreds, saying you should be traded. It makes me so angry. I want to go to their houses and punch them in the face. Like these armchair analysts even know shit about hockey."

I eyed her. "You read what they say in the sports section?"

She scoffed at me. "Minnesotan! I love hockey, you know that. Also, I may have a Google alert set up for you," she muttered that last part under her breath.

I raised an eyebrow. "I'm sorry, what?"

"I have a Google alert set up for you. I care about your career, about you."

"You do?"

"Of course!" she exclaimed. "You worked your ass off to get where you are; it's something I always admired about you. I always wanted to know where you ended up."

"I hate that our careers kept us apart so much."

She grimaced. "It wasn't just our careers, you know that."

I was honestly surprised she admitted that. It had been clear to me that her ex didn't like me and didn't want us spending time together. When she told me he refused to have a summer wedding, I knew it was because he didn't want me to show up.

"He really didn't want us to be friends."

"I'm sorry; I should have fought him more. You're my best and oldest friend; I couldn't bear to lose you."

I grumbled and drained the rest of my wine. I was really glad she didn't marry that douche. I was pretty sure I would have never seen my best friend again if she did. Just the thought of it put an ache in my chest.

"You don't have to worry about that now. I'm here, and I'm not going anywhere," I reassured her.

She gave me a small smile in return.

The waiter came and dropped off the check, so I picked it up to take care of it while she sipped on her water. "Come on, let's get out of here," I said to her once the check was all squared away.

I felt warmth fill my chest when she reached out for my hand and slid her small fingers between my larger ones. Maybe I could score her heart after all.

CHAPTER SEVEN

FIONA

*I*t might have been the wine, but I felt a warm sensation in my chest by the time dinner was over and we got back to the hotel. I walked into the bedroom and kicked off my heels, then sat on the bed and rubbed my feet. I'm not sure why I even wore them in the first place when they hurt so much.

Riley sauntered into the room and started taking his tie off and shrugging out of his suit. He looked damn good in a suit, I knew that, but it was nice that he dressed up to take me out to dinner.

"What time is our flight, again?" I asked, too lazy to look at the email he had sent me earlier.

He unbuttoned his shirt and untucked it from his pants, and all thoughts left my brain as my eyes scanned across his body. Geez, what was wrong with me? Well, it wasn't weird to ogle the guy so much if you were technically married to him, right?

"It's early. Sorry, that was the best I could do," he offered. "I need to be back for practice."

When Riley looked at me, I felt like that timid seventeen-year-old girl in her parents' basement again. I put a hand to my lip, and my thoughts drifted back to the plans for my book that I had gotten while we were at dinner. The words were still rolling around in my brain, and I needed to release them now, or I would lose them. The problem was, I also needed to pack up all my things and shower if we were going to leave early.

I jumped when I felt Riley's hand on my arm. "Sorry," he said and rubbed his hand on the back of his neck.

I shook my head and looked up at him. He was still shirtless, damn him, but now he was wearing a pair of pajama pants. He looked down at me but then planted a tender kiss on my forehead. "Go on," he urged.

"What?" I asked and raised an eyebrow in confusion.

He took my hands in his. "You've got that look in your eyes like you need to write."

"But I need to pack."

"I'll handle it," he offered.

"You sure?" I asked hesitantly.

He cupped my face in his hands and kissed me so softly his lips barely ghosted over mine. "Go."

I didn't need to ask him twice. I rushed into the adjoining room where my computer was, sat at the counter in front of my computer, cracked my knuckles, and poured out my soul onto the keyboard.

❄

Later, when I finished and had packed my computer into my carry-on bag, I returned to the bedroom to find Riley already asleep in the bed. I inspected the room and assessed that he did a good job of getting everything together. It was sweet that he did that for me so I could get some writing done. I always knew he cared about me, we were best friends after all, but it was like he was going out of his way to show it to me.

I didn't want to keep comparing him to Eric, but the differences between the two men were eye-opening. I was wondering if I really had been happy with Eric before it all went to shit yesterday. Maybe we had both settled? I didn't want to think about it right now.

I dug into my carry-on for my pajamas and slipped into the bathroom to take a quick shower. While I was washing my hair, I realized the kindness Riley had shown me tonight was probably the sexiest thing he could have done. It made me want him even more than I already did. Maybe it was the honeymoon thing, but I definitely wanted to jump his bones again.

I towel-dried my hair, afraid the hairdryer would be too loud, and I didn't want to wake Riley. I tip-toed back into the bedroom and put my dirty clothes in the top section of my suitcase. I looked for comfy clothes to lay out on the chair next to the bed so I could quickly change into them tomorrow morning. I then slid into the bed beside Riley and felt him shift onto his side so he was facing me.

"Did you get everything done?" he asked sleepily, his eyes still closed.

"I thought you were asleep," I mused and brushed his hair out of his eyes.

"I've been in and out."

"Hmm. Thanks for letting me go write. I needed to get that out."

His blue eyes popped open, and he wrapped his arms around my waist, trapping me in my position lying on my back.

"I knew you needed to," he told me, nuzzling my neck sleepily. It was kind of cute, and I never thought that Riley and cute would be in the same sentence. He was so big and manly. Kittens were cute; a six-foot-tall, two-hundred-pound hockey player, not so much.

I struggled in his arms, and he laughed until he released his grip, and I shifted so I was facing him. I pulled him to me and kissed him softly. I sighed into him, and he kissed me back. I deepened the kiss by flicking my tongue across his bottom lip. I think I pouted when he pulled away and didn't let it go any further.

"Thank you," I told him.

"For what?" he asked, brushing a piece of red hair behind my ear. His calloused fingers lingered on my cheek and stroked in a soft and gentle pattern.

"For letting me write. Even though I knew you would rather be doing something else."

"You had that twinkle in your eye; I wasn't going to keep you from that. I know your writing's important to you, and I'll always support that."

Not sure what melted at that, my heart or my ovaries.

"Oh, Aaron," I whispered.

He smiled down at me with a soft, small curve of his lips. The way he looked at me, like he was looking into my soul, made me want to push him away. His blue eyes searched mine, and then they closed slowly, and he kissed me again. A small, soft kiss, but one that made me feel safe and secure.

I found myself disappointed when he rolled me onto my side instead of tearing off my clothes and getting on top of me again. He pushed my hair on top of the pillow so he didn't lay on it, and then he clutched me against his chest, holding me tightly around the waist. I wrapped my arm around his larger forearm, circling the red and gold artwork on his arm.

He lightly nipped my neck. "Stop, that tickles," he whispered.

A smile played across my lips. "I know that. It's fun."

"You're a naughty girl, Fiona Riley."

I turned around in his arms to fix him with a glare. "Um...I'm not changing my name!" I protested.

He smiled at me, and I knew he was trying to hold in his laugh. I shoved him away, realizing he'd said it just to annoy me. He leaned down to chastely kiss my cheek. "Oh, sweetheart, I know you won't ever change your name, and I would never ask you to."

"I'm not fucking property!"

"No, sweetheart, you're my equal, my partner," he agreed.

Something unlocked inside my heart at his words, but I swallowed and tried to shove it down. I wanted what he was offering, but could Riley really deliver? I pushed down the feelings that were trying to bubble up to the surface. The feelings of optimism, that maybe, just maybe, my best friend and I could make this marriage work.

Instead, I stroked my hand across his chiseled jaw and kissed him again. He kissed me back, and soon I lost myself in the feel of my husband's tongue tangling with mine while his hands roamed across my body. Our legs entwined while we kissed until we were burning up the sheets and I had a fire inside me, raging to get as close to this man as I possibly could.

I straddled his hips, and his hands gripped my waist while he groaned against my lips. I smiled into the kiss and made my way down his jaw to that spot behind his ear. I loved the sound of him sighing in pleasure underneath me. I felt the stiffness of his erection beneath me, straining to be inside me again while I kissed my way from his ear to the column of his throat.

"Fi," Riley hissed.

I pulled back to look down at him, his piercing blue eyes alight with desire. Wordlessly I pulled my t-shirt over my head and ran my hands down his bare chest. I played with the dusting of blond hair across the hard muscular planes of his chest. My husband was a work of art, but I knew he worked his ass off to be in peak physical condition. He needed to be for his job. A job he'd worked his entire life for. I had watched him work so hard only for it to pay off when he left for the NHL.

When he finally left me.

"Fi," he said again, and this time it sounded like he was pleading.

"What?" I snapped in annoyance.

"We don't have to have sex tonight," he said.

My face fell. "You don't want to?" I asked. I felt an ache in my chest at that. Why didn't he want me?

He reached a hand up and pushed a strand of my hair out of my face. "I didn't say that. I just don't expect you to—"

He cut himself off with a groan because I took his hand and shoved it into my pants so he felt my arousal. His big fingers dipped inside me and barely touched my aching clit.

"Touch me," I demanded. "Feel how much I want you right now. Don't you want that?"

He sighed. "Fuck, sweetheart, you're so wet already."

I nodded vigorously and ground against his hand shamelessly. "Please, baby," I begged. I never thought I would be straddling a man and begging him for sex while his fingers grazed my swollen clit. Or that I would be calling that man 'baby.' Or that that man would be my childhood best friend.

He shoved me off of him and pinned me down on the bed, hovering over me. I bit my lip in anticipation. His eyes were ablaze with passion. "Of course I want that, you silly woman. I don't want you to feel like we have to because I told you to go write tonight instead of coming to bed with me."

"Oh," I whispered.

He was on to me. I was trying to have sex with him as a thank you to him for not complaining that I needed to get writing done. Eric always complained I loved my books more than I loved him. A part of me wondered if maybe he had been right.

"Fiona," Riley breathed, his breath hot on my neck. "I really want this to work between us. I want a partner, and I know that has a give and take."

"I want that too," I admitted.

I really did. A partner who felt like I was an equal was exactly what I wanted. But I was afraid that even though Riley said that was what he wanted, it wasn't going to last. He would get bored of me; the fame and the women were what he wanted more than a quiet life with me. Because that was what he would have with me. I'm a quiet person, a private person, who buried themselves in fictional characters and didn't have a lot of friends. I may have a loud personality, but I'm more of a hermit than people understood.

He caressed my face gently. "Fi..."

"Take what you want, Aaron. Take me, please," I begged while I squirmed out of my pajama pants, leaving myself naked and on display for him.

He grinned at me and shed himself of his own clothes. "Oh? Is that what you want? You want me to take charge?"

"Aaron, please stop talking and get your dick inside me."

"Christ, Fiona," he said with a chuckle. Then he kissed me hard again, pinning my arms above my head with one of his big hands. His other hand toyed between my legs, teasing me until I was writhing in pain from not getting what I desired.

I kissed him back roughly, biting his lip and growling. He pulled away and pulled his fingers out of me. I whimpered at the loss, but then he flipped me over and swatted my ass. "Grab the headboard, Fiona," he ordered in a low sexy growl.

I scrambled up onto all fours and grabbed the headboard of the bed while he grabbed a condom. I heard the crinkle of the package behind me, but when I turned to look over my shoulder, he pushed my head back to look at the wall. I heard the creak of the cap from the travel-sized bottle of lube next, and I bit back a moan when his finger rubbed the excess lubrication across my entrance.

Riley certainly was a considerate lover. What man actually was thoughtful enough to use lube? Not any of the ones I had been with before.

He slapped my ass again, playfully, and I gasped in response but secretly loved it. "Disobedient girl, you better grab that headboard and hold on," he snarled.

Holy fuck, I loved this shit. This was exactly what I wanted in a man! An alpha-male who would be rough and passionate with me, and that was exactly what Riley was like in bed.

Shit, maybe this marriage would work after all.

I groaned when his cock pressed inside me from behind, and I shamelessly rocked back into him. Riley held onto my hips and thrust inside me deep and rough. I gripped the headboard tight and cried out while he hit all my good spots and swatted at my ass here and there.

"Yes, fuck, Aaron, so good," I cried into the pillows, burying my head to muffle the sounds of my oncoming orgasm.

"This is what you want, Fiona?" he growled behind me. He placed soft kisses up my spine until he was at my ear. "You want me to be rough with you? Go all growly alpha-male?"

I nodded in response, rocking back into him, feeling him deep inside of me. "Please," I begged.

"Turn around," he growled, and I pouted when I felt him pull out of me. "I want to see your face when you come all over my cock."

OH MY GOD!

He flipped me onto my back and spread my legs before entering again. I wrapped my legs around his waist, and he nuzzled his head into my neck, kissing me while my nails dug into his strong, muscular back. Our bodies slapped together, and the bed groaned in protest from him grunting and groaning on top of me. I squeezed my legs tighter around his middle and met his thrusts with cries of delight. He was hitting me hard and deep, giving it to me rough just like I liked it. I dug my nails harder into his skin, but if it hurt him, he didn't complain.

"I'm close," I gasped while he rocked harder on top of me.

His hands went to my face, and he kissed me harder. "Come for me, sweetheart."

I nodded in agreement and thrashed under him, slipping my hand down to finger my clit in unison with his hard thrusts. "Yes, baby, so good," I moaned.

He gave me that cocky grin that I loved and kissed me through my orgasm. From the way he bucked almost angrily on top of me, I knew he was close behind me.

"Fuck, Fiona," he grunted out while he went faster and faster, pulling me apart and making me come undone again until he was roaring out his own orgasm moments later.

I sighed in relief at the release, and he laid his head across my chest. I lightly stroked his blond hair while he tried to catch his breath.

"So, what time is our flight?" I asked from beneath him.

He lifted his head up and laughed at me. "Early," he said again with a sigh and got off of me. "We should get to bed."

He got rid of the condom while I went to pee. He was back in his pajama pants when I came back to bed. He was lying on his back with his arms behind his head while I found my pajamas and slipped back into them. I slid back into the bed and smiled when he wrapped an arm around me and held me to his chest.

"Goodnight, Fi."

"Night, Riley."

I snuggled down into the bed, feeling cozy and not just from the warm bed sheets but because of the warm chest of the man holding me. The man who was my best friend in the entire world. When did my life get so weird?

CHAPTER EIGHT

RILEY

*W*e woke the next morning, tired from the late-night sex. I honestly hadn't been expecting Fi to slide into bed last night and practically offer herself up to me. It had been awesome, and I one hundred percent would fuck her as rough and hard as I did last night again, but now I was exhausted. Which meant practice today was going to be awful.

Waking up at the ass crack of dawn had never been fun. I thought one day I would get used to it, but even after all the early wake-ups playing hockey as a kid, I was still not a morning person.

When I looked at Fi, my heart pounded in my head, and the sense of dread was starting to kick in again. A part of me knew Fi still wasn't convinced of this marriage, but I must have been doing something right if she had practically begged for me to be inside her again yesterday.

The ride to the airport was quiet, but it was a quiet where we were both too tired to even speak. Once we were through security and waiting at the gate for our plane, I went to go get us breakfast and coffee. She had already snapped at me once, so I knew she needed some caffeine in her. She was probably also super hangry. I stopped at the bookstore in the airport and was surprised they actually had her book in stock, so I picked that up too.

Her eyes lit up when I waved the coffee in her face. "Oh, I really need that," she told me with relief as she took it out of my hands. She took a sip of it and practically moaned at the taste. I had to adjust myself in my jeans at that sound, the man downstairs perked up in interest at that noise.

I raised my eyebrows and nodded while taking a small sip of my own coffee. "Uh huh," I grunted.

"Sorry, I'm being a bitch," she offered.

I put an arm around the back of her neck and lightly massaged her there. I felt her straighten up at the neck grip, and I filed that away for later. "It's fine."

I handed her the egg and cheese bagel, keeping the yogurt for myself. She had her computer out again and was typing away at something, so I tried not to bother her. I cracked open the big hardback and started to read the second book in her sci-fi series. It kind of amazed me that every word she wrote was something that popped into her head. Her name was here on the cover, and she would have that forever. Pride beamed in my chest at this woman accomplishing her dreams. I was so damn proud of her.

I flipped to the dedication page.

To all the girls with stars in your eyes, this one's for you.

I sipped my coffee and flipped to the first chapter, but

felt her nudge me with her shoulder. I looked at her with a questioning look. "Is that my book?" she asked, nervously.

"Yes. How did you come up with this stuff?"

She shrugged. "It's a gift."

I cocked my head at her. "That's not an explanation, Fi."

She shrugged again. "I don't know, man. It's easy to come up with stories inside your head when that's all you have."

I didn't know what she meant by that.

She went back to her computer for a few minutes but then reluctantly closed it down and put it back in her carry-on bag. I looked up at the gate when I heard them start to call for boarding. I closed the book and held out my hand to take her bag from her.

She glared daggers at me. "I'm fine, Riley."

I held up my hands in surrender and let her be on her own. Nobody ever got to tell Fiona Gallagher what to do, not even me, her husband. Once we got settled on the plane, she dived into writing again. I was still tired, so I ended up falling asleep for a little bit. I woke to the sound of her sighing in frustration.

"What's wrong?" I asked, rubbing the sleep from my eyes.

"I think this is awful," she explained.

I frowned. "I thought you figured out the problems yesterday?"

She gripped a pen in her hand angrily. "Ugh! Everything I write is a pile of garbage. Why did I even try to do this? It's not like I am fooling anyone here!"

"I think maybe you could use a break. Take a nap. We still have a couple hours left until we get home," I suggested.

I totally expected her to blow up on me, but she saved

her doc and shut the lid to her laptop. She reached down below the seat in front of her and put it away. "Maybe you're right," she sighed.

"C'mere," I ordered.

I pushed the armrest between us up and pulled her into my chest, wrapping my arm around her shoulder. Her head rested on me, and I stroked her hair until she fell asleep. She claimed she didn't sleep on planes, but I called bullshit. Or else she was really tired. I couldn't remember what time she had climbed into bed last night, but it had been pretty late, and we got preoccupied for a while. I was not sorry about that.

The flight attendant walked by asking if we wanted any drinks, and she smiled as I whispered, trying not to wake Fi. She eyed the ring on my hand and then looked at Fi. "Vegas wedding?" she asked.

I nodded and absent-mindedly continued to stroke Fi's vibrant red hair.

She smiled. "You two look cute together. I hope it works out."

Me too. I hoped that as soon as we landed in Philly, my new wife wouldn't throw it all away and decide a divorce was the right course of action for us. I wanted forever with this woman, but I didn't know how to prove that to her.

As soon as we landed in Philly, I felt something shift between us. The tension was in the air again. Just like on the morning after our wedding when she ambushed me into asking for a divorce. It was like the past couple days had been a vacation from real life, and now we had to face the consequences that we were married. There were a lot of logistics to work out, and I wasn't sure how to broach the subject with her yet. I had already tried about the living arrangements, and she nearly bit my head off about that.

She was distant and texting on her phone as we waited for our bags to come around the carousel. When she looked up from her phone, she asked, "So what's your schedule like this week?"

I grimaced and scratched my face. "Practice today. We travel tomorrow, game in Minnesota Tuesday, back here for a home game on Thursday, off Friday, but I have another home game on Saturday."

"Oh."

"Will you come to the game on Saturday?" I asked before thinking about it.

She eyed me cautiously. "You want me to?"

"It would be nice if you could come to my game."

She put her phone away. "I don't know if I can. I'm still on deadline and have a lot of work to do."

I nodded, understanding her reasons even if I didn't like them.

"Well...how about next Saturday night? My teammates Noah and TJ usually have people over."

"Maybe."

Our bags finally came around on the carousel, and I grabbed hers for her. "Are you sure you don't want me to drive you home? It's not that far."

She shook her head and waved me off. "It's fine; Katie's coming to get me."

"Okay...so I guess we'll plan for something Thursday or Friday?" I asked, hopeful that I wouldn't come back from Minnesota with divorce papers waiting for me in the mail.

She nodded. "Sure." She had a smile on her face, but I knew her well enough to know it was a smile she reserved for her mom. She was faking it, and I couldn't understand why.

"I can wait with you," I offered while we walked outside to the pick-up area.

"Oh, Riley, that's sweet, but you don't have to do that."

I nodded. She seemed firm on this, and I didn't want to push it. I turned to her and snaked my hands up behind her neck, sliding one hand to grip her there as if to say she was mine. She looked at me like I had knocked the wind out of her, and then I leaned down to plant a long and lingering kiss on her lips.

I rested my forehead against hers when I pulled away. "I wasn't lying, Fi. I want this marriage to work."

"O-okay," she stuttered out but avoided meeting my eyes.

I brushed my hand over her cheek and grasped her jaw in my hand. I kissed her again, and I smiled against her lips when I felt her hand slide to the back of my neck. She lightly stroked my short blond hair while we kissed goodbye.

"See you later, okay, sweetheart?"

She nodded but stared at me wordlessly as I walked away. A part of me wanted to stay with her and make sure Katie got there okay, but I didn't want to be late for practice. Once I got home, all I wanted to do was drop down into my bed and take the longest nap ever, but I had to get to practice, and since Benny lived close by, he swung by to take me to the rink.

"DUDE!" he exclaimed when he saw my wedding ring glint under the light in my kitchen. "You seriously got married?"

I nodded but fidgeted with the wedding band around my finger. I hadn't taken it off since Fi slipped it on my finger a couple days ago. I was a hockey player, so I was superstitious, and taking it off made me think she would know and she would want this to be over. I didn't want to ever take it off, but I knew I had to when I was playing. Like most teams, the bulldogs had banned wearing rings when we were on the ice. It was too risky to take a puck to the hand that at best led to you having to get the ring cut off, but at worst led to a gruesome, career-ending injury. No way I would risk an injury like that.

"So where's your new bride anyway?" he asked. I flipped off the lights in my condo, and we walked out to the parking garage together.

I scratched the back of my head. "Um..."

"Did you agree to a divorce already?"

I shook my head and climbed into his SUV. "It's complicated."

He put the car into drive and started off. "How so?"

"Well, for one, she was with someone else for five years and then up and married me," I explained with a sigh.

"Okay..." he trailed off and frowned.

It was clear that Benny didn't have words for this situation, and I honestly didn't blame him. Who marries someone after the person they were supposed to marry left them high and dry? Me. That's who.

We drove to the practice facility in the suburbs in silence for a few minutes. I ran a hand across my still unshaven jaw, now rough from stubble since I didn't have time to shave. "She asked for a divorce the next morning," I revealed.

"Oh, Ri. I'm sorry."

"I convinced her to give me a couple months. I can make her happy."

He furrowed his brow as he got on 95. "Okay...so why isn't she with you now?"

I sighed. "She was really distant when we landed. She wants to keep her apartment," I explained with a grumble.

I wasn't happy that Fi didn't want to move in with me. How was our marriage supposed to work if we lived separately?

"She probably wants to have it to fall back on it. I know you don't want to hear that, but maybe she's scared it won't work out. Marriage is a huge deal, man."

"Says the man who never wants to get married," I scoffed.

A frown etched across Benny's face. Benny's girl had been dropping mad hints that she was ready for the next step, but he was like the president of the anti-marriage club. And the anti-kids club. Stephanie was a sweet girl, but when you had fundamental differences, it wasn't going to work out, and I thought Benny knew that but didn't know what to do about it. I thought he really cared about her but knew they wanted different things.

Honestly? I didn't think she was the right girl for him. I thought there was a curvy Canadian woman who was perfect for him, but they were stuck in a three-year feud neither of them would stop. A dumb feud because he took one look at the woman and was star-struck by her beauty. Okay, he might have said, "Holy shit, are those real?" and stared at her tits and maybe drooled a little bit, which was super bad, but he apologized for it. Too bad that Roxanne Desjardins knew how to hold a grudge like nobody's business and was also our teammate TJ's twin sister. Family members tended to be off-limits, but I've never seen two people more suited for each other than Roxanne and Benny. If they ever figured out how to stop fighting over nothing.

"I've never seen you this twisted up over a girl," he mused.

I sighed. "It's not just some girl; it's Fiona Gallagher."

"You're so messed up over this woman!" he laughed.

"I know."

He grinned. "But the sex is good?"

"Oh, for sure."

"Damn. Well, she might be interested in you, you never know. This marriage of yours might actually work."

I didn't know about that. I wanted her as my life partner, my equal, the person I told everything to. Once upon a time, we were inseparable, and I knew even when I was seventeen that she was the girl for me. I wished she saw the potential of *us*. I wished I hadn't been such a coward back then, and instead of asking Stacey Graves out, I asked Fiona out instead. Maybe we would have been married with a couple kids already.

I ran a hand over my jaw again. "I don't know. Her and her ex hadn't had sex for a while, so maybe she just needs it right now."

It certainly would have explained why she basically woke me up last night and begged for sex. I kind of felt like a dick about it because I felt like she was thanking me for giving her time to write. Her work was important to her, which made it important to me. I've seen Fi lose her writing track by getting distracted, and last night, I didn't want to be that distraction. I didn't want her to feel like she owed me or some shit because I was being a nice guy either, though. I was starting to wonder how bad her last relationship had been.

Benny laughed. "Are you saying that your new wife doesn't really like you but just craves your dick?"

I smiled at him and shrugged.

"I always thought you would never settle down."

I furrowed my brow at him. "What does that mean?"

"You seem to enjoy the single life."

"I did, but it got tiring. It's nice to come home to some-one, but most women can't handle me being away half the year. Don't you want someone to come home to?"

"Yeah, but it doesn't mean that I have to get married. You think Fi could handle it? Do you wonder if maybe that's why she thinks this is a bad idea?"

I shrugged. She didn't seem like the type of woman that would be bothered by it. Fi was more the woman that actually liked to be left alone most of the time.

"No. Fi has been there since before I made it in the league. She knows how important hockey is to me, how important my career is."

Benny clapped me on the shoulder. "Maybe you should talk to her before we leave for the road," he suggested.

I sighed. "Yeah, maybe you're right. Anyway, how are things with Stephanie?"

He gave me an annoyed look, and I held my hands up in surrender. He'd talk about it when he wanted, which was definitely not right now.

I couldn't badger him anyway because we had arrived at the practice rink, and it was time to get to business. I pushed all thoughts of my wife out of my head as we got down to practice, team meetings, and reviewing game tape. I had to be ready to defend Metz in this upcoming stretch on the road.

I had to be better. I just had to.

CHAPTER NINE

FIONA

I hadn't lied to Riley when I said that Katie was going to pick me up from the airport, but she was doing it because her brother still wasn't out of my apartment yet. I was planning on crashing on Katie's couch in the meantime because I was pretty sure my husband would not be happy if he found out I was staying in my one-bedroom apartment with my ex. I was kind of miffed about it, but I also hadn't given Eric a lot of time to get out. I knew I shouldn't let him walk all over me, especially considering that the apartment was in my name. At the same time, I knew trying to find an apartment in a couple days in this city was hard. So maybe I wasn't exactly being fair.

I dropped down into the passenger seat of Katie's car, and she drove off to her place in Mt. Airy. It was technically still Philly, but outside enough that only suburbanites lived there to say that they still lived in Philly. Her place was small, but the rent was cheap. Once we got to her apartment, I dumped my bags on her floor and sunk into her couch.

She sat on the loveseat next to me. "I tried to get my brother to come here while he looked for a new place, but no go," she explained with a sad smile. "I'm sorry. I always knew my brother was an asshole, but I never knew how much."

I sighed and ran a hand through my hair. It was all tangled from having slept with it a little damp last night. But also probably from the way Riley had manhandled me while we fucked last night. Not that I was complaining about that; Riley and I seemed to be on the same level when it came to that. I pulled my hair on top of my head and found a hair tie in my bag to secure it in a messy bun.

"Thanks for trying," I told her, and honestly, I was thankful that she was trying. Katie was a good friend.

She eyed my left hand, where I still wore the plain silver wedding band. "So, what's going on?" she asked.

"I don't even know. I asked him for a divorce."

She looked surprised at that. "Really? Why?"

I gave her a dirty look. "Why? We got married on a whim after your brother, who I dated for five years, left me at the altar!"

"You know I don't approve of what he did. He told me you talked, and I think maybe it was better you didn't end up together. He never was supportive of your work, and that always pissed me off."

I nodded and was reminded again of how in two days, my new husband was already more supportive of my writing than my ex of half a decade had been. Was that because Riley and I had been friends since before we could talk? We knew a lot about each other, so maybe that was why he was so supportive. I mean, I had a freaking Google alert set for him. I wanted him to succeed. He worked so hard to be good at hockey, and I always kept tabs on him. I think my heart had soared with pride when he signed his big contract with the Bulldogs.

"So, are you gonna get divorced?" she asked with a cock of her eyebrow. "I would think no since you're still wearing that ring. By the way, sorry I got you the plainest thing ever."

I shook my head. "This is fine; you really helped us out. It was a little impulsive, though. I still can't believe we got married. But he wants to give it a shot."

She glared at me. "Then what the fuck are you doing here complaining to me about it? I don't understand why you're not with him now."

I sighed again. "I don't know if this was a good idea. Maybe we should get a clean divorce and go back to being friends."

"Okay, but you're still wearing your ring, so I feel like a part of you wants it to be a good idea," she argued. "You, um...spent your wedding night tonight, right?" She waggled her eyebrows at me.

I put my hands over my face. "Um...yeah, you could say that," I said between my fingers.

She barked out a laugh. "Oh my God, how many times?"

I squinted at her. "Like the night of our wedding? Or since we've been married?"

Her eyes were wide. "Oh my God, are you admitting that Aaron Riley has enough stamina to go more than once in a night? Okay, girl, I need details."

I laughed at her. "Um...yeah, we had sex like three times on our wedding night. And twice yesterday."

She howled with laughter. "Get it, girl! Damn, does he have any single teammates? I could use a man who can go all night. So...I'm guessing it was good, huh?"

"Really good," I admitted.

She laughed again. "Feel free to not answer this, but what's a big guy like him like between the sheets?"

I glared at her but surprised both of us when I answered, "Gentle at times and really attentive, but also like a total aggressive alpha-male. Which I'm totally into. I mean, shit girl, he knows where the clit is and how to pay attention to it."

Her eyebrows quirked up, and she nudged my shoulder. "Seriously, why are you still here? What are you so afraid of? This guy comes in, saves your wedding day, knows how to fuck you, and seems to want to honestly try to have a marriage with you. Why not give it a shot?"

"I'm afraid it was all a whim, and he'll get bored of me. He's been living the single life for a long time, and I don't think he's a one-woman guy. Riley has been the king of hookups for a long time; why would he want to be married to me? Also...I don't love him. I don't want him to be in a loveless marriage with me and be trapped."

She eyed me again and crossed her arms over her chest. "You know lots of people get married and don't love each other, but love finds a way. Also, I totally call bullshit because your face lights up when you talk about him."

I gave her the finger. She was definitely wrong about that.

"Fi, I know you don't want to hear it, but you two looked happy together in Vegas."

I groaned, digging the heel of my hand into my cheek. "Maybe it was because it was Vegas. And we drank a lot of whiskey, that does it to us Irish people."

She threw up her hands in defeat. "Okay, fine, you can stay here as long as you like, but my couch is not very comfortable."

"It's fine," I tried to convince both of us.

She crossed her arms and stared me down. "Would it be so bad to really try it with this guy? It might be unorthodox, but maybe you can find happiness together."

"Ugh fine! He's about to leave for a couple days for some road games anyway," I gave in and pulled out my phone.

She gave me a dirty look. "Then go be with your husband before he heads out! Oh my God, girl, I love you, but you don't make smart decisions."

I gave her the finger again while I put the phone to my ear and dialed Riley's number. He answered on the second ring. "Hey, so listen," I started without even saying hello.

"I'm pissed you didn't come home with me. Damnit, Fiona, I want this marriage to work, but it can't work if we're not living together."

I was taken aback by the venom in his voice. "I didn't know it bothered you so much," I snapped back.

"Of course it fucking bothers me," he huffed out. "I want this marriage to work, Fi. I want *us* to work."

"I'm sorry."

"Fuck, I'm sorry too. I didn't mean to yell at you."

His voice was soft like he really was sorry, and I felt bad that I pushed him to yell. I also knew Riley, and I had a feeling his anger wasn't about me not coming to live with him.

"I have a problem," I admitted. "Eric's not moved out yet."

"Come home with me."

"That's why I'm calling!"

"Oh," he said in a quiet voice.

"I've got to go pick up some of my things."

"I've got to run into a team meeting, so you can take your time," he said. "I'll come get you."

I closed my eyes and cringed. I had completely forgotten that he had to rush to practice this morning. No wonder he was in such a shit mood. The Bulldogs season was tanking, and I didn't think they were making it to the playoffs.

"Shit, I'm sorry, I forgot you had practice. Forget it; I can stay at Katie's in the meantime."

"Fi, it's fine. I'll come get you when I'm done, okay?"

"Okay," I said in a small voice. His tone was so irritated that I was sure he was still mad at me. Especially since he hung up without saying goodbye.

I got a bad feeling in my gut. He said he wanted to prove to me that this could work, that he could make me happy, but I wasn't exactly happy with him right now. Maybe I should have pushed for the divorce.

I slid my phone into the back pocket of my jeans and walked into Katie's kitchen, where she was scrolling on her phone and pretending she hadn't been eavesdropping.

"I need to go get some things at my apartment," I told her.

Her brown eyes lit up. "Are you going to go to your husband's?"

I gritted my teeth. "Yes, even though he's irritated with me right now."

She smirked. "I'm sure you can make it up to him."

"Don't start."

"With your mouth!" she teased.

I laughed into my hands. "Katie, shut up."

She laughed and grabbed her keys. "Come on, girl, let's go."

We went back down to her car and headed to Fishtown, where Eric and I used to live together. I don't know how my life took this weird turn, but somehow it did. My ex was still living in the apartment I shared with him, but I was married to someone else. Katie dropped me off and asked me three times if I was okay, but I waved her off each time. Thankfully, Eric was out, which I was kind of surprised by since it was a Sunday. I didn't care, as long as he wasn't here.

I walked into the apartment and didn't notice a change in it at all. It was as if nothing had happened this past weekend, like Eric and I were still living here happily like we had been for the past couple of years. I bit my lip. Now I was starting to wonder if maybe I should move out and let Eric have the apartment.

I was still scared about what the future held and if this marriage with Riley could really last. Katie's words were haunting me. Could we be happy together? Is that what Riley really wanted? Or would he stick it out with me because he was loyal to a fault? He was my best and oldest friend, and I wanted him to be happy, even if that meant this marriage was a failure. I never wanted to be the cause of his unhappiness. I cared about him too much for that.

I carried my suitcase into the bedroom and opened it up. I dumped all my dirty clothes in the hamper in the closet. Except for the white wedding gown that was still in the garment bag. I smiled, thinking about how gentle Riley had been with it even though we had both been hammered out of our minds. He had taken the care to help me out of it and not damage it, even if he wanted to rip me out of it. I wondered if Eric would have done the same. I could kick myself for comparing the two men yet again.

I opened my closet and assessed what clothes I had hanging up there. I threw a couple dresses and blouses into my suitcase before packing up some of my casual jeans and t-shirts from the dresser across the room. I packed enough to have clothes at Riley's place for a few weeks since I wasn't sure what was going to happen.

I glanced around the room at the rumpled bedclothes on the bed. I vaguely remembered making the bed before we left for Vegas, which meant Eric was still sleeping here. I spied something black underneath the bed and got even more annoyed because he couldn't bother to pick up his dirty clothes off the floor. I bent down and felt myself throw up in my mouth a little bit. It was a black lacy thong. I did not wear black lacy thongs, so it definitely was not mine.

Unbelievable.

We were broken up now, so I couldn't be angry at him for sleeping with someone else, but to do it in my bed when I told him to get out of my apartment made my skin crawl.

I snapped a picture of it and sent it to Katie.

ME: *OMG! These aren't mine!*

KATIE: *Ewwwww!!! My eyes!*

ME: *KATIE!!! I don't think your brother has any intention of letting me keep this apartment!*

KATIE: *Girl, get out and move in with your hot husband!*

I sighed and glanced around the room; there were no boxes anywhere or even the appearance of Eric trying to move his stuff out. I sunk down to the floor because the bed now skeeved me out. I would never be able to sleep there again, knowing he had fucked some other woman in it. This was so totally fucked.

I felt my phone buzz again next to me on the carpet.

"Hey," I said into the phone when I saw it was Riley.

"Sorry, I'm just getting back to my place now. One of my teammates drove me to practice, but I know you're not far," he apologized.

I honestly didn't even notice he was late because I was still reeling from the fact that Eric had completely violated my personal space. I felt like he did it on purpose, and I wondered if those underwear were left there on purpose. A part of me also wondered how long they had been there. Was it just in the last couple days? Maybe Eric didn't notice we hadn't had sex in months because he was going to someone else for it. I felt sick to my stomach.

"Fi?" I heard Riley call, and he had definitely called my name more than once.

I shook my head. "Sorry, what?"

"Do you need some time?" he asked again.

"Uh huh," I answered noncommittally.

"Are you okay?"

"Nope!" I admitted with a shaky laugh.

He cleared his throat on the other line. "Hey, what's going on?"

"I don't think I can keep my apartment," I blurted.

"Oh...okay? Are you sure?" he asked.

Now I wasn't so sure if this was a good idea, but I knew there was no way I could stay here and sleep in this bed if I knew what Eric had done in it. To be honest, I also wasn't sure I could afford the rent on my author pay either. Riley didn't sound relieved like I thought he would, though; he sounded uncertain. My heart tightened in my chest. Now I was even more unsure about what I was about to do. Did I just invite myself to move in with Riley when we were already uncertain if we were going to stay married or not? Fuck, I should have gone back to Katie's. But Riley called my name again, and I blurted it all out.

"I think he fucked someone in my bed. After I told him to get out and he told me he would find a new place."

I cringed at the string of curses that flew out of Riley's mouth. I had to hold the phone away because of how loud he was yelling. "Okay, you have boxes?" he finally asked.

"Uh..." I looked around and then walked into the living room and searched the hall closet. "That's a big nope."

He sighed. "Okay, hang tight, I've got this. Get together what you can, and I'll be there soon."

The phone clicked, and I stared at my phone as the call log blinked. I then marched out of the apartment and down to the landlord's apartment on the first floor. She was a nice old Asian lady, who loved me but straight up hated Eric, so this was going to be hard.

"Fiona!" Mrs. Lee greeted me, and then her face turned down into a frown. "I've heard. But good for you. I never liked that man."

I sighed. "Okay, then you're not going to like what I say next."

"What is it?"

"I'm moving out, but Eric isn't. I know everything is in my name, but can we sign new lease papers so I can sign it over to him?" I asked.

"For you, I do. Otherwise, I would say no," she answered. Her black-brown eyes darted to my wedding ring. "You're wearing a wedding ring even though he didn't show up?"

Shit. "Um...I married someone else. When in Vegas, right?"

She barked out a laugh. "Come in and tell me all about it. Then we'll draft up those papers for you."

I really didn't want to explain the whole thing to my landlady, but she was a lonely old lady, and she had always been nice to me. I also really needed to get her to agree to this so I could get out of the lease without paying her any rent for the next month. So I sipped on green tea with her and told her the whole messy thing. Mrs. Lee was awesome about it when I angry-cried, and she patted my hand and gave me more tea.

"You know, I had an arranged marriage," she told me and sipped on her tea.

I cocked an eyebrow. "Oh?"

She nodded. "My parents were immigrants, very traditional Chinese, so they picked my husband. He was a good man."

"Did you love him?" I asked, genuinely curious. My landlady never talked about her husband; he died before I became a tenant.

Her eyes crinkled at her temples when she smiled. "I did, eventually. At first, we had to learn to be with each other, and the love stuff came later. You said you are friends?"

"The best of friends. We grew up together."

She smiled at me and patted my hand again. "I think you two will be fine."

I hoped she was right.

CHAPTER TEN

RILEY

When Fiona called me about wanting to come stay with me, I should have been ecstatic. Instead, I was pissy and snippy with her, even though it wasn't her I was mad at. Another meeting about how shit the team's penalty kill was and how I needed to stop it with the dumb penalties put me in a sour mood. I spent a lot of time in the media room with my defensive partner Jonesy going over the tape. Our special teams needed a lot of work, especially if we were going to dig ourselves out of this hole and get a spot in the playoffs. I liked to be optimistic, but I was looking at the stats, and I had my doubts.

When I had calmed down later and called Fi, and she told me what was going on, I immediately jumped into action. Luckily for her, I was a planner, and I kept moving boxes in my hall closet. I never knew with my career if I was going to be shipped off to another city, so I liked to be prepared. Especially since my contract was up come July, and I would become a free agent. The trade deadline was over, so I didn't have a fear of getting traded, but if the Bulldogs didn't want to re-sign me this summer, I had another problem. It was another reason why I was so worried about the team's standing this year. I had to stay in Philly, not for me, but for my wife. This was her home too, and I couldn't wrench her away from it. Not when I still needed to convince her that this thing between us was real.

I called Benny back. "Listen, buddy," I began. "I need your help."

"Okay, I'm turning around now. What's up?" he asked without hesitation.

That was the great thing about Michael Bennett. He was a good guy, and if you called him asking for help, he would be there in a heartbeat. Probably the same went for a lot of my teammates; if I didn't call Benny, my next call would have been Noah Kennedy. I swear, those two were in a battle to win the Lady Byng.

"I hate to ask this, but Fi's gotta move out of her apartment like today," I explained in a rush.

"Okay."

"Okay?" I asked in disbelief.

He laughed on the other line. "I'll be there in a few."

I owed him a drink or several. Plus, he was the biggest guy on the team, so even though I was pretty fit and muscular, I needed his muscles to help even more. At six-foot-four and two-hundred pounds of muscle, the guy was a beast.

I flipped off the lights in my condo and went downstairs to meet Benny. He rolled down the window of his SUV. "You sent me the address, right?" he asked.

I hitched a thumb back to my own SUV. "You want to

follow me? I have no idea how much stuff she has. Actually, girl has a shit ton of books."

He nodded. "No worries."

"Thanks for doing this, man. You're a real life-saver."

He smiled. "You owe me a beer."

I shook my head with a laugh in agreement. I got into my own SUV and drove to Fi's place in Fishtown. With the traffic, and there was always traffic in Philly, it took us a bit to get there, but I was sure she didn't mind the extra time. Benny and I both had to drive around the block a couple times to find parking, but I waited outside her building for him so we could walk up together. I hit the buzzer for her apartment, and she let us inside.

The apartment was a one-bedroom with a small living room/kitchen area. She was shoving clothes into suitcases when I followed her back into her bedroom. She shoved her hands into her hair in frustration and audibly groaned. "I don't know if we can get this all done today," she confessed with a pained look on her face.

"C'mere," I told her and pulled her into a hug. She sighed into my chest, and I stroked her hair. "It's gonna be fine; we'll do what we can. Plus, I have help."

She glanced over at Benny in the living room, already putting together the packing boxes. He waved a hand at her. "Hi. Michael Bennett," he called over.

She pulled away from me and crossed into the living room. She held her hand out to him. "I know. It's Benny, right? Fiona Gallagher."

Benny raised an eyebrow but shook her hand. His six-foot-four frame towered over everyone, so it was amusing to see my five-foot-nine wife look small next to him. Fi was not a tiny woman, but Benny made everyone else look petite.

"I hear you're Mrs. Riley now," Benny teased.

She made an annoyed face, and I covered my face in embarrassment. She shook off the look. "I guess I am, but I'm not changing my name."

I smiled at that. That, at least, was not a surprise. "Okay, what all in here needs to get packed away?" I asked, changing the subject.

"The books." She pointed at a standing bookshelf in the corner.

"All of them?" Benny asked.

She grinned. "All of them."

I took a box and started packing books into it. "Okay, let's get to work."

It took nearly all day, and it was around dinner time when we got all of Fi's stuff into the SUVs. In the end, she left behind her old bookcase because it was in really bad shape and her writing desk. I had a pretty decent desk in the second bedroom that I used as my office/guest room, and I told her I could get her some nice bookshelves. The majority of the stuff she had was books and some glassware that she wanted to keep. I noticed she left a pair of underwear and some paperwork on the kitchen counter, but I'd ask her about that later.

She ordered a pizza when we got back to my condo and started bringing in all the boxes. Benny was a champ and such a good friend for helping us out today; I think I owed him three beers.

I saw her starting to unpack all her boxes while Benny and I chowed down on the pizza. "Sweetheart, come on, leave it for tomorrow," I chastised her.

Benny gave me a sly look at the pet-name that had slipped out, but I ignored him.

She glared at me. "I need to get all my research books out."

"Fiona," I warned sternly.

"Aaron," she snapped back in the same tone of voice.

Seemed like she liked to use my first name either in bed or when she was mad at me. This was very confusing for me. Especially since my dick thought the angry tone of her voice meant it was time to come out and play. I shifted in my seat, uncomfortably.

Benny raised his eyebrows up at the sound of my first name. No one really used it, like no one ever really called him Michael. I wasn't even sure his girlfriend called him by his first name.

Benny scowled at his phone, so I nudged him. "What's up?"

He shook his head. "Fucking Stephanie."

I raised my eyebrows at that. "Huh."

He glared dark eyes at me. "What does that 'huh' mean?"

I shrugged. "I thought you broke up."

"No...it was just a disagreement."

I nodded and decided not to butt my nose into it anymore. I had already given him my opinion on that, and he didn't want to hear it anymore.

Fi stood up from her crouched position on the floor, where the moving boxes were now scattered around my living room. She walked over to the table in the kitchen and finally took a seat, and grabbed a slice of pizza.

"Who's Stephanie?" she asked Benny.

"My girlfriend...I think?" he explained with an unsure shrug.

Fi eyed me in question, but I shrugged. At this point, her guess was as good as mine. "You guess?" she asked.

Benny ran a brown hand down his face and stroked his beard. "We've been fighting. A lot. It's complicated."

"Buddy, you need to stay here tonight?" I asked.

Benny's brown eyes slid over to Fi, who was shoveling pizza in her mouth. "Um...no. Also, maybe you should talk to your wife before you ask me that?"

Fi shrugged. "It's his place."

"Sweetheart..." I sighed. I didn't want it to just be my place anymore.

She shrugged. "What? It is. What's going on with the girlfriend, Benny?"

Benny tipped back his head and laughed. "You two are perfect for each other, annoying and all up in my business."

Fi held her hands up in surrender. "Hey, I just met you. I don't even know your girlfriend."

He sighed. "Sorry, you're right. We got into another argument. I should probably get home and defuse the situation."

I gave Fi a warning look to drop it. If I couldn't get Benny to talk about his weird relationship, I didn't think she could either.

Benny went to go clear his plate, but Fi waved her hand at him. "No, leave it; you were such a big help today." She put a hand on his arm. "Thank you."

He smiled at her. "It was nice meeting you, Fi."

She waved at him through mouthfuls of pizza.

I laughed and stood up to walk Benny to the door. He grinned at me. "I guess you're all in, huh?" he asked.

I nodded and fist-bumped him. "Thanks, man. I really owe you."

He pointed at me. "Several beers."

"You got it. Are you sure you don't need to stay here tonight?" I offered again.

Sometimes Stephanie needed time to cool down, so Benny stayed in the guest room. It had been happening with more frequency, and I didn't understand why they were still together.

He shook his head. "Nah, but maybe you should clear that with your wife before offering in the future. You're not a bachelor anymore."

I nodded. He was right about that. I had to remember that it wasn't just me anymore. I had Fi here now, and I didn't like that she referred to it as my place. I wanted it to be her home too. I didn't want her thinking that this was temporary. Not when she had been living rent-free in my heart since we were seventeen.

He was out the door without another word, and I started cleaning up the empty plates and boxes.

"Oh, leave it," Fi said to me. "Or at least let me help."

"No," I argued and looked at her pointedly. "I got it. Finish your food."

She frowned at me. "You already helped me out so much today. I have to imagine you're as exhausted as I am. More so since I know you had practice today."

She didn't push the issue further but helped clean up once she was done.

"So, Benny seems nice," she started.

I grinned. "He's kind of my best friend."

She put her hands on her hips. "I thought I was your best friend."

"Oh, Fi, you are, but Benny's like my best bud on the team."

She laughed. "I was just teasing you. So what's the deal with his girlfriend?"

I sighed. "I don't know. I think they're about to break up."

Her face got sad at that. "Oh...that's too bad."

I shrugged. "I don't think they're meant to be."

She hummed as she rinsed off the plates and loaded up my dishwasher. I didn't try to tell her not to do it because I didn't want to get into another fight.

I leaned against the counter. "Hey, I want to talk to you about something."

She closed the lid of the dishwasher and started it. "What's up?"

I reached out to push her hair behind her ear. My hand lingered on her cheek, and I wanted to kiss her again. I wanted to do a lot of things to her, but I was exhausted from not getting a lot of sleep last night and a rough practice today. "Fi, this is not just my place."

She pulled away from me and crossed her arms. "It is, and I feel bad moving in here so soon."

"Sweetheart, I want you here. I want my wife to live with me, not live in hipster Fishtown away from me."

She rolled her eyes at my hipster comment, but we both knew it was true. Not that I could say anything; I lived in the ritzy side of the city.

"What are you trying to say?" she asked.

"I want this to be your home, too. I should have asked you if it was okay to offer Benny to stay here."

"I wouldn't have minded."

"I know, sweetheart, but I should have asked you first."

She nodded. "Okay."

I ran a hand through my hair. "I need a shower."

"Yeah, you stink!" she teased.

I headed into my bedroom to take a shower. When I came out, she was on the floor in the bedroom, trying to figure out where to put all her clothes.

"Oh, leave it for the night," I told her.

I dropped the towel from around my waist and put on a clean pair of boxers and pajama bottoms to sleep in. I hated sleeping with a shirt on, and it seemed like Fi didn't mind it by the way her gaze scanned over my body. I grinned at her, but as much as I wanted nothing more than to wrestle with her on my bed and hear that sexy moan of hers again, I was too damn tired for that. I slid into the bed and patted the empty side next to me. She closed the lid of her suitcase and walked over to the bed. She sat on the side next to me timidly, and then swung her legs over the length of the bed and finally laid down. I flicked the lamp off and plunged us into darkness.

She shifted onto her side, and I ran my hand down the length of her arm to finally rest against her hip. "Night, Fi," I breathed on her neck.

She craned her head to look up at me. "Night, Riley."

I bent down to kiss her softly goodnight. "I'm glad you came home with me. I really want this to work between us. Though I'm sorry about your ex."

"That's not your fault," she sighed.

I shifted so I was leaning over her and brushed her hair out of her eyes. My dick was definitely lifting up in interest again, but I was way too tired for that, and by the look on her face, I knew she was too. We had a lifetime of that ahead of us; I could wait.

I smiled at seeing my wedding ring on my finger as I caressed her cheek.

"Sweetheart, I know it's not my fault, but I was glad to be there for you."

She smiled, but it didn't reach her eyes. She leaned into my hand and kissed it sweetly. "Thank you."

"Fiona, I'm going to do everything in my power to make you happy. I promise you that."

She didn't look convinced. "Ri, can we talk about all this heavy stuff later? It's been a long day."

I cupped her face in my hands and kissed her gently goodnight. "Okay, sweetheart, let's get some sleep. I have to fly out tomorrow, and there was a Succubus who kept me up all night last night," I joked.

She playfully slapped my arm, and this time her smile was for real. I rolled her onto her side and pulled her towards me. I fell asleep, cradling her smaller form in my arms. I could get used to this. If only she would let me.

CHAPTER ELEVEN

FIONA

I woke to a rustling of the drawers and slid my eyes open to see Riley getting dressed in the dark. I still felt like a stranger here in his entirely way too modern and nice condo. It was like his wealth was smacking me in the face, and I didn't think I deserved to live here with him. Even if the ring on my finger told me that I should.

My hand went to my phone to check the time, and it wasn't that early. I probably should have already been awake. I had some more drafting to do, and I needed to get going on all the unpacking. I wanted everything to be done when he got back into town.

I sat up in bed. "Why are you getting dressed in the dark like a weirdo?" I asked.

He flinched at my voice. "Jesus, Fi, you scared the shit out of me."

I smirked but flipped on the lamp on the bedside table next to me. "Turn on a light!" I got out of bed and walked over to him. He stood in front of his massive walk-in closet, trying to pick out a tie to wear.

"Help me pick," he urged. He held up the red tie to his crisp white dress shirt and then the blue striped one.

I took the blue one in my hands and put it up against his chest. "Blue," I said and handed it back to him with a yawn. "Blue's your color. It brings out your eyes."

"I made coffee. Wasn't sure if you were going to wake up, or I would have made you breakfast," he told me.

My heart sang in my chest at that. This big strong man trying to take care of me was confusing to me. "Wait, you cook?" I asked, astonished.

He furrowed his brow at me. "Yeah...had to learn to be on my own. Truth be told, Benny taught me."

"Really?"

"He's a good cook."

I stretched my arms over my head and yawned again. I pretended not to notice his crystal blue eyes gazing at my chest. I adjusted my tank top, as it had been knocked askew during sleep, and my tits were practically falling out of it. He was a man, so of course, he noticed. Not that there was that much to notice; I wasn't exactly top-heavy.

"I guess it's time to tell you that marrying me was a bad decision because I'm not really good at cooking."

He laughed. "Oh, I remember home ec."

I frowned. "Sometimes, I forget how much you know about me. Sometimes it's nice, but other times, I wish you would forget."

"Go get your coffee. You seem grumpy this morning."

He wasn't wrong about that.

I walked out of the room and into the sparkling kitchen, with its stainless steel appliances and granite countertops. I was seriously out of my element when it came to his man. At the same time, I felt a sense of pride swell in my chest.

I spent many years cheering Riley on in the stands when we were kids. Especially after his dad left and my mom helped take him to his hockey games while his single-mother worked two jobs to provide. I admired our moms for their fierce friendship and the way my parents had helped out Paula. No wonder they were pleased when Riley stepped in and married me. He had already been a part of the family for a long time. Now it was official.

At least until he realized that this was all a mistake and decided to divorce me. I wouldn't blame him when he finally came to his senses. He left my life for hockey before, and I couldn't imagine he wanted me like this in his life permanently. It was only a matter of time.

I poured myself a cup of coffee and found a greek yogurt in his fridge, then parked myself on one of the barstools at the island. I put my coffee cup down when Riley walked into the kitchen. He bent over to land a soft and tender kiss on my lips. I hadn't been expecting that, but I melted into the feeling of his soft lips gently pressed up against mine. Now I regretted being so tired last night and not having my way with him before he was back on the road.

"I've got to get going," he apologized.

I waved a hand at him. "Go on, then."

He looked around at all the boxes in his condo and looked at me again. Then he went into a drawer in the kitchen and handed me a single key. "Here. You need your own key now."

I stared him down. "What makes you think I'm actually going to leave this place? I've got a lot of stuff to do."

He shook his head. "Don't hole yourself up while I'm gone, okay? Also, I'm sorry to leave you in the lurch to unpack everything by yourself."

"It's fine; you helped enough. It's just a couple days. I'll be fine. Go, before you're late."

"We can go get you some new bookshelves when I get back, okay?"

I waved him off again. "Go, you're gonna be late."

His hand cupped my face, and I felt the cold metal of his wedding ring against my cheek as he kissed me again. Honestly, if this was what being married to him was going to be like, I thought maybe I could get used to it. The deep kisses goodbye were some of the best kisses I had ever received. When he pulled away and left the condo, I felt an odd pang in my heart. I didn't know what to make of it.

Riley being away for his job didn't really bother me all that much. I was kind of a recluse, so I liked being alone. But him being on the road being surrounded by women at bars who were more beautiful than me did have me a little worried. I mean, was it a thing that athletes cheated on their wives while they were on the road? Was that something we should have talked about? I knew how he felt about cheaters, but I was still scared to ask. I also didn't know why I was so worried when I was the one who asked for a divorce, and Riley had convinced me to give this marriage a chance.

Maybe it was finding that thong under my bed yesterday that was making me feel this way. It also made me wonder if that had been the first time Eric had someone else in our bed. It made my skin crawl, so I had to busy myself with unpacking all of my things. I didn't want to think about it because, in the back of my mind, it explained how Eric didn't realize that we hadn't had sex in three months.

I was honestly surprised I hadn't heard from Eric like at all. He must have come home yesterday surprised to see I had moved all my things out and left the apartment to him. I was still mad about it because it had been my apartment in the first place, but I couldn't stay there. Not hearing from him solidified that not marrying him had been the right choice. I think our relationship had ended a long time ago, but we kept going through the motions. The not having sex thing should have been the first sign, but I guess being so busy working on my book, I didn't notice. That didn't mean it didn't still hurt, though. It made me actually kind of glad Riley wasn't here because I could be alone with my thoughts for a couple days and really consider whether jumping into this marriage was a good idea.

I spent all morning unpacking my things, but I still didn't have a bookcase, so I ended up putting my books in piles in Riley's office. He said he wanted to get me a nice bookshelf because the one I had in my old apartment was pretty much trashed. It wasn't ideal, but I could live with it for now.

Around lunchtime, Katie called to check in on me. I ran a hand through my hair in frustration when I saw her name across my phone screen. I picked it up. "Are you checking up on me?" I asked, even though I knew the answer.

She laughed on the other end. "Sorry...yes. How are you doing?"

"Okay...I guess. Riley left for the road this morning, so I've kind of just been unpacking. I haven't even written today yet."

"Girl, get to writing!"

"I will. Other things are more important right now," I

told her. I wedged the phone between my ear and shoulder and walked over to the dishwasher so I could start unloading it. I might not be a good cook, but the least I could do while Riley was gone was manage the household. I set the phone down on the counter and put it on speaker. "Hang on, I'm putting you on speaker so I can unload the dishes."

She chuckled on the other line. "Ha! Look at you being a housewife."

"Shut it. I can't cook, so at least I can clean."

"Fi, how are you doing really? I know everything has been hard for you."

I sighed and unloaded the plates into Riley's cabinet. This man was surprisingly organized. And clean. Like so fucking clean. He wasn't the messy teenaged Riley I remembered. "I'm fine. I guess? I don't know."

"Things with Riley are good? Are you happy you're sticking things out with him?"

"I'm not sure yet. One of his teammates came to help me move in here, so most of yesterday was spent getting all my stuff out of the apartment in Fishtown. I think we both were exhausted last night from the packing and from jet lag. We ended up going to sleep early."

"Uh huh."

I finished unloading the dishwasher and took the phone with me into the bedroom, where I found Riley's hamper. It was full, and I wasn't sure when was the last time he changed the sheets. I stripped those off the bed and started sorting the wash.

"Don't worry about me," I reassured Katie.

Since I had started dating her brother, Katie and I had really bonded. Maybe it was because I was a writer and she was an English professor at UPenn. We had a lot in common, and I had been excited at the prospect that we would be sisters, but that wasn't a good enough reason for me to marry her brother. When her marriage had broken up, I had been the shoulder she cried on while Eric told her to just suck it up. I guess I should have known then that he was a complete and utter dickweed.

She sighed into the phone on her line. "Look, I need to tell you something."

Fear struck my heart at the tone of her voice. Now I was worried. "What's wrong? Are you okay?" I asked.

"No, it's not about me. It's just..." She trailed off, and I could almost see her face on the other line scrunching up with anxiety.

"Katie, what?" I asked, frustrated now.

"I ran into Brock on Campus today."

Oh.

Katie's ex-husband was a professor of history at UPenn. It was a big campus, so it wasn't like she was constantly bumping into him. Although, from what Katie had told me, they had a very amicable divorce. No cheating or anything; it just wasn't working out for them. I think part of it was because he wanted kids, and Katie had always been a part of the no-kids club, just like her brother.

"Hey, I can practically see the pity look on your face right now, but it's fine. Brock and I didn't work out, but we're still friends."

"Okay, so why are you telling me about this?"

She sighed. "You know the underwear you found?"

I made a gagging sound. "Don't remind me."

"Well...it probably wasn't the first time."

"What?" I nearly screeched.

"Brock told me he heard about you and Eric breaking up, and then he told me he wasn't surprised because he saw

Eric out one night with a leggy blonde that looked like one of Brock's students."

I dropped the detergent into the washer and slammed the lid shut with an angry bang. "What the actual fuck?"

"I'm sorry."

"Your brother's a Grade A asshole."

"Can confirm. I'm sorry again."

I sighed and turned the dial on the machine to get it going. "Thanks for telling me. I really dodged a bullet, huh?"

"Fi, I'm so sorry about what happened with my brother, but I'm really glad you two didn't get married."

"Yeah, me too. I better go; I've been procrastinating on writing."

"Sure. You want to get dinner tomorrow?"

"Definitely."

After hanging up with Katie, I ran around the condo doing more chores, but mostly it was because I was still procrastinating. It was late when I finally sat down at my computer to work on the novel. I only ended up procrastinating more on Twitter; after all, if you weren't dicking around on Twitter with all the other writers, could you even call yourself a writer?

I was so close with this draft, but I saw the deadline looming ahead, and the panic was starting to set in. I really needed to finish this final chapter so I had time to proofread it and send it off to my publisher. I ended up banging out the words, but I didn't really like it. I knew I needed to come at it with fresh eyes in the morning, so I closed my laptop and headed into the bedroom for some much-needed rest.

Sliding into the sheets of Riley's big bed felt oddly cold without his warm body there beside me. We had spent three whole days being married and sharing a bed together, and I had gotten used to him being next to me. There was a pang in my chest at being without him, and as I was nodding off into dreamland, I realized it was because I missed him. Good God, it hadn't even been a full day. What was wrong with me?

CHAPTER TWELVE

RILEY

*A*s soon as I got on the plane heading to Minnesota, of all places, my heart yearned for Fi. I hated that I had to leave her all alone in my condo for the next couple days. We had only been married for a couple days, and we didn't really get to talk about the expectations.

I wanted this to work because I had loved her since I was a teen, and I didn't want to let her go again. I was also slightly worried that I would get back from the road to find she had disappeared, leaving me with divorce papers. I felt like we clicked so perfectly. Being married to that woman seemed right to me. Why else had she agreed to marry me so quickly? I wanted to text her and tell her I missed her already, but that seemed so desperate. Fiona was like a stray cat, she spooked easily, and I wanted to coax her inside and take care of her. If she let me.

I put my earbuds in and cracked open the pages of her

second book from where I had bookmarked it yesterday. I had to kind of look up what happened in the first book because I read it so long ago that I forgot what happened. I had read the very first draft of it when she was still in college, so I couldn't remember what had changed.

I was amazed at how much she had improved in her writing. I beamed, thinking about how proud I was of her and all she had accomplished. It made me grit my teeth more that her family and the man she was supposed to marry instead of me had been wholly unsupportive of her work. I didn't get it. Fi was amazing, and she only quit her job because that first book sold so well.

I must have been absent-mindedly rubbing the ring on my left hand because Girard, our captain, nudged my shoulder. "What's with you?" he asked.

I marked my page in the book and turned to him. "Huh?" I asked.

G cocked his head at me. "Ri, is that a wedding ring?" he asked, and his eyes got wide.

I sighed. It wasn't like I was planning on keeping it a secret. Benny already knew, but he wasn't a big gossip and knew when to keep things close to the vest. G was like the dad of the team, even though he was only a few years older than me. I felt like he was going to berate me for my weird marriage. I hadn't even told my agent yet because I knew what he was going to say, that I should have gotten a prenup, but I was definitely not going to have that conversation with Fi. If she really wanted to move forward with the divorce, she could have whatever she wanted from me. But I knew her, and I knew she wouldn't take any of my money. She only moved in with me because her ex basically refused to move out of her apartment.

I ran a hand through my hair and twisted the ring around on my finger again. "Um, yeah, it is," I confessed.

"I didn't even know you were engaged," he commented.

"Uh...I wasn't," I admitted.

He eyed me with a confused look and raised both of his eyebrows. "Okay, you need to explain right now."

I sighed and told him the whole story. When I was done, he was looking at me as if I was certifiable. "Don't judge me!" I exclaimed.

G pursed his lips. "So let me get this straight. You married your best friend, she asked for a divorce, but now you have a couple of months to convince her that you should stay married?"

I hung my head. "You know, when you say it out loud, it sounds even worse."

He chuckled and clapped me on the shoulder. "What's this woman like? I've never seen you hung up on someone before." He turned around in his seat to call over to Hallsy, who sat behind us. "Yo, Hallsy, I owe you twenty bucks."

"For what?" Hallsy asked, and I looked up at him, standing up and leaning over my seat.

Hallsy was a dark-skinned Black guy from Canada and probably one of the best forwards I had ever skated alongside. Actually, there were a lot of amazing players on this team, but we weren't gelling right this season. Hallsy's dark brown eyes sparkled with mirth at the current conversation.

G grinned. "Our boy Riley over here has gone and fallen in love!"

Hallsy laughed, and his dark corkscrew coiled hair bounced with the motion. "Ooh, I knew they would get you soon! TJ's next!"

"HARD PASS!" TJ yelled from a couple seats in front of us.

I punched G lightly in the shoulder, but I grinned. "Dicks!" I swore at them.

G dramatically rubbed his shoulder, but I knew it didn't hurt. "You're gonna tell me all about her," he demanded.

I held up my book. "She's fiercely private. Now let me read my wife's book in peace."

I laughed at his confused expression and spent the rest of the plane ride to my home state devouring Fi's book. I was completely amazed that the things on print had come out of her head. I would be lying if I didn't say I flipped to the back jacket flap a couple times to see her author photo staring back at me because damn, did I miss my wife of three days already, and I wondered if she would ever miss me like that too.

Depending on travel plans, we usually got to a city a day before game day, which was nice because it gave us time to get settled into the hotel, do any meetings, and then be fresh for game day skate and all the pre-game rituals. So once we all got settled into the hotel, I went to go visit my mom. Mom tried to come to games when we played the Minnesota Tundra, but it didn't always work out. Sometimes she was too busy grading papers.

Even though I told her I would pay off the house for her and take care of her, she wouldn't hear of it. She loved her job as a high school English teacher, and even though she complained about the bad pay, I knew it was what she wanted. At least she was only working one job these days. Guilt had wrapped around my chest every day as a teen, knowing she was working herself into an early grave when Dad left.

Dad was basically dead to me. We hadn't talked in years. That was kind of what happened when you were the one to find your dad in a compromising position with his secretary, and then he left your mom for her. I didn't think I would ever forgive him for that, so I never returned any of his calls. Ever. Fuck that guy.

After Dad left, things were hard for my mom, and the Gallaghers really stepped in to help. It's why Fi and I had gotten so close in the first place. I worried about my mom; it had just been me and her for so long that I was a wreck when I left for the NHL as an eighteen-year-old. When Mom got remarried a few years ago to Ted, I felt a sigh of relief, but I was uneasy about it. Ted was a good guy, and he made her happy, but I was a bit wary of him. I used to think my dad was a good guy too.

Mom lived in a small split-level in the suburbs of St. Paul, so it was lucky for me that the Tundra played in that city, and I was able to make the trip out to see her. I opened the door to my childhood home and was greeted by my mom and step-dad Ted, who were in the living room watching TV. Being six-foot-tall, I had to bend down to my mom's five foot nothing frame to hug her and kiss her on the cheek.

"Oh, honey, it's good to see you," she greeted me with a smile. "Did you eat yet?"

I smirked. "Yeah, Mom. I'm good."

Ted shook my hand, and I took it firmly, keeping eye contact with him the whole time. "Ted," I stated flatly.

"Riley, good to see you," he greeted and pretended not to hear the tension in my voice.

I followed my mom into her kitchen and took a seat at the table, hunching my big frame into the wood-backed chair. Mom made a cup of tea and sat in the chair across from me.

She had this funny look on her face that I couldn't place. "What?" I asked, annoyed that I was about to get a lecture.

She set her teacup down and sighed. "I have to ask. Why did you do it?"

"Do what?"

"Marry Fiona."

I looked down at my shoes. "What do you mean 'why?' She's my best friend; it felt right."

She looked unsure and ran a hand through her short-cropped, pale blond hair. She gave me a sympathetic smile and put her hand on top of mine. "Baby, I love you, and I want to see you happy, but...is your marriage real?"

"What?" I scoffed. "What are you talking about? Of course it's real."

She dropped her gaze from me and ran a hand over the rim of her teacup. She breathed out and looked back up at me. "Look, I love you, and I love Fiona, and I would love it if you two were really together. But I know you only did this because you couldn't stand to see her so hurt."

I stared back at her, my jaw twitching in annoyance. That was only partly true, but I didn't want to admit to my mom that the reason I did it was that Fiona was the love of my life.

"You married her immediately after she was left at the altar; she didn't even get a chance to grieve over the end of her five-year relationship," she explained. She must have seen the sea of torment spread across my face because she squeezed my hand. "I'm sorry, but I felt like you rushed into a marriage neither of you was really prepared for."

I scratched the back of my neck because I didn't know what to say. This was exactly why Fi had asked me for a divorce the next day. We had rushed into this marriage, and now I had trapped her in it with my ridiculous romantic notions that I could get her to fall in love with me. Maybe she should have kept her apartment. Fuck, now I felt like an asshole.

We were quiet for a minute because I honestly didn't know what to say. My mom was right; I had made a mess of things, and it might have been at the cost of the best friendship I ever had.

"She asked for a divorce," I admitted.

My mom's eyes softened. "Oh, baby, I'm so sorry."

I cringed, knowing now I had to explain the next part to my mom. "But we're not getting one. At least not yet."

She narrowed her eyes at me. "What do you mean not yet? Aaron Michael Riley! Did you get Fiona pregnant already?"

My face went as white as a ghost. "What? No! We always use—" I cut myself off and shook my head. I was not getting into my sex life with my mom, that was for sure. "I think it's too early to tell for that, but no. We agreed to give it a shot. I have a couple months to prove to her that this marriage is gonna work."

I hid my hands behind my face but noticed she wasn't saying anything. When I pulled my hands away from my face, my mom stared back at me with the most amused look I'd ever seen on her face. Then she tipped back her head and laughed like a hyena.

"Okay..." I trailed off, utterly confused.

Mom kept laughing until she had to wipe tears from her eyes. "I'm pretty sure I read a romance book with this same exact plot."

I gave her a sour look. I didn't even want to think about

my mom reading romance books. Ew, gross. Nope, not going to think about that one at all. Moms don't have sex, nope, never.

Mom leaned back in her chair and cocked her head at me. "So, I'm gonna ask you again," she began. "Why did you marry Fiona?"

I ran a hand down my face and sighed in defeat. "Because I'm tired of the single life, and I think Fi and I could be really great together."

"Aaron," she warned sternly.

"Fine! It's because I'm in love with her."

Mom patted my hand. "There you go. Glad you finally admitted it."

I looked at her dumbfounded. "You knew?"

"Since you were teens, but then you started going out with that one girl." Mom looked up at the ceiling, trying to remember, but I knew.

Stacey Graves. Or better known as the biggest mistake of my life.

Fi and I had been fooling around a lot back then, but then she heard that Stacey really liked me. She encouraged me to ask her out, and since I thought Fi didn't see me as anything more than a fuck buddy, I did. Stacey was nothing like Fi; she was dramatic and high-maintenance, but she was also hot, and I was a horny teenager. Fi had started dating the captain of the hockey team, Jackson. It may have caused him and me to not be friends anymore when I threatened to straight-up murder him if he messed around on her.

"Stacey! I didn't like that girl."

"I was a kid!" I protested.

"I know, baby. So are you gonna fight for your marriage or what?"

I shrugged. "I don't even know how!"

My mom smiled widely at me. "Start by telling her how you feel."

"What if she doesn't feel the same way?"

Mom shrugged. "Well, you won't know if you don't try."

CHAPTER THIRTEEN

FIONA

I dropped down into a seat at a table in the coffee house in Rittenhouse Square, where I was meeting my agent, Brad. I didn't know how I got so lucky to find a lit agent that was local to me. Brad had just moved back to Philly from NYC, and I was so glad because making the trip to get together with him could be tiresome. Also, he knew I didn't like to leave my apartment.

I hadn't told anyone in my literary circle about my busted up wedding day and had planned to hole myself up in Riley's condo until I finished my book. But Brad saw my stories on Instagram and figured out quickly that I was not on my honeymoon. He basically harassed me into getting coffee with him. Plus, he knew I was procrastinating if I was on Instagram.

Riley had gotten in late last night, and then he had to go to morning skate before I woke up, so we kept missing each other. I remembered waking up last night to him, shifting into the bed and slinging his arm across my waist to hold me close, but otherwise, it felt like he was a ghost.

I set down my purse and my cup of coffee at the table. I glared at my agent. "You suck, you know that?" I asked.

Brad stuck out his tongue, ever the professional, but also why I was so glad he was my agent. He wore his thick dark hair in twists again. His dark brown, almost black eyes drifted down to the ring on my finger, and he looked pointedly at it. "Okay, you have to explain everything to me," he urged.

I sighed and twisted the simple band around my finger. Katie had picked out some pretty simple wedding bands, which was perfectly okay with me. I had examined the simple band with the mil-grain detail and knew it felt like the right ring for me.

"Um...so I got married?"

"Yes, I gathered that, but someone told me not to your partner of five years!" he exclaimed and waved his hand around, all flustered. Someone named Katie probably.

I sighed and put my head in my hands. "Yeah...Eric didn't bother to show up. You remember my friend Riley, right?"

"The hockey player? The hot one with the muscles as big as my head?"

"His muscles aren't that big," I muttered, but Brad laughed.

It was so a lie; he did have really big muscles. Shit, now I was thinking about those muscles lifting me up and fucking me against the wall. Hello, hormones. Why did my best friend/husband have to be so hot? And why hadn't we had sex since our honeymoon?

"Okay, let me get this straight. The guy you were dating

for five years left, you hanging, and you married someone else instead?" he asked.

"I know, it's wild! I asked for a divorce, but he wants to stick it out. He thinks we could be happy together," I explained.

"Oh, honey," Brad lamented. "I think you married the right man."

I took a drink of my black coffee so I didn't have to respond. "Can we please stop talking about this and focus on this book that I still don't know how to finish?"

Brad shook his head. "Um, no, I need more details. Like first, what did he do to convince you? Also, are you still living with your ex?"

I sighed and ran a shaky hand through my hair. I thought this was going to be a meeting to focus on my writing, not about my very weird marriage to my best friend. "He asked me to give him a couple months to prove it. And no, I ended up moving in with Riley. Mostly because I found a pair of underwear that weren't mine under my bed!"

Brad scrunched up his face. "Ew!"

"Right? Eric's sister found out he had been cheating on me."

A scowl appeared across Brad's face. Brad was in his mid-forties and had been in this business for a while. He was also so totally a dad. He was Papa Bear to all his clients, which was one of the things I loved about him. "What an asshole!"

I laughed and nodded.

"So, I want to talk about your book...but are you okay?"

"Riley's been on the road this week, so I've had some time to think, and I think it's a blessing I didn't marry Eric. I think our relationship was over a long time ago, and maybe we were just holding on. But enough about that. Can we please talk about my writing?"

"Okay, fine. Where are you at?"

"I need to proofread, but almost done."

His eyes cut across to me suspiciously. "Okay, but what's the problem?"

I took another gulp of my drink and put a hand to my chin.

What was the problem?

That I thought it was hot garbage and everyone would want to dump the book right in the trash. That I wasn't actually as skilled as I thought at stringing words into complete sentences. I thought that I was a fraud, and my publisher was going to figure that out when they read the stinking pile of crap that flew into their inbox.

"I think it's bad," I admitted.

Brad drummed his hands on the table in front of me. "Why?"

I shrugged. "Everything I do is awful. It feels like I have the thoughts inside my brain, but my hands turn them into ash on the keyboard."

Brad raised an eyebrow. "Okay...I think this is your imposter syndrome rearing its ugly head again."

I frowned and took another sip of my coffee. He might have been onto something. I had inked a three-book deal with my publisher, and they were so far happy with my results. Book two had hit lists, not great, but it did okay, but I was so worried that this last book was going to tank. Or that everyone was going to hate it.

"Fi, turn in the book. It's a first draft; stop holding on to it," Brad urged.

"I'm not ready!" I whined.

"You'll never be ready!" he exclaimed. "Again, it's a first draft."

I pouted and crossed my arms. "Okay, fine, but I need to proofread it before turning it in."

I saw my phone light up with a notification, and I couldn't help the smile from spreading across my face when I saw it was a text from Riley.

RILEY: *Get off Twitter, and finish your book!*

Brad nudged me with his foot. "Okay, what is that face? Who just texted you?"

My face fell in horror. "What? Nothing, no one!"

Brad's face had a grin so mischievous that I wanted to slap it off of him.

"Oh my God, is it your husband? I need to meet this guy because your boring ex never made you smile like that!"

I sipped at my coffee and pretended not to hear that last part. It didn't stop me from texting Riley under the table while Brad and I talked about my plans for stories after this trilogy was done. I had a few ideas but couldn't really settle on one.

ME: *Don't tell me what to do!*

RILEY: *Just words of encouragement, sweetheart.*

ME: *Gah, I think it sucks real bad.*

RILEY: *I can't wait to get home so I can read it.*

ME: *You want to read it?*

RILEY: *I NEED to know what happens next.*

ME: *You read the second book?*

RILEY: *Yes!!! Gimme the next one!*

ME: *Ugh, don't you have some pre-game rituals you need to do?*

RILEY: *Yeah, I was wondering where you were. I just got home, about to take my pre-game nap.*

ME: *Work thing. I'll see you later.*

I looked up from my phone when I realized Brad had stopped talking and I hadn't been paying attention. He glared at me and threw a napkin at my head. "You're texting him, aren't you?"

"No..."

Brad grinned again. "Okay, you're so in love."

"What?" I balked.

I bit my nails and thought. Could I be? With Riley? Could you fall in love with someone that quickly? Was that even possible? I definitely had been lying in his bed alone the past couple nights with a sense of yearning. Jury was still out on if that yearning came from my heart or from between my legs. I wasn't sure I was ready for the answer yet.

I directed my attention back to my agent and shook my head vigorously. "I don't know about that."

Brad raised his eyebrows, and I put my phone away so I wouldn't be distracted any longer. Brad was still smiling at me. "So...I've never been to a hockey game before. You think you can teach me?"

"Do you want to come over and watch the game with me?"

He nodded. "Yes, because I really think you need a break from writing tonight. You need to relax."

One thing my agent Brad didn't understand was that watching hockey was the least relaxing thing in the world for me. Especially when I was a rabid fan, and I was watching my husband take too many goddamn penalties and getting checked into the boards a little too hard. I took a swig of my beer, and my eyes darted across the flatscreen TV, watching the players shuffle down the ice.

Brad took another slice of pizza from off the coffee table. I had invited Katie over too, and they were arguing about whether my life was playing out like a fake marriage trope or a marriage of convenience trope.

Dicks.

"What position does your man play again?" Brad asked with a sparkle in his eyes.

I flicked him off. "Riley's a D-man."

"I'm sorry, what?" Brad asked with a laugh.

I shook my head. "Defense or blueliner."

"It's why he's so big," Katie joked.

I laughed.

Riley was a solid mass of muscle in front of the net, but he wasn't the biggest guy on the team. He was a skilled skater and good at getting in front of the offense. I watched number twenty-two skate across the ice into the face-off circle. Benny was the biggest player on the team, and on skates, he looked way taller than his six-foot-four height.

I pointed at the screen. "Riley's not even the biggest guy on the team; Benny is."

"He's dreamy," Katie cooed.

I shook my head at her. "Calm your tits; he's taken. I think. He's the one who helped me move in here. He seems like a total sweetheart. He's Riley's best friend on the team."

Brad whistled as he looked around the place again. I was aware that Riley's condo was impressive. From the granite countertops to the wide windows with the nice city view, he did live in luxury. It was so weird that I was also living here now.

"He's worked really hard all his life for these millions," I defended him.

Brad held up his hands. "Hey, I didn't say anything. So explain it again, how do you have an offsides in hockey if it's like, you know, on ice?"

I ignored his question because I saw Riley get checked hard into the boards. Right in the fucking numbers. Where was that fucking penalty?

"Shit!" I yelled.

Brad and Katie scanned the TV to see what I was seeing. "What happened?" Katie asked.

"Riley took a bad hit," I yelled, not particularly at them.

I chewed on my nails. I loved this sport, but I worried so much about the damage it could do on the players. Especially now that one of those players was my husband. Riley had minor injuries throughout his career, but being the person on the sidelines watching him wreck his body, I was afraid for him.

"Is he gonna be okay?" Katie asked.

I nodded, but I wasn't that confident as I watched Riley hop onto the bench for the shift change.

I loved watching Riley play hockey. I spent most of my life watching him on the ice, and it always made me so proud to see his accomplishments. I watched his big body tear across the ice, and I could almost hear the delicious sound of his skates biting into the surface. I loved the sounds of the game, that scritchy-scratchy noise of blades and the thwack of the puck into the netting. Watching hockey on TV was fine, but it was nothing like live hockey. I could have asked Riley for tickets tonight, but I didn't want to overstep my bounds. I knew I was a wife now, and I should be in the wife's room or whatever, but I wasn't sure if his teammates even knew he was married. Maybe he took his ring off when he left. We hadn't really talked about it.

I jumped and cheered when I saw Riley block the shot

and the Bulldogs get possession of the puck. Noah Kennedy had the breakaway and scored the game-winning goal. "Fucking right, baby, that's how you do it!" I exclaimed.

Katie and Brad laughed at me. Brad shook his head. "You really are a hockey fan."

"I'm from Minnesota; it's kind of not a choice!"

"Oh, I almost forgot!" Brad exclaimed and reached down into his bag to pull out a paperback book. He handed it to me, and I nearly peed myself with laughter at the cover with the half-naked man with ice skates in his hand. "My wife really liked this one and thought you might like it."

"Oh yeah, I think I read the first one in this series. They are very steamy."

Brad smiled. "I've met Ruby a couple times. She does the whole self-pub thing."

I thought about doing the self-pub thing before, and despite what people said about it being easier, it was not. You had all the control, which was great, but also bad because you were in charge of everything yourself. It was a lot of work. I didn't think I was built for that.

I peered at the name on the cover in interest and flipped to the back, where a brunette in cat-eye glasses stared back at me.

Katie's eyes sparkled. "I know! You should write a steamy romance book next!"

Brad had his agent face on. "You could do it under a pen name if you want; it might be a good idea."

"Hmmm...I don't know. But I will definitely enjoy reading this," I said evenly. I finished the rest of my beer and took it into the bin in the kitchen. "You guys okay to drive?" I asked.

I didn't have a car because I never needed one with public transportation, even though SEPTA was reliably unreliable. Just because I didn't drive didn't mean I didn't want my friends to get home safe.

"I'll take an UBER," Katie assured me.

"You sure? I mean, we do have a bed in the office if you want it," I suggested. Katie's apartment in Mt. Airy was a bit of a hike from Center City, and I worried about her being alone at night.

"I'll drive you home," Brad offered. Brad didn't drink, so I knew he was okay to go.

"Oh, no, it's out of your way," she said.

"Katie, take the ride. Mt. Airy isn't that far from Chestnut Hill. Thanks, Brad."

Brad gave me a thumbs up, and he helped me clean up. I hugged both of them goodbye and thanked them for coming over. Brad was right, I did need to relax, and then I could work on my book with fresh eyes tomorrow.

I put away the leftover pizza and changed into pajamas. I then parked myself on the couch with the sports news channel still on while I dived into the very sexy book that Brad's wife had recommended. She always had the best tastes in the smuttiest romances. I freaking loved it.

CHAPTER FOURTEEN

RILEY

I had hoped I would see Fi before leaving for the game, but she was nowhere to be found when I came home for my pre-game nap. I had slid into bed late last night, and she had curled into my side, but then I had to get up early for morning skate. Leaving my bed warm with her next to me had been torture.

I wanted to give her space, but I also really wanted to talk to her. I still felt like maybe I trapped her in this marriage by proposing to give me a couple months to prove to her it was worth it. At the same time, I was hopelessly in love with her, and I wanted her to feel that way about me too.

How did you woo the woman you were already married to? And hopelessly in love with?

It had only been a couple days since I last saw her, but damn did I miss that woman. I didn't question what work thing she was doing but instead suited up for my game. I drove myself to the arena but walked in with Hallsy. We fist-bumped each other and then went our separate ways to start our pre-game rituals. I taped and re-taped my stick three times before it was time to get dressed. I dressed in my particular weird order, saving my jersey for last, always. I heard the music from down the tunnel and was ready to get out on the ice.

I shut my brain off from thoughts about Fi and focused on the game. I visualized skating backward to block the puck and being on the breakaway while I took practice shots on Metzy during warm-ups. I felt good, and we were coming off a win, so we had a loose feeling to our game. That didn't mean the pressure wasn't on, though. We all felt like every game needed to be played like a playoff game. It would all be worth it in the end if we could climb out of the bottom of the standings to secure that wild card spot. I had my doubts, though, because I had been studying the stats religiously. It didn't look good for us.

The game started, and I got my head into it, thinking about nothing but getting the puck on my stick and protecting the slot in front of Metzy. I took to the ice on the first shift change and watched Noah take the face-off while I backed him up and trash-talked the opposing defenseman. I was ready for this game to be a battle.

I was an offensive defenseman. I was good at protecting the net and blocking shots, but I also knew when to get up in my opponent's zone. It was all good because my defensive partner Jonesy played his game close to the old-school blueliner way. He was a stay at home defensemen, so when I rushed the net, he knew to cover the other end of the zone. We worked well together, but I had to admit his game had been a little off lately. I wasn't sure what that was about;

Jonesy usually had his shit together. We were gonna need to spend more time reviewing tape together this week, but I couldn't think about that right now. I had to focus on the task at hand.

I eyed the opposing defenseman while Noah took the next face-off in their zone. Noah's face-off skills were legit; it also helped that he had Benny and TJ on his wings tonight. Noah won the draw and went to the net. He flicked the puck back to me to distract our opponents; I took the shot without hesitating and scrambled as it hit the post. Benny fought in the trapezoid with our opponent, and as if graced by the hockey gods themselves, he scored the wraparound goal.

The siren sounded, and the red light lit up behind the net while the goalie threw down his stick in annoyance. Ha! Goalies were the weirdest guy on the team.

Benny skated right over to me and threw me into a great big hug. I returned it, cheering and excited that we scored the first goal of the game. It was going to be a good game; I could feel it.

I looked up into the stands and saw the spot where all the WAGs usually sat together. Noah's girl Dinah was cheering with Hallsy's girl Mia. I waved and smiled at them as I headed towards the bench.

"Yo, why isn't your wife here?" Benny asked as I slid onto the pine next to him and grabbed a water bottle.

I shrugged. That was a good question. I hadn't thought about asking her to come, but when I looked at the other girls smiling and cheering on their men, I felt a pang of regret. Fi always loved coming to my games when we were younger. It was nice that she always had my back. She stopped coming after I started dating Stacey in high school, though. I was going to regret that for the rest of my life.

"Why isn't *your* girl here?" I countered.

He made a face, but at least it shut him up. I really didn't understand why he was still with Stephanie. I never had any particular animosity towards her, but the woman did not like me. I think she thought Benny's anti-marriage shit was because I was a guy who had a lot of casual sex. Nope, that was one hundred percent on him.

I cleaned my visor with a towel and watched my teammates try to start up another scoring chance. My mind should have been on the game in front of me, but it kept wandering back to Benny's question.

Why hadn't I asked Fi to come to the game tonight? I asked her to come to Saturday's game, but I wasn't sure why I didn't ask her to come tonight.

I shook my thoughts away when the change-up came, and I was back on the ice again. I would think about all that stuff later, right now I needed to help my team win this game.

Somehow, we managed to win the game. I liked to think it was because we played our hearts out and skated our balls off, but really it was because the other team had the worst penalty kill in the league right now. The superstitious part of me was thanking the hockey gods for our good luck. I rubbed my shoulder as I put my wedding ring back on.

"You okay?" Benny asked from his spot beside me at his own cubby. He was combing back his hair, still wet from his shower, while I stripped off my gear.

I rolled my shoulder again. I had gotten boarded during the second period, and there was no fucking penalty. The refs pretended like it didn't happen, but I felt okay. Doc

Franklin even made me do a baseline test during the inter-
mission, and then he wanted to look at me again after the
game. I felt fine, but I'd never had a concussion before, so I
wasn't sure how I was supposed to feel if I was concussed.
They wanted me to keep an eye on it, but I thought they
were freaking out over nothing.

"All good," I told him.

Benny raised a dark eyebrow. "You sure?"

"Benny, get off my dick. I passed the baseline test."

He hummed at me.

"Boys!" G cheered. "Tonight's win calls for a drink! No
one gets out of it, except you underage rookies. You can
beat it!"

I sighed. As much as I could use a drink, I really wanted
to get home to Fi, but I knew that shit was important to G. It
was important that there wasn't lingering drama in the
locker room and that we were a team in sync with each
other. I had played on other teams where the locker room
was a toxic waste dump, but so far, the Bulldogs had been a
good place for me for the past three years. I was sure some
of the boys' significant others would show up, at least those
that came to the games, and I itched to call Fi, but I knew
she wasn't ready for being around this part of my life. I
wondered if she ever would be.

Benny nudged me. "What's with you?"

"I miss Fi."

He laughed. "Ask G if you can get out of it."

I shook my head and wrapped my towel around my
waist. "It's fine. I'll see you over there."

He gave me a little sarcastic salute while he changed
back into his suit.

"Yo man." Hallsy slapped me on the back after I was
showered and dressed to head to the bar. He fixed his tie

and ran a hand across his recently shaved jaw. His girlfriend Mia wasn't much for facial hair, and the man obliged her.

"Hey, man. What's up?" I asked and kept stride with him as we walked outside the arena and to our respective vehicles.

He looked down at his phone and frowned. "Why do you keep retweeting stuff from this one writer? I didn't even know you could read."

"Har har har," I muttered.

Hallsy's brown eyes widened, and I realized he saw my left hand. "G wasn't kidding. Did you get married?"

"Yup. It's my wife, by the way."

He looked confused. "Who is?"

I rolled my eyes. "The author I keep on retweeting. She's my wife."

Hallsy stared down at his phone and smirked. "Damn, your wife's smoking! I didn't know you were seeing anyone."

Didn't I know it? I punched him in the arm. "Still my wife, Hallsy. And I wasn't." I waved my hand away when he gave me a 'go on' sort of look. "It's a long story."

He shook his head and laughed, his dark curly hair bouncing around. I watched him get into his car and speed away. I sat in my SUV for a minute, debating whether I could go home and get out of having a drink with the boys. The boys were great, they were my pals and my teammates, but my heart ached to see Fi.

I dropped my head onto the steering wheel with a sigh. This was bad. I loved her so much, but I didn't think it was love for her. Oh, she was very much attracted to me, that was clear, but I thought it was just sex for her. I liked sex, a lot, so it was great, but I never knew how much it could hurt to be with someone who didn't love you back.

Which was why I hadn't initiated being intimate with her since we got back from Vegas. I didn't want her to think that was the only reason I married her. If she wanted this bod, she was going to have to ask for it.

So on that depressing note, I drove off in my SUV to meet the guys at the bar and grab a drink or two. I sat at the bar and drank my whiskey while my mind was preoccupied with how to fix my weird marriage.

A blonde with legs for days sidled up on the stool beside me. "So what position do you play?" she asked with a seductive smile.

"Defense," I stated flatly.

When I brought my glass up to my mouth, she must have seen the ring on my hand because next thing I knew, she was cozying up to TJ. Good for him, because I was only interested in one woman right now, and she was home alone and probably in my bed. With that thought, I finished my drink.

I clapped G on the shoulder. "See you, man. I gotta get home."

He eyed me confused, and then his eyes widened. "Oh, I totally forgot you have a wife now."

I smirked, but it was faked because I hadn't heard from Fi since this afternoon, and I was starting to wonder if I did still have a wife.

It was kind of late when I got home but not crazy late for a night-owl like Fi. When I walked into the condo, I heard the TV on but saw that she had fallen asleep on the couch with a paperback book on her lap, looking like she was ready to curl up into bed. I flicked off the TV with the remote and picked the book up off her lap. My eyes widened at what appeared to be a pretty intense sex scene. I glanced at the cover, a little surprised to see a naked man's chest on the front of it. Okay...didn't expect that from Fi. I found her bookmark on the coffee table and put it in the book before setting it down on the table. There was no way I was dealing with her wrath if I dog-eared her book.

The couch was comfortable, but I knew our bed would be way more comfortable to sleep in. Plus, I really missed having her next to me. Which was wild because we had barely been married for a week!

I bent down next to her ear. "Fi," I whispered, but she didn't move.

I wasn't a stupid man, so I wasn't about to shake her awake. Instead, I kneeled down and slid my arms underneath her body. I pulled her tight against my chest, gripping the back of her knees under one arm and her shoulders with the other arm.

I felt her stir against me, and she wrapped her hands around my neck, so I wouldn't drop her. Like I ever would have done that. I felt her eyelashes flicker across my neck, giving me ticklish butterfly kisses. "Riley?" she asked sleepily. "What are you doing?"

"Shush," I whispered to her. "Go back to sleep."

I crossed the doorway of the bedroom and gently laid her down on her side of the bed. I felt warmth spread across my body at the sight. Before we recklessly got married, I didn't sleep on one side of the bed but rather sprawled out like a starfish, stretching my big body across the bed. Now, with her here, she had wormed a place into my home and into my heart, and I didn't want her to leave.

She was still half-asleep, and I couldn't help but think about how cute she looked. I tip-toed into the bathroom to do my normal night-time routine. When I came back into the bedroom, she was asleep again. I pulled my shirt over my head and changed into a pair of pajama pants before I quietly sunk down onto the bed next to my beautiful wife.

"Riley?" she whispered, still half-asleep.

"Shush, go back to sleep," I whispered back.

"Are you okay?" she asked. Her green eyes opened in the dark of the bedroom, but she peered at me seriously.

"What do you mean?"

"That asshole hit you right in the numbers!"

I chuckled. "What are you gonna do, fight him?"

"Maybe," she mumbled. "Fucking asshole better stay away from my man."

"Your man?" I asked with a laugh.

She lifted her left hand up to my jaw and pulled me down towards her lips. I grinned at the feeling of her wedding ring on my face as I kissed her properly. She pulled away sleepily.

"Missed you, baby," she sighed sleepily.

"Yeah?" I asked.

She nodded but then promptly turned on her other side and fell back asleep. I had a feeling she wasn't going to remember this conversation in the morning. I would, though. I was gonna keep that in the back of my mind. It was one step toward wooing my gorgeous trial wife.

I took off my watch and set it on the nightstand next to my side of the bed. My eyes lingered on the ring on my finger, but I kept that on. If it wasn't for the risk of breaking my finger while I played, I would never take off my ring.

I scooted closer to Fi and wrapped my arm around her waist. She shifted in her sleep, and I smelled her shampoo, breathing it in. I had definitely missed her scent and her presence in my arms at night.

I was so totally screwed when it came to my wife.

CHAPTER FIFTEEN

FIONA

$\mathcal{M}$y eyes slanted open in confusion as I stared up at the ceiling of Riley's bedroom. I didn't remember coming to bed last night, which was weird for me. The last thing I remembered after Katie and Brad left was sinking down onto the couch to read that hockey romance that Brad's wife had recommended. Shit, Riley was so going to make fun of me for that.

I ran my hands down my face to rub away the sleep, and my eyes wandered over to the lump on the other side of the bed. On Riley's side of the bed. I must have fallen asleep on the couch, and he brought me to bed last night.

I found myself staring at him for too long, watching the rise and fall of his chest as he breathed in and out while he slept soundly in the bed next to me. I wanted to slink out of the bed, but something about his warm body being beside

144

me hypnotized me into wanting to lay back on the bed and snuggle up with him. I sat up on the bed, at a crossroad, unsure what to do next.

"Stop staring at me," I heard his gruff voice say.

It scared me so much I nearly yelped, and I almost saw the sheepish grin on his face without having to look at him. Sometimes it surprised me after all these years how well I still knew the man beside me.

His strong arms pulled me back down so my head was lying on his chest, and his hand stroked my hair. I loved when a man played with or stroked my hair like this. It was so intimate and sweet.

"Hey!" I exclaimed indignantly. It shouldn't have felt this good being in my best friend's arms.

His chest vibrated underneath me as he laughed. "Shush, the baby's sleeping."

I glared at him, and his blue eyes twinkled with a smile. "What baby?"

"Me!"

I pulled away from him and shoved his shoulder, but he laughed again. "Yeah, you're a big old baby, that's for sure," I scoffed.

His eyes slid closed again. "What time is it?" he asked through a yawn.

I sat up and swung my legs over the side of the bed. "Time for me to get up and get some writing done."

"So, I didn't know you were into romance books," he commented and popped open one blue eye.

The blush rose from my neck and spread across my pale face. He *had* seen what I was reading last night. God, I hope he hadn't read the page I was on because there was steamy action about to go down. I couldn't believe I fell asleep before getting to that! Also, it was a good thing Katie and Brad had been over last night because otherwise, I would have been reading in the bed with my vibrator out on the nightstand, ready to go. God, I hope he didn't know I had that. Or how much I had used it in the few days he had been gone.

"I read lots of books," I argued. "Do you want to sleep in for a little longer? I can wake you in a little bit."

He reached out a hand and found mine on the bed. My chest felt warm at his touch, but I tried to ignore it. "Please. Give me another hour?" he asked.

I pulled away from him quickly and nodded. I practically ran out of the bedroom and quietly shut the door behind me. I had to get out of there, or I would have done something irrational, like make love to my husband.

Make love? Geez, I must have been reading too many romance books lately.

I went into the kitchen to start making my coffee for the day, but I felt out of breath and frustrated. I didn't know what was wrong with me. Maybe I was in the wrong head-space to finish proofreading today. I had calmed down by the time I had a second cup of coffee in me and was sitting down at my desk to proofread the rest of this book. I was at the halfway mark when I heard the creak of the bedroom door. I looked at the clock on my computer and silently cursed. I had told Riley I would wake him in an hour, but I had immersed myself in my book for so long, it had been nearly two. I was finishing my edits on one last chapter when I heard footsteps behind me.

I saw Riley's shadow in the screen of my laptop. He surveyed the piles of books that were in stacks on the floor and grunted. I cringed and hunched my shoulders, afraid of how mad he might be about the mess I made of his office.

I felt his hands on my shoulders suddenly. "Hey, what is that for?" he asked with a hint of concern at my tense reaction.

I turned to him and tried to form a coherent thought, which was hard when he stood there without his shirt, showing off his lean muscles and his abs for days. The words melted right out of my brain. His finger titled my chin up to look at him from my seated position.

I shook my head and batted his hand away. "Sorry, it's such a mess. And sorry for not waking you; I got lost in the words."

He studied me for a moment but didn't say anything at first. "Okay, I think we need to go get you some new bookshelves."

"You don't need to buy me bookcases."

He smiled. "I have the day off and no practice, so let me do something nice for you."

Normally, I would have put up a fight, but the way he looked so earnestly at me, I couldn't say no. I nodded. "Fine, yeah, okay."

"Come on. You know you're excited to buy new bookshelves."

"Maybe..." I trailed off but grinned from ear-to-ear. Riley totally knew the right things to say to me. "I would totally marry the Beast to get that sick-ass library."

"Are you saying I'm a beast?" He laughed and flexed his muscles.

I visibly rolled my eyes at him, but I smiled.

"Come on," he urged. "I'll make breakfast, and then we can go get you something better than the floor to put your books on. Damn, you have a lot of books."

I cringed but stood up to follow him out of the office and into the kitchen. "Sorry."

He kissed the top of my head. "Don't be. I'm just teasing."

I watched him make another pot of coffee and start cooking up some eggs for omelettes. I had asked him if he wanted help, but he absolutely refused. It was almost like he was trying to woo me, which I guess made sense if he really wanted this marriage to work. There was that old saying that a way to a man's heart was their stomach, but I think they were talking about me.

He opened the kitchen cabinet looking for plates and looked back at me with a smile. "Did you do dishes while I was gone?"

"Yeah..." I trailed off like it was the dumbest question I had heard all week. "And the laundry."

"I thought the sheets smelled fresh. That's—you didn't have to do that," he stuttered.

I shrugged. "You weren't here. Shouldn't I help around here? I am your wife, after all."

Riley set a plate down in front of me and handed me a fork, then he came around to the barstool next to me and took his own plate. He shoveled some food in his mouth, and I did too. I almost moaned at the taste. We were both quiet while we ate. More like Riley devoured his food, and I took my time eating because I was thinking too hard. When we were done, I took the empty plates and loaded up the dishwasher. He tried to protest, but I glared with a killing look, and he held up his hands in surrender.

When I finished the clean-up, I saw he was sitting on the couch and furrowing his brow while reading the book I had been reading last night. Embarrassment colored my face as I walked over to him and sat on the couch next to him.

He turned to me with the biggest smirk I had ever seen

on his face. "I can't believe they let people write books like this."

I barked out a long laugh. "Oh, honey, you don't even know. That's not even like a BDSM book. That one's pretty tame."

He flipped to the back to read the summary. "Wait a second...this is a hockey romance?"

I put my face in my hands but laughed. It was kind of ironic to be reading a hockey romance book when my life was currently feeling like one. Riley closed the book, leaving my bookmark where I left off last night and putting the book back on the coffee table. I would definitely be picking that back up when he was back on the road.

He sighed. "So I think we should talk about things."

I swear I could hear my heart, it started beating so hard. No one ever wanted to hear that sentence, and I was worried about what he wanted to talk about. But I nodded and calmly said, "Okay."

He twisted his ring around on his left hand, and subconsciously I started to fidget with my own. Even though I had asked to get divorced the day after we got married, I hadn't taken off my ring, not once. I was a little confused about what that meant. I watched him sigh and run a hand down his chiseled jaw. He hadn't shaved in a couple days, and I couldn't help but think the rugged look was damn sexy on him.

"Look, I'm done with the single life. I want something real, and I think...I want something real with you." I was sensing a 'but' coming here, but I stayed quiet and let him continue. "I feel like I trapped you into this marriage, so if you really want a divorce and to not give this a shot with me, I'll understand."

I did want that...or at least I thought that was what I

wanted. But I had really missed him while he had been away. And now, seeing this man before me so vulnerable and so caring, I wasn't sure what I wanted.

"I don't know what I want," I admitted. "I do feel like this marriage was a bit rushed, but I told you I would give you a couple months to prove to me that this could work between us."

He turned to me with a surprised look on his face. "I think we could have a happy life together, but if you're not happy, I don't want that. You're right, though, and Mom said the same thing, that we rushed into this too quickly after what happened to you."

I nodded. "She's not wrong, but I think my relationship with Eric had ended a long time ago. Him not showing up was the final straw. Katie thinks he had been cheating on me the whole time."

Riley's jaw clenched, and I noticed his fists did too. I knew how he felt about cheaters after what his dad did to his mom. I felt the anger rolling off of him, so I reached out a hand to calm him down. "Hey, it's okay. Good thing I didn't marry him. Good thing I married you instead."

Riley nodded, but he still seemed cautious and unsure, which was strange to me because I wanted him to lean over and slant his mouth onto mine. There was a torrent of emotions clouding his eyes, and it filled me with dread. I really thought we had made a mistake in getting married, but when I looked at him sitting here bearing his soul to me, something in my heart flipped over. I told myself it was just my lust for his hot bod, but I wasn't exactly sure about that. Maybe it wasn't just sexual attraction between us. There were too many years between us for it to just be platonic love between friends. That's what scared me the most.

He grabbed my hand suddenly and kissed the back of it. Oh, he was so smooth. I think my heart melted at that sweet gesture a little bit. "You know my schedule's crazy," he warned.

"I know."

"We have a road stretch next week, and I'll be gone all week."

"I know," I said again. I had checked his schedule the other day, wanting to know how much we would get to see each other. In a couple months, the season would be over unless they made the playoffs, which I kind of doubted they would.

"A lot of women can't handle the pressure of having an absent partner. So I would understand if it gets to be too much for you."

I cocked my head at him and studied his profile for a moment. "Riley, I know the deal, and...I can't believe I'm saying this, but okay, let's try this. What did I say when we went to get our marriage license?"

He smirked. "I believe you said YOLO."

"Do you think anyone will ever buy that we got married?"

He laughed. "I have gotten a lot of questions from my teammates."

I paused for a second. I knew hockey was important to him and his teammates were important to him, but the idea of being a WAG and having my whole identity based on him rubbed me the wrong way. So it was really strange to me when my mouth opened on its own accord and I asked, "So do you want me to meet your teammates?"

He reached a hand up and pushed my hair out of my face. "Only if you want to."

"I do."

He smiled back at me and pulled his hand away. I found myself slightly disappointed when he didn't kiss me.

"Come on, girl, let's go get you some new bookcases."

He did not have to tell me twice.

CHAPTER SIXTEEN

RILEY

"What about this one?" I asked Fi.

She peered up at the cherry-wood book-cases that would look perfect in the office. She looked down at her phone, her long fiery-red hair sliding up her back at the movement. My hand itched to wrap around her hair, to feel her in my arms again, but I wasn't going to press her right now. After our talk today, I was more aware that if this marriage was going to work, I needed to really woo her. So, as much as I had no desire to shop for furniture in the maze that was IKEA on my day off, I did want to spend time with her.

She put a finger on her chin. "I think it could work..."

"Sweetheart, it would fit perfectly!" I argued.

I pretended not to notice the color on her face at the pet-name or the way one corner of her lips upturned at it. She wasn't as good at hiding her feelings as she thought. My job was to read people, to figure out what the other guy was thinking, so of course, I saw that she was fighting her feelings. Also, she had been my best friend before becoming my wife, so I knew her in and out. Probably better than she knew herself.

She nodded. "Okay, let's get it. I'm sorry this is probably really boring for you." She took a picture of the id number on the bookcase and walked away.

I followed her through the maze of the showroom. I caught up to her as she weaved her way through people trying to get to the bottom floor where we could get the boxes for the bookshelves. I reached out and grabbed her hand, smiling to myself as her fingers threaded through mine almost on instinct. Being away from her sucked, but I had a feeling that I was starting to chip through the wall she put up between us.

"You don't have to buy this for me," she finally said when we got to the lower level and were searching through the aisles to find the box for the bookshelf.

"You're so frustrating. Let me take care of you," I growled while I pushed our cart down the aisle to the row we needed.

I could afford to buy her a nicer bookshelf at a fancier furniture store, but Fi insisted that IKEA could do the job. I wasn't about to have a pointless argument with my wife over where to buy her bookshelf. Maybe I should have thought about building them into the wall themselves. I didn't really have time for that project and a half, though. Although I knew Benny and Noah would have helped in a heartbeat, and Noah grew up in the middle of nowhere Winnipeg and was really good with his hands.

She put her hands on her hips and stared at me with a cocked red eyebrow as if challenging me. I took the pushcart and pulled the box we needed on top of it. It was heavy, but nothing I couldn't handle. I glanced up and saw she was still giving me that furious look.

"Don't be like that, Fi."

She sighed and ran a hand across her face. "I'm sorry. You know how I don't like to ask for help."

"No? You?" I asked sarcastically.

She glared. "Riley, you don't have to be this guy. You don't have to feel like you need to take care of me."

I pulled her toward me by her slender waist and grinned as she blushed at the public display of affection. I gave her a quick kiss. "Shush. I want to. I'm your husband. Let me provide for you."

"But you don't have to," she argued.

I gave her another kiss to soften her edges. "But I *want* to."

That seemed to shut her up, so we went to the checkout, and she didn't refuse this time when I paid for her damn bookshelves. I loaded the SUV with the boxes, not really looking forward to having to put it together, but I would do this for her with no complaints. She was being so stubborn today, and I couldn't stand it. Didn't we literally talk about trying to make this thing work? She was really gonna make me work to woo her.

Fi was looking at her phone when I got into the driver's seat. I checked the clock and saw it was around lunchtime. Fi looked up when I started the engine. She put a gentle hand on my arm. "Thank you. For doing this for me. I know this isn't exactly how you want to spend your day off."

I grabbed her hand in my bigger one and brought it to my lips to kiss it. "I want to spend time with you."

Her eyes crinkled when she smiled at me. "In that case, do you want to go to South Street today? I wanted to stop in the comic book store. There's a good Italian restaurant next door where we could go for lunch."

"Sounds like a date."

"Is it?" she asked cautiously and bit her lip.

"What?"

"Is it a date?"

"Yes. Is that a problem?"

She shook her head. I kissed her hand one last time before letting her go and putting both hands back on the steering wheel.

We found a parking garage and then walked several blocks down to South Street. I didn't mind, because walking in the city with her hand in mine was the best feeling in the world.

I had always dated women who were smaller than me - being six feet tall, that was a given - but Fi's five-foot-nine height made her just a tiny bit shorter than me. I liked a tall, lean woman like Fi with legs for days and a nice ass. I had never really been a big breast-man, but I liked Fi's. Not too small but not too big. They didn't necessarily fit in the palm of my big hands, but they were nice. And shit, I was thinking about my wife's tits in the middle of a public street. The tightening in my jeans reminded me that I should stop that right now.

She cocked an eyebrow at me while she stepped up into the comic book store. "What's that face for?" she asked.

I let her drag me inside. "What face?"

"You have your horny face on."

"I'm sorry, what?" I asked with a laugh.

She laughed. "You do! You make a face when you're horny. Has no one ever told you that?"

She was still laughing as she pulled me into the back of the shop. There were rows upon rows of thick collections of comics from the floor to the ceiling. She eyed the thick, hard-back binding of what looked like an entire comic run in one book. I didn't know shit about comics or any of this nerd shit, but the look on her face when she searched was enough to make me want to watch her look at books all day.

Was that weird?

Probably.

She crouched down to look at the bottom shelf, and I would be lying if I said I didn't turn my head a little and stare at her ass. God, my wife was hot. She pulled a couple of soft-cover comics out of the stacks and stood back up. A red eyebrow arched at me again, and I realized I was still staring.

She reached her hand up to grip my jaw between her fingers. "Eyes up here, buddy," she teased.

"Come on, Fi. You know you're hot," I tried to argue.

She bristled at that but shoved me out of the way and walked up to the counter. I followed behind her, ready to whip out my credit card again, but she already had hers out. She chatted with the blue-haired guy at the counter about the comics she was buying. I couldn't help but notice his eyes sweeping across her chest. My eyes narrowed to tiny slits in his direction. Fi didn't pay it any mind but waved goodbye to him with her bag in hand, and I quickly grabbed her other hand into mine. Fi squeezed my hand in warning, but soon we were out on the street and about to walk into the place she wanted to go for lunch. Only to walk straight into Stephanie—Benny's girl—and Cindy, one of my exes.

"Riley!" Cindy exclaimed in surprise.

Her dark olive skin-tone shone in the sun, and her dark eyes narrowed in confusion at Fi standing next to me. Cindy was a great girl, but she was one of the few relationships that didn't work out because she couldn't handle me never being around. There were no hard feelings; I got that it was hard on the girls when their partner was gone most of the time. Not every break-up had to be terrible.

Stephanie narrowed her grey eyes at me in confusion and flipped her black hair behind her shoulder. She hated me. Don't know why; I was always nice to her.

"Hey, Cin, Steph, how are you?" I greeted them.

Stephanie's eyes scanned from me to Fi, who was looking at me with a confused look. "Fine," Stephanie answered coolly. "Who's this?"

Fi opened her mouth to make a snarky comment, and this time I squeezed her hand to warn her and say 'be nice.' "This is my wife, Fiona. Fi, this is Benny's girl, Stephanie, and...Cindy's my—"

"His ex," she cut me off to explain. Cindy's smile was genuine. She was such a great girl. I hoped she would find someone soon.

"Benny said you got married; I thought it was a joke," Stephanie snarked.

Oh, there was definitely something up with him and her again, and I had a feeling it was the fact that he didn't want to get serious again. Shit. Fi kinda already knew about their frequent fights and that Benny sometimes crashed in my guest room, but maybe I had to tell him he needed to escape somewhere else. I think he eluded to that when I offered to let him stay when he helped move Fi into my place.

"It was nice to meet both of you," Fi offered, and I could tell she meant it.

"Riley, I'm so happy for you!" Cindy beamed. "You both look so happy together!"

"We won't keep you," Stephanie told us with a grimace.

"Nice seeing you," I told them and then steered Fi into the restaurant.

We got situated in the restaurant and ordered before Fi finally asked about the elephant in the room. I had been texting Benny to ask what was up and had to look up.

"So Benny's girlfriend doesn't like you. What did you ever do to her?" she asked.

I shrugged. "Nothing. Benny and her are having problems."

"Oh. What does that have to do with you?"

"He's not really big on the whole marriage thing."

"Oh. And that Asian girl was your ex? She seemed nice."

"Yeah, Cindy's a great girl, but she couldn't handle me traveling all the time."

She sipped her water in thought.

I put my phone down, and I reached out to take her hand. "Tell me about your progress with the book."

Her smile was a thousand-watt, and I wanted to see it on her face for the rest of my life. "Brad thinks I have imposter syndrome and that I need to release the first draft."

"Who's Brad?" I asked with narrowed eyes.

She waved her hand at my jealousy. "My agent. I had him and Katie over to watch the game last night."

I frowned. "You could have come to the game; I could have gotten you tickets."

She looked down at her hands in her lap. "I didn't want to impose."

"Sweetheart, it's not a big deal. Just give me notice next time, and I can get you tickets. I want you to come to my games. Will you come tomorrow?"

Our food came, so the question sort of hung in the air for a bit. Fi laughed as she watched me eat more pasta than I knew what to do with. She stirred around the spaghetti on her eggplant parm, lost in thought. She still hadn't answered my question.

"So will you?" I asked again.

"Depends on where I'm at with my book."

I nodded. "If you're busy, I understand. I don't want to impose on your work. It would mean a lot to me, though."

She seemed to mull it around. "Well...maybe I can work on it tonight."

I smiled up at her. I didn't think she understood how much that meant to me. How much she meant to me.

CHAPTER SEVENTEEN

FIONA

I never understood when I read romance books and the heroine went on and on about wanting to lick the hot hero's abs...until Riley was putting together my bookshelves with no shirt on. Why did he have to take his shirt off? I tried to write, but watching the cut man put together furniture was too distracting for me. I couldn't focus, and it felt a bit too hot in here. I wanted to run my hands down his ripped body and kiss the length of his forearm tattoo.

I was very horny and was deprived of sex from my hot best friend/husband, but I didn't know how to bring up the conversation with him. I was really bad at asking for sex. Even when I was so uncomfortably horny.

"Sweetheart?" Riley's voice came back to me, but it felt like he was far away.

"Hmm?" I asked but was still slack-jawed, staring at his insanely ripped torso. When did my best friend get so cut?

"Eyes on your writing."

BUSTED.

My face flushed, and he laughed. This man made my blood pump and my panties get wet. I wanted to jump him, but at the same time, he hadn't exactly been open to us getting physical again. Why was he keeping me at arm's length? He said he wanted this to work, but he hadn't broached sex with me again, and I was starting to get self-conscious about it. Did he not want me anymore? Did he just want a wife to come home to? But he would continue to fuck whomever he wanted when he wasn't here? We should have talked about this stuff, but I was too scared to know the answers. If I found out Riley had been fucking other women, it would have broken me.

Riley swore under his breath.

"What?" I asked.

He looked down at his phone. "Do you care if Benny comes over tonight? He might need to crash here." He gestured to the twin-sized bed that was shoved up on the back wall. I eyed it. I wasn't exactly sure if six-foot-four Benny was going to fit in the spare bed.

"It's your condo!" I told him with a shrug.

He stared at me and rubbed the bridge of his nose between two fingers. He crossed the room and knelt down so we were at eye-level. He brushed my hair out of my face and tucked it behind my ear. I nearly melted at the gentle gesture.

"Fiona, I thought we talked about this. I'm all in for this to be a true partnership. This is our home, not just mine, so of course I'm going to ask you if it's okay with you if my friend comes over because he got into another fight with his girlfriend."

"It's fine with me, but I think I need to move into the bedroom. You shirtless is a distraction."

"Oh yeah?" he asked with a twinkle in his eye.

I shoved him away and took my laptop into our bedroom. I put headphones on and drowned out the rest of the world. I only came out to the smell of some really good food a few hours later.

I stepped into the kitchen to find Benny behind the stove, stirring some sort of meat in one of the frying pans. It smelled amazing. Riley was sitting at one of the barstools nursing a beer.

"Um...hi?" I asked.

Benny looked over his shoulder and smiled at me. "Hi, Fi. Figured I'd make myself useful by making dinner since Riley said I could crash here tonight."

"What are you making?" I asked.

"Chicken tinga tacos. It's nothing special," Benny replied with a shrug of his wide-set shoulders.

Riley smiled while he peeled the label off his beer bottle. "He's so modest."

"It smells awesome. Riley, you should have asked Benny to marry you instead. I think he'd be a better hockey wife."

Riley laughed.

That got us both the finger from the big man in the kitchen.

"How's the writing going?" Riley asked.

I wrung my hands. "Don't ask! Ugh, it's terrible. Everything sucks, and I'm sure my publisher's gonna ask for my advance back."

I pretended not to notice the two men share an uneasy

glance. "What did your agent say again?" Riley asked, trying to be helpful.

I grumbled, "To send it over."

"Sweetheart, turn it in."

Benny turned off the burner. He turned to the three plates he had laid out on the counter with a soft tortilla shell laid out on each. He spooned the meat filling onto all three, along with diced avocado, onion, and some sort of soft cheese I didn't recognize, and squeezed lime onto them. He handed me the first plate. "Here, ladies first."

I took my plate to the dining room table Riley had set up in the space in front of the big window. The two big men joined me. I took the first bite and moaned in ecstasy. "Holy shit!" I exclaimed.

"Good, right?" Riley said with a grin. "That's why the ladies all love Benny here."

Benny frowned. "Damn, this is still not as good as my abuela's."

"So your grandmother taught you how to cook?" I asked

I didn't really know anything about Riley's teammates. I had met TJ Desjardins last year in passing; he seemed like a fun guy, and he definitely hit on me, but I think he only did it to annoy Riley. Benny was Riley's best friend, outside of me, so I did want to get to know the big man sitting next to me.

He nodded. "I'm not close to my parents or my dad's parents, but my mom's parents have always been really loving and supportive. I used to hate it as a kid, but Abuela always said I would win some nice girl over with my cooking."

"Hasn't worked yet, though," Riley joked.

I glared at my husband for being insensitive. Man, he

must not like this Stephanie girl. "So what's the deal with the girlfriend?" I asked.

"Oh no you don't. Go finish your writing, and then you can play therapist," Riley warned.

I gave him the finger, and Benny tipped back his head with a loud laugh. "Man, you two are something else. Not much to say, honestly. She wants the whole marriage and family thing, and that's never been me."

"You don't want kids?" I asked.

He shook his head. "Nope. I like being the fun uncle! Kids aren't for me; it's hard to find women who are okay with that. Some say they are but end up changing their mind."

Riley drained the rest of his beer. "So did you finally break up for good this time?"

Benny shrugged. "No idea, but I knew I couldn't stay there tonight. Thanks, Fi, for putting up with me."

I shook my head. "If you cook me dinner every time you need to crash here, it's fine by me."

Both men laughed, but Benny looked sad, and that made me sad too. "No, really. I know you two are still in the newly-wed phase, and I feel bad being a cock-block," he apologized.

I averted my gaze and finished eating my tacos. Riley took the empty plates into the kitchen and started doing the dishes. He didn't say anything either. Benny couldn't really be a cockblock if we weren't having sex.

Benny's brown eyes bored into me. "Fi, you better not break his heart," he whispered.

"What?" I asked because I had zero idea what he was actually talking about.

"Riley. That man loves you."

I stared at him for a second and then excused myself to go finish working on my book. Riley rolled into bed around eleven while I was still proofreading, sitting up against the headboard of our bed. I lifted the headphones off of my head and smiled at him. He undressed for bed and slid into the covers next to me.

"Sweetheart," he sighed. "Send it in."

I groaned. "I don't think I'm ready."

"When's your deadline?"

"Tomorrow," I mumbled.

He groaned next to me but reached out a hand to stroke across my thigh exposed from the shorts I wore to bed. "Fi, turn it in. It will be okay."

Somehow the reassuring words from the man next to me actually worked, and I found myself emailing the first draft over. I closed the lid to my laptop and put it on the bedside table, then started getting ready for bed. When I slid between the sheets next to Riley, he was already passed out. That didn't stop me from curling up against him as sleep took hold of me.

"It's Fiona, right?" the thin, blond-haired woman said to me when I sat in my seat right up in front of the glass. "I'm Brianna Girard."

She reached a hand out to me, and I shook it. "Fi's fine. You're the captain's wife, right?"

She nodded and looked to the ice where the boys were starting warm-ups. I looked over and saw Riley laughing with Benny as they raced across the ice and lobbed practice shots at the goaltender, Seamus Metz. Riley's normally short-cropped blond hair was starting to grow past his ears. It reminded me of when we were kids, and he had that typical long hockey-flow look. I was kind of a fan of it.

He skated by the glass and tapped it with a smile. I waved at him, and there was something deep inside me that was beaming as if to say, "He's mine."

"First hockey game?" Brianna asked.

I shook my head. "Oh, no, Minnesota born and raised. I spent so much time at the rink cheering Riley on."

"Oh? I didn't realize you knew each other growing up."

I laughed. "All our lives. Our moms are best friends; it was unavoidable."

She looked at me with a curious glance. "Huh," she finally said noncommittally.

"He's my best friend," I explained.

She smiled and pointed to the blond guy wearing the 'C' on his jersey and stretching on the ice with TJ Desjardins. "I understand that; I have one of those."

I smiled back but couldn't say anything else because I felt the weight of the seat next to me dip in. I turned to see the brunette from yesterday sitting down next to me, Stephanie. Huh. I guessed she and Benny made up. She was holding a half-drunk beer in her hand, and there was a sour look on her face.

Oh okkayyy then.

"So you and Riley, huh?" she asked without any greeting.

I nodded. Although all I could think about was what her boyfriend had said to me last night. And how I felt about it. Of course, Riley loved me; we were best friends. This marriage was a partnership, but that didn't mean we were in love with each other. I mean, we loved each other.

Of course, I loved Riley. He was my best friend, the person I trusted most when I discovered my sexuality, the person I told everything to. That didn't mean we were madly in love with each other, though. A marriage could just be a partnership; it didn't have to be for love. Right?

Stephanie drained the rest of the beer and fixed me with a dirty look. I crossed eyes with Brianna, who gave me some sort of warning look. Shit. I had heard that sometimes the WAGs could be toxic, and there could be some drama. I was not a dramatic person! But a lot of people thought I was cold and distant because I never let myself get close to people. I assumed everyone would abandon me, so what was the point?

I tried to be the bigger person here. "It's Stephanie, right? Did uhh...you and Benny make up?"

"I guess," she snapped.

Okkayyy.

"Stephanie," Brianna warned.

Stephanie cut her eyes to me. "Is your marriage even real?"

I arched an eyebrow at her. "Excuse me?"

"You know what I mean. Riley's the biggest whore on the team. Do you honestly expect him to not cheat when he's on the road?"

It was something I had been wondering about, but I wasn't about to admit that to this woman who clearly was taking her issues with her own relationship out on me. Riley might sleep around a lot, and that was totally fine, but I knew how he felt about cheating after what happened with his own parents. We never discussed if this marriage meant we would only sleep with each other. Did he assume I was okay with him hooking up with other women? Fuck, we should have talked about that the day after the wedding when I asked him to divorce me.

I dug my nails into the palm of my skin in a fist and tried to bite my tongue. I didn't need to be that woman who caused issues.

"Stephanie, that's enough," Brianna snapped. She gave me a small, sympathetic smile.

I took that as my leave. "I'm going to get a beer. Anyone want anything?"

"I'll come with you," offered the young Black girl with long braids who was sitting on my other side. I thought her name was Lacey. We walked to the concessions. "Sorry about Stephanie; she really doesn't like Riley," she told me.

"Right."

She gave me a small smile. "Riley's a great guy. I think the other girls slut-shame him because he's kind of into casual hookups. Not that—shit, am I making it worse?"

I laughed as I took my beer from the cashier and handed him my money. "Slightly, but I know all of Riley's history. We're best friends. I had him first, so suck it bitches!"

She laughed. "Really? And now you're married! That's so cute. You must have been the one that got away."

I shrugged.

Was I?

We walked back to our seats as the puck was about to drop. Stephanie was now talking to another one of the younger blonde girls; Mia, I think her name was. She seemed nice, so I think she was just trying to let the other woman vent.

We watched Girard take the first face-off at center ice and groaned together when the puck got turned over to the other team. But the Bulldogs goaltender Metzy showed them the leather and issued the stoppage of play.

Lacey cheered. "Yeah, baby, that's how you do it!"

I smiled at her and sipped my beer. "Yours?" I asked.

She nodded. "How could you tell?"

"Just a feeling."

We watched Noah Kennedy take the face-off with TJ and Hallsy on his wings. Riley was on the ice with his defensive partner Jonesy lined up next to him. A smile formed across my lips because I knew Riley was sizing up his opponent and trash-talking him. He could be a bit of a chirper, but I thought it was all a part of his strategy to make the other d-man mess up.

"Seamus was born for this job," Lacey said next to me. "He's homegrown, practically grew up in this arena too. I was so stoked when they called him up from the farm team."

"Oh yeah?" I asked, genuinely curious.

I was a Tundra fan because, duh, Minnesota. But I loved hockey, so I was always interested in how the Philly team was doing. Now that I was married to one of their defensemen, I was more invested. Seamus Metz was the latest goaltender to be between the pipes for the team this season. Make that the eighth in rotation. It was not a good look for the team. It hadn't been a great season, but this young kid was good.

She beamed. "He's a hometown boy, so the fans love him."

"I bet."

The next question died on my lips because I watched Noah dive onto the ice to cover the crease and then get hit in the face with the puck. What was the big center doing blocking shots? That was Riley and Jonesy's jobs!

"Fuck! He better not have a concussion!" I yelled.

"That was bad!" Lacey agreed.

We shared a look of concern.

"Dinah's gotta be going out of her mind," she muttered.

"Who's that?" I asked.

"Oh, Noah's new girlfriend. I heard you're a writer, so you might know her. Dinah Lace."

"Oh! I think we have the same publisher. Petite, dark-hair?"

Lacey nodded. "Yup, that's D."

I chewed on my lip until the recognition dawned on me. She wrote cute YA romances about hockey. "Yeah, I'm pretty sure we've met before. Noah's a bit younger than her, huh?"

Lacey nodded. "Even before those two got together, she always worried about Noah. I'm not sure why she's not here today." The younger girl had a guilty look on her face. "I may have actually scared her off."

"How so?" I asked.

She grimaced. "I don't think she knew that Noah was already in love with her, and I might have spilled the beans on that."

I cringed but squeezed her hand in support. I hadn't met Noah yet, but Riley had kind of mentioned something similar to me. He even told me he had goaded the kid into asking her out by telling him if Noah didn't, he would. Riley was just trying to push him, though; he wasn't interested in Dinah.

The play was still stopped on the ice, so I turned my attention back to what was going on in front of us. It was scary when a player got injured. Especially when they weren't getting up off the ice. You never wanted to see a guy get hurt, even if you hated his guts.

TJ Desjardins and the team doctor were trying to get the kid up. Eventually, his six-foot-two frame lifted off the ice, and the doctor held a towel to the side of his face, which was now bleeding. My eyes flicked to Riley on the ice, looking like he was having some words with one of the Pittsburgh Miners. By words, of course, I meant it looked like he was about to drop the gloves. Riley didn't fight much, but I think as one of the older players on this team, he felt like it was his duty to protect his boys.

He must have felt my gaze on him because he looked up and saw me giving him a warning look and mouthing, "Don't," from the other side of the glass.

He winked and blew me a kiss. To which I rolled my eyes.

"Aw! You guys are so cute!" Lacey squealed.

I chewed my lip in worry while I watched Noah get taken down the tunnel. I would have been losing my mind if that was Riley, so maybe it was a good thing that Dinah wasn't here to see her man like that. Especially when he never returned to the ice.

Noah getting taken out of the game must have rallied up the rest of the boys because, after the second period, they were out for blood. TJ Desjardins, in particular, was ready to go; I saw the chirps coming out of his mouth when he was on the ice. Riley was trying to be safe and not trying to take too many penalties but was getting in the corners and protecting the net as much as possible. I loved watching that big man play the game he loved, and seeing him do it in person again made my heart soar with pride. Watching him be successful at the sport he loved made my soul do a little dance. I was so proud of my best friend for all he had accomplished. When the Bulldogs won the game, I was practically beaming.

"Are you going to come to Noah and TJ's place tonight?" Lacey asked.

I nodded.

She squeezed my hand. "You know, us WAGs aren't all scary."

I smiled at the younger girl. "Thanks, Lace."

"If it makes you feel better, none of us like Stephanie."

I smiled at her. As petty as it was, it did make me feel a little better.

CHAPTER EIGHTEEN

RILEY

"Are you sure you want to come with me to Noah and TJ's? We could have a night in," I suggested to Fi when I got home after my game.

I had actually been surprised last night when she sent in her book and said she was going to come to the game and then later to TJ and Noah's place with me. I was also secretly really glad because I had heard from G that Stephanie was trying to start drama with her at the game, and Fi was so cool and collected about it. Metzy's girl Lacey ended up hanging with her all night, and that made me happy. Lacey was a great girl and smart like Fi.

I was also happy Fi was at the game tonight because we actually had a win! Mostly because Noah got taken out of the game early when he took a puck to the face, so we all fought to win the game for him. And, of course, the big goof's first question was if he blocked the shot or not. Sometimes us hockey players could be a bit thick.

Fi stood in front of the mirror in the bathroom, applying dark lipstick on her lips. I felt my pants tighten at it. Damn, did my wife look hot.

"I already put lipstick on; we're going," she replied with a stern look on her face.

The lipstick was good because it kept me from pulling her into my arms and spending the night in bed with her. Not that I didn't want to, the tent in my pants definitely wanted that, but after our talk the other day, I didn't want her to think I only married her for the great sex. Although it occurred to me that keeping her at arm's length might not be the best. There had to be a reason she had been reading that very steamy romance novel the other night. I was hoping she would make a move on me again, but so far, it was like we were each holding out for each other.

I wanted this marriage to be a real partnership, a real relationship, but it still felt like she was holding it in her head as a business relationship. We were just roommates who had fucked a couple times and now chastely shared a bed. I didn't know what to do about it.

I watched her part her lips and then rub them together; my mouth went dry at seeing her do that. Once satisfied, she flicked off the light and walked out of the bathroom. She was still wearing the Philadelphia Bulldogs jersey with my name on the back. Something dug into my heart at that...like her wearing my jersey meant she was finally mine. She might be wearing her wedding ring, but it didn't feel like she was mine yet. Not by a long shot.

She turned around when she saw I wasn't following her. "Hey, am I going by myself?" she asked, amused.

I shook my head and took a deep breath. I was totally caught foaming at the mouth while I stared at her delicious ass. I adjusted myself in my pants when I noticed a stack of papers on my bedside table. I picked it up. "Hey, what's this?" I asked.

She looked back at me and had a nervous look on her face. "Um, book three? You said you wanted to read it."

I set it back down and walked over to her. I slid my hand in hers, and we walked together out of the condo. "I do. How are you feeling about it?"

She grimaced. "I'm not satisfied with it."

I led her out the door and down to my SUV in the underground parking garage. "I'm sure it's fine."

She bit her lip and was quiet the whole ride to my teammates' place. When we got there, TJ greeted us at the door since Noah was still at Dinah's next door. We slapped hands in greeting. "Yo, dude," I greeted.

"Wild game today. You ready to get lit?" he asked.

I shook my head. "I'm driving tonight, so you can."

Fi's face fell. "Oh, Riley, I can drive if you want."

I squeezed her hand. "No, it's okay; I know you need to celebrate finishing your first draft." TJ's head kept wiping back and forth between the two of us, and I realized that I was rude and hadn't introduced them. "Fi, this is my teammate, TJ. TJ, this is my wife, Fiona."

I swear TJ's eyes bugged out of his head, and he stared down at my left hand. "I thought you wearing a ring was new. Wait, haven't we met before?"

Fi nodded. "Yeah, we did! Nice meeting you again."

TJ shook his head. "Riley, man, never thought I would see you of all people settle down."

I glared at him when I saw the sour look that crossed Fi's face. She shifted to neutral when I turned to her, but I saw it, and I wanted to know so badly what she was thinking inside that brain of hers. Probably nothing good.

I guided Fi into the kitchen to get a drink, where we bumped into Noah, who was coming back from next door. He was just as surprised as TJ was when I introduced Fi as my wife, but he slunk away when Benny came over to us.

"Hi, Fi," Benny greeted her.

"Hey. So you and your girl got back together?" she asked.

Benny nodded, but I noticed Stephanie wasn't with him. "Sorry, I heard she was really rude to you."

Fi waved him off. "It's okay. I ended up hanging with Metzy's girl, Lacey."

Benny frowned. "Still, I'm sorry."

Fi shook her head at him.

Benny wandered off when Hallsy called him over to the other side of the room, and I walked off when Noah's girl Dinah came in, and she and Fi got to talking shop. I walked over to TJ and Noah with a grimace on my face, not really wanting to explain the situation to my younger teammates. Noah and I got to talking about my weird marriage, and when I looked across the room, I shook my head at seeing Mia, Fi, and Dinah all doing shots together.

"Oh, no. I smell trouble," I groaned out loud.

Noah glanced in the direction I was looking in. "Was it a good idea to leave those two together?"

"Hence, why I offered to drive tonight," I commented and raised my glass of water to him.

Noah shook his head and clapped me on the back. "I don't understand this whole marriage of yours. "

I shrugged. "I don't think either of us do."

I heard TJ groan as he sunk a ping-pong ball into a red

solo cup. "You two are kind of insufferable lovesick puppies."

I gave him the finger. I wondered if TJ would ever come to the dark side with us, but he seemed like a guy who would never settle down. Although, I guess a lot of people said that about me too.

After our game of beer pong, I watched Dinah come over to the couch, where she and Noah looked so disgustingly cute. He pulled the tiny woman into his lap and whispered sweetly to her. I had never seen the kid look happier. I wanted what they had, but I wasn't sure if Fi would ever feel like that about me. I went into the kitchen to find her alone and nursing a glass of water, which I guessed was good. She side-eyed me from behind the glass and put it down on the counter.

"You were right," she stated.

"Yeah? What was I right about this time?"

Her eyes slanted into slits of annoyance at my cockiness. "That I would get along with Dinah. I'm not good at friendships."

My heart softened at that, and I grabbed her hand. "We're friends."

"True, but I'm not good at keeping friends," she explained with a sigh, and she squeezed my hand. I smelled the alcohol on her breath, so I wondered if these were melancholy drunk thoughts. "I guess that's why it really hurt when Eric didn't show up. It was yet another person who left."

I cupped her face in my hands and looked into her eyes. "You know I'm not going to abandon you, right?"

She shook her head. "You already did."

"When I left for the NHL?" I asked.

She nodded. "Everyone always abandons me. So what's the point in getting close to anyone?"

My heart broke for the woman standing in front of me. I couldn't believe she thought that I would ghost her out of my life. I didn't realize it bothered her that we weren't as close as when I left for the NHL and she left for college. She had wormed her way inside my heart when we were seventeen. Probably even way before that. She wasn't just always on my mind; she practically lived inside my brain. It now made a lot of sense why she was so hesitant about this marriage between us. She was convinced that I was going to leave her. I didn't know how to explain to her that was never going to happen.

"Hey," I said to her softly. "I'm sorry you felt like I abandoned you. I'm sorry we haven't been as close."

She shook her head at me and looked down at the floor.

"Fi, that's not going to happen again, okay?"

She refused to look at me and pulled away to sip her water almost coldly. Maybe keeping her at a distance had been a bad idea. She shook her head suddenly and looked up at me with a worried look. "I'm sorry."

"What are you sorry for?"

She shrugged.

I glanced at my watch and noticed it wasn't too late, but I could see the party starting to peter out. "Do you want to head home?" I asked.

Her eyes got shiny then. "Do you mean to your home?"

"Fi, we talked about this. It's our home. I want it to be our home, okay?"

She nodded. "Okay, yeah. I think vodka was a bad idea; it put me in a bad mood."

I smiled and raised my eyebrows but didn't say anything. We headed home in silence, Fiona thinking about whatever was rolling around in her brain, and me silent because I didn't even know what to say. What did you say to your wife, who didn't even want to give your marriage a shot because she was afraid she was going to lose you in the end? I never meant for her to feel like I abandoned her when I got drafted into the NHL. I knew we weren't as close as we used to be, but part of that had been because her ex hated me and never wanted me around.

Upon our return to the condo, she got ready for bed while I cracked a beer in the kitchen. She sauntered back into the kitchen in shorts and a tank top that did nothing to hide her figure and grabbed another glass of water.

"I think I drank too much; I'm still a little drunk," she mused.

I raised one eyebrow in response. "You want to go to bed?"

She yawned. "Yeah. I kind of have the spins."

I abandoned my beer and led her into the bedroom. "Let's go to bed."

She climbed into bed while I got undressed. I slipped into the bed beside her, and I smiled when she crawled over to rest her head on my chest.

"Baby?" she whispered.

"What's wrong, sweetheart?"

"I'm sorry."

"For what?"

"For getting too drunk tonight and picking a fight."

I tilted her chin up to look at me, and it crushed me to see the downcast look etched across her face. "I'm sorry if you felt abandoned when my career took me away from you." I lifted my left hand up for her to see. "You see this?"

"Your wedding ring?"

"It means I'm not going anywhere. Okay?"

"Promise?"

"Promise, sweetheart."

"I'm sorry you always have to take care of me."

I cupped her face and pressed a quick kiss to her lips. "I like taking care of you. I'm always gonna do that, okay?"

She nodded and curled up against me again. I stroked her hair while we cuddled in our bed, loving the feeling of this woman at my side.

I should have told her then that I loved her. It would have assuaged the insecurities that were bubbling to the surface for her. I didn't know she felt that way when I left for the NHL, and I had a feeling that being left at the altar had brought back those feelings. I had to do everything in my power to prove to this woman that I wasn't gonna be like him. That I was here to stay and I was gonna fight for her.

"Fiona," I whispered, but when I looked down at her, she was already asleep in my arms.

I needed to tell her how I felt, but I wasn't sure if I was ready yet. I wasn't sure if either of us were ready for that. Deep down, I was scared that if I told her, she would ask for a divorce again because I was afraid she didn't feel the same way. I couldn't bear it if I lost my best friend.

CHAPTER NINETEEN

FIONA

J was sexually frustrated. Riley had been gone playing hockey for an entire week on the road. It was the longest we had been apart since we got married a few short weeks ago. It wasn't until he was gone that I realized we hadn't had sex since Vegas. I knew I was in more trouble than before because my whole body ached for him. I was not good about letting a man know when I wanted him, but it was clear to me that he was leaving everything in my court.

In Vegas, we had been so in-tuned to each other's bodies. It felt like even though we were living together, there was a wall in between us. I'd be lying if I said I hadn't been reading a lot of smutty romance books while he was gone. Or that I didn't dial the pink telephone a lot thinking about his hands on me. Or his mouth. Or his co—

"FIONA!" Katie yelled at me and threw her straw wrapper at me.

I blushed at the thoughts in my head and turned to Katie, who sat on the couch beside me. I had holed myself up in here all week, working on outlining new stories while my editor worked on notes for my third novel. It had gotten so bad that Katie texted Riley to ask him to make me respond to her texts.

"Sorry, what?" I asked.

She rolled her eyes at me. "Girl! What are you thinking about?"

"Um..."

She laughed. "Oh my God! The sex must be real good if you're daydreaming about it. Isn't Riley supposed to come home tonight?"

I sighed. "We haven't had sex since Vegas."

She sat up and looked at me in shock. "Seriously? Why?"

I threw my hands up in the air. "I don't know!"

"Have you asked?"

I blanched. "No."

"Fi! Sometimes guys don't get subtlety. He's probably worried you think he wants sex all the time. You have to talk to him."

I shrugged and put my hands in my hair with a sigh. "I don't know how!"

She patted my knee. "In all the years you dated my brother, I've never seen you like this before. If you two want this thing to work, you really need to work at it and talk to each other. You need to communicate your needs."

I stared at her, impressed by her advice.

She shrugged. "Brock and I were in therapy for a long time."

"Katie, I had no idea."

"We didn't work, but I see the smile on your face whenever Riley texts you, and I can see how much you miss him."

I bit my lip. "Is it that obvious?"

She smiled at me. "Why are you so hesitant to admit that you actually like your husband?"

I shrunk down on the couch. "Because it's a marriage of convenience. Yeah, he's my best friend, but why should I think he's not out there fucking other women?"

"Honey, have you two talked about that?"

I went to open my mouth to answer, but then the front door opened, which alarmed both of us because I always made sure to lock it. I leaned over the couch to see Riley drop his bag down at the front door. We locked gazes, and I saw the fire in his blue eyes. Heat pooled low in my belly at the sight of him in that immaculately tailored suit. My husband was FIIINE. His eyes shifted slightly to the left of me to see Katie on the couch beside me. His face shifted in confusion, but then he smiled.

"Hi, Katie!" he greeted.

"Hi, Riley!" she greeted back cheerfully. She turned to me with a smirk. "I think that's my cue to leave."

I grabbed her arm. "What? No, you don't have to leave."

Her eyes glanced between me, and Riley and then she laughed. "Um, yeah, I think I do."

She gathered her things and patted Riley's arm on the way-out. "Bye, Riley!"

He smirked. "Leaving so soon?"

She laughed her way out the door. I slunk down into the couch, but Riley crossed over to me and sat beside me. He put his arm around me and pulled me toward him. I swear I nearly purred. I had missed his strong arms pulling me towards him and the smell of his scent on the sheets. Shit, I had really missed him. Like I missed him so much, I was sleeping in his old t-shirts at night to feel like he was there. Shit, maybe Katie was right. Maybe Riley wasn't just my best friend anymore; maybe he was something much more, and that scared me.

I leaned my head on his shoulder, and he stroked my hair. "How was your week?" he asked.

"Fine. Waiting on edits, trying to work on new things," I answered truthfully. Not what I wanted to say, which was, "Shitty, because you weren't here, and I'm mad that we haven't had sex since we got married, and can you please throw me down and tear off my clothes?" Although, if I said those things out loud, he probably would have loved it.

I pulled my head off his chest and saw he was looking at me intensely. I opened my mouth to say something, but I was stopped by his mouth, crushing up against mine roughly. His hands were in my hair, and I pulled at the collar of his shirt with both of my hands. I kissed him back urgently like I needed his tongue in my mouth in order to breathe air. We pulled away from each other as suddenly as the kiss started, both of our chests heaving from being out of breath.

He leaned his forehead against mine. "Would it be bad if I told you I missed you?"

"No," I whispered back. "I missed you, too." My hands clutched the lapels of his dress shirt, and I wanted to tear it off of him.

His hands covered my own, and he pushed my hands off of him. I pouted, and he laughed at me while he squeezed out of the suit jacket. "I need a beer. Do you want a beer?" he asked.

Instead of answering his question, I blurted out the first thing that came into my head. "No, I want you."

He froze mid-getting up from the couch, but then he sat back down. He reached down to grab onto my thighs and swung me around, so I was straddling his hips on the couch. I melted at his touch while his hands roamed down my back until he firmly squeezed my ass.

I placed my hands on his chest. "Why haven't we had sex since Vegas?" I asked.

"I didn't want you to think that was all I wanted," he answered with a grunt as I ground myself against the hard bulge in his pants. Oh, his dick certainly was happy that I was on top of him.

"You say you want this marriage to work, but you've been keeping me at arm's length. Riley, I have needs, too."

He sighed. "Shit, I'm sorry. I promised you that I wouldn't be like him. That I wouldn't forget we hadn't had sex in months."

"It hasn't been months."

"Not the point, Fiona," he growled.

Mmm, I loved that growly alpha-male shit.

"Oh. Well, you can make it up to me now," I whispered into his ear.

"Tell me what you want," he demanded.

I gripped the back of his neck hard, digging my fingernails roughly into his skin. "I want you to touch me, please."

"Where?" he asked huskily.

"Everywhere," I breathed.

In a split-second, he stood, and I had my legs wrapped around his waist. We kissed like that while he slowly backed us into the bedroom. I loved the way he could lift me up like it was nothing. He tossed me on the bed and frantically started undoing his tie. I ripped my t-shirt off and was unbuttoning my jeans while he slowly undid the buttons on his crisp dress shirt. I slid my jeans down my thighs, but my mouth watered watching him reveal the hard planes of his chest with each button. I glared up at him because he was doing that on purpose.

"Stop being a tease!"

He went slower on the last button with a wicked grin. He gestured to his six-pack. "You thirsty for this bod, sweetheart?"

"Baby! Get over here and fuck my brains out!"

He laughed and finally pulled the shirt off his body and dropped it to the floor. I was too eager for this, arousal pooling low in my belly. I unclasped my bra and kicked my panties off, then leaned back on the bed, naked and ready for him. I watched him hungrily undo his belt buckle and kick his pants onto the floor. Damn, he was fucking hot. I ran my thumb over my bottom lip as the boxers fell too.

"Hey, my eyes are up here," he joked.

"Get over here," I urged.

"Happy wife, happy life," he muttered and stretched out on his side next to me.

His hand ran down my cheek and cupped my face pulling me towards him in another urgent kiss. I moaned while his other hand trailed down my chest, and he rolled one of my nipples in between his fingers. I felt both nipples get hard at his touch. He moved away from my mouth and kissed my neck, my chest, and finally rolled the hard bud of one of my nipples into his mouth. I moaned and closed my eyes while he used his tongue and his hands on my breasts. I was getting so into it that I kind of forgot he was actually here, and I wasn't daydreaming. My hand slipped down between my legs to touch myself.

"God, that's so hot," he breathed onto my chest. "Love watching you touch yourself. But let me do it."

My eyes flew open, and I felt the blush on my face.

He smirked at me before he took my hand and slowly sucked my finger. "Mmm," he moaned. "I love tasting you."

Before I could respond, he slipped a finger inside me and pumped into me slowly. "Don't be embarrassed, sweetheart," he said before he planted another kiss on my lips. "I love thinking about you touching yourself in our bed. What do you think about while you do it?"

"You," I whispered. "I think about what you're doing right now. Sometimes I use my vibrator."

"Fuck, that's so fucking hot," he breathed. "I'm filing that away for when I'm on the road."

"What do you mean?" I asked.

He kissed the side of my neck. "I think of you when I'm alone in my hotel room and horny," he whispered into my ear. "Which is all the time when I'm on the road and away from you."

I gasped when another finger pumped inside me, and I kind of lost the ability to speak for a little bit as he fingered me and sucked one of my tits simultaneously. It put me over the edge when his thumb touched my clit at the same time.

"Fuck, Aaron," I whined. I needed his hard cock pumping inside my pussy right now. I didn't want his fucking fingers; I wanted the real deal.

"Fuck yeah. Love hearing my name on your lips," he growled at me.

"Baby...I need you inside me, like yesterday," I urged.

I fumbled around behind me in the drawer of the bedside table for a condom. I handed the package to him and hungrily watched him roll it onto his swelling erection.

He reached into the drawer for the lube, and I watched as he slid it across his cock, pumping it in his hand a few times. He slowly entered me, giving me time to adjust to the feel of him. He was being too gentle; I wanted him to slam into me and be aggressive. I was starting to get into it when he stopped suddenly.

He ran his hand down my face and kissed me tenderly. "Tell me what you want." Before I could answer, he wrapped his fingers around my throat. "Oh, but you like it when I'm in charge, don't you?"

I could only whimper and nod in response. I really liked the possessive grip of his hands on me like this.

His lips curled up into a wolfish grin. "I want you to beg for it, Fiona. Beg for my cock."

"Oh, yeah?" I asked and arched an eyebrow at him.

"I don't hear you begging," he growled.

I yelped in surprise when he released his grip on my neck, pulled out, and flipped me over onto my stomach, pressing me against the mattress. His lips made a tortuous path up my back until he was at my neck, his breath hot in my ear. "I'm gonna ride you hard and spank your perfect ass."

I groaned into the pillow. Oh my God, this man so had my number when it came to sex.

His hands slid down my sides and gripped my hips. "You want that, sweetheart? You want to get spanked?"

"Yes," I groaned in frustration.

Why is he torturing me?

I leaned up on my elbows and grinned at him from over my shoulder. He smirked at me as he smacked my ass. I moaned at the stinging sensation and gripped the sheets below me, and he wasn't even inside me again yet. His hands rubbed across my ass, soothing the spot he had just struck, then he traveled up my back, caressing me in slow, gentle circles. He pressed his front against my back and kissed my neck.

"You want it?" he whispered huskily in my ear, lightly tweaking my hair. The tingling sensation on my scalp went all through my body, and yes, I very much wanted what he was offering to me right now.

"Please," I begged.

He kissed my neck and slid his hand onto the back of it softly but in a possessive grip. "You really want it, you better beg for it."

"Please, Aaron," I whimpered.

"Please, what?" he growled into my ear, and I felt a shiver run along my whole body. Riley was so large and in charge, such an alpha-male. I was so fucking into it.

"Baby, please, I need you."

"Need me to what?"

"I need you to dominate me. Please."

"Holy fuck, you're gonna get it so good," he growled and slapped my ass again.

He positioned himself behind me, spreading my legs, and then he gripped my hips in his strong hands and crashed into me. He jackknifed deviously hard inside of me, so hard that I had to grab the headboard so I didn't fall to pieces onto the mattress. Every once in a while, he paired a thrust with a nice slap on my ass, and I tumbled further and further into ecstasy while he continued to give me what I wanted. I squeezed my eyes shut, taking the feeling up and up inside myself until I was moaning his name as I came. My limbs felt like jelly as I dropped down on my stomach onto the mattress, and Riley continued thrusting hard inside me.

"I'm gonna come," he growled, his hand sliding up my back to grip my hair in his hand.

Fuck yes!

"Do it!" I growled back.

He thrust hard and fast, and I smiled into the pillow when my name ended as a moan on his lips.

CHAPTER TWENTY

RILEY

"Fuck me," I breathed and dropped down onto the bed on my back when I returned from throwing out the condom.

"I think I just did," Fi joked with a smirk and leaned into my chest. I pulled my arm around her back, and she snuggled into me further. I had loved this woman for a long time, but her need for me to be aggressive with her in bed was such a fucking turn on for me. She really liked that alpha-male shit in bed, and I loved giving it to her. I liked to be in charge, and fuck, it was sexy that she let me.

"Remind me to never go that long without sex," I mused.

"Oh? Has it been as long for you as it has been for me?" she asked.

I pushed her onto her back, and her eyes went wide

when she obviously realized what she had said. "What do you mean?" I seethed.

She shook her head. "Nothing. Forget it."

"Fiona, what do you mean? Tell me."

She let out a frustrated noise from deep in her throat. "Well...you're a professional athlete."

"Can confirm."

"Who has beautiful women throwing themselves at you all the time."

"Okay. What's your point?" I asked, even more confused. What the hell was she saying to me?

She furrowed her brow at me and sighed. "Riley! I know that athletes cheat on their wives all the time! I've come to accept that's going to be part of this deal."

"WHAT.THE.ACTUAL.FUCK?" I bellowed.

She shrank away at my raised voice. I sat up on the bed and ran a frustrated hand down my face. The scared look on her face broke my heart. "You think...you think I've been cheating on you? What, do you think I wanted an open marriage or some shit?"

"Well, we never talked about it! I mean, our marriage is kinda...fake."

"Fiona, you know how I feel about cheating. You know what my dad did to my mom," I snapped at her. "And what do you mean our marriage is 'fake'?"

"Well, we didn't exactly get married for love."

That hit me right in the chest. I got married for love, but she definitely did not.

"Fi..."

She sat up on the bed, clutching the sheet to her chest. "I'm sorry. I mean, I would be okay...if you want to have an arrangement like that."

"Fiona, what the fuck? Why would I want an open marriage?"

"So you can fuck other people. And not feel guilty about cheating on me."

"Sweetheart, I don't want that," I seethed at her. "Why would you think that?"

"I didn't mean—"

"Did you seriously think I would cheat on you?"

She looked taken aback. "What do you mean?"

"Do you think so little of me?"

She reached out at hand and touched my arm. "Hey, hey, I'm sorry. I should have talked to you about it. I assumed the worst. Forgive me?"

My head was in my hands, but I pulled my hands away to look at her. Her green eyes looked up at me with a sadness and insecurity I hadn't seen in them before. "Fiona, you know I would never do that. I'm not my dad."

She leaned over, gripped the back of my neck, and pulled my lips to hers. I didn't kiss her back, because honestly, I was really hurt at the accusations. I knew our marriage was weird and rushed, but I married her for real. This was a real marriage to me. I knew she didn't love me like I did her, and maybe I should have told her how I felt so she didn't jump to this conclusion. I was still too chicken-shit to tell her that I loved her because I was afraid she would ask for a divorce again. It hurt that she thought I was off out there sleeping with other women just because I knew she would be fine with that. I didn't want a marriage like that.

"I'm sorry. Please, Aaron, please forgive me," she begged.

Oh, she so knew what to say to get me to forgive her. The sound of her voice so soft and small did me in. "You know how I feel about that. We're exclusive, right? You haven't..." But I couldn't complete the question. The idea that Fi had been sleeping with another man while I was traveling for my job ripped my heart in two.

She looked at me in horror. "No! I married you! Why do you think I nearly jumped you when you got home? I have been so sexually frustrated; my vibrator isn't good enough sometimes."

I laughed at that. "Again, I'm going to have to file that imagery away for when I'm on the road."

She laughed with me. "Oh my God! Were you being serious earlier?"

I smiled and kissed her, this time pulling her back down to me so she was straddling my hips again. "Only you," I told her when I pulled away. "I married you, only you. I know this is kind of like a trial marriage, but you get all of me in this."

She ran her hands down my chest, raking her nails on my skin. "When did you get so seriously ripped?" she asked.

"It's kind of my job to be in peak physical condition."

Her eyes scanned down the hard lines of my chest, and her hands gripped the thick muscles of my biceps. "I never thought I would be into big muscles," she said so softly that I didn't think I was supposed to hear her.

I pulled her down to kiss me again and loved the feeling of her hands all over me. When I pulled away, her eyes widened, probably at feeling my cock beneath her.

"Seriously?" she asked but had a smile on her face.

I smirked. "We do have to make up for some lost time. Also, you're right. Using my hand just isn't the same thing."

She laughed, but then I had her on her back again and moaning my name while I spent some much needed time with my head between her legs. I ached for this woman and was hungry to please her. It was especially nice when she returned the favor without me having to ask. Damn, if I hadn't already married her, I probably would have said she was wife material.

Fi laid her head on my chest again, and I pulled my arm around her to hold her tight against me. A sheen of sweat covered both of us from our recent activities, but neither of us was complaining. Being on the road for half the year could be tough, but I didn't realize how tough until I married my best friend and she came to live with me. It swelled my heart to know that she had missed me as much as I missed her, and I wondered if maybe, just maybe, she was falling in love with me too. Lying here naked in bed with her and holding her against me was the best feeling in the world.

I flinched a little when I felt her small hand trace the lines of the red-gold phoenix tattoo on my forearm. She looked up at me with a cheeky smile. "Sorry."

I smiled down at her and kissed the top of her vibrant red hair. "It tickles," I admitted.

"I always loved this tattoo."

I stroked her hair and closed my eyes. "Remember how nervous I was when I got it?"

I felt her laugh on my chest. "Didn't Stacey break up with you because of it?"

"Don't remind me," I groaned. "Why did you ever let me go out with her?"

"I thought you liked her!"

I sighed. "I was a kid, and she was hot, but her personality not so much. I wish—" But I couldn't finish my thought because I heard something vibrating on the floor where I had discarded my pants. "Shit!"

Fi moved from off my chest with a look of concern in her eyes. "What's wrong?"

I reluctantly glided out of bed and started rushing around to get dressed again. "I was supposed to meet my agent," I explained. I picked up my phone and saw all the missed calls. Steve was going to kill me, especially since it was so not like me to be late for a meeting.

"Oh my God, you're never late for anything in your life, ever. I'm sorry."

I tucked my shirt into my pants and walked back over to the bed, where she was now sitting up against the headboard but had the sheet wrapped around her chest. That amused me because I just had my mouth all over her body. I leaned down and kissed her goodbye.

"Sorry, I really have to go."

She waved me off. "Go on. I feel bad I made you late."

I smirked. "I'll tell my agent I was too busy eating out my wife to be on time for the meeting."

Her eyes widened. "Riley! Don't you dare!"

I laughed. "I'm just kidding." I tilted her chin up and kissed her again one last time before booking it out of there. I pulled my cell out and called Steve back while I rushed down to my SUV in the parking garage.

"Riley!" he greeted me. "I've been trying to get a hold of you."

I put the vehicle in gear. "Sorry, man."

"You're never late for anything; I was kind of worried," Steve admitted.

Steve had been my agent since I was drafted into the NHL as a kid. He had been in the business for a long time, and he knew what he was doing. He was kind of a father figure to me when I was coming up and was always there for guidance. He was also TJ's agent, so I knew that was why he was in town. Also, with our season almost over, there was some worry about my contract being up in July. I liked Philly, but I was even more nervous about the possibility that the Bulldogs might not want to re-sign me now that I had Fi with me. I didn't want to have to uproot her entire life because of my career. I knew that was something she was worried about, too, even if she never voiced it. I was afraid if Philly didn't sign me and I had to go somewhere else, ripping Fi from her life here could cause her to rethink giving this marriage a chance.

"I'm sorry, man. I'm on my way now."

I ran a hand through my blond hair and hung up the phone. It was not like me to forget about a meeting, but when I walked in today and saw Fi sitting there on the couch, all rational thoughts fell out of my head. All I wanted was to take her in my arms and show her what she had been missing. Which I totally did, so it was worth it being late for this meeting. I just had to think up a good excuse for my agent. The "sorry, I was too busy pleasuring my new wife" wasn't exactly the type of thing I could lead with. Plus, Fi probably would have murdered me if I told Steve that. Steve had been Cillian Gallagher's roommate in college, and he'd known both of us since we were small children.

I got to the restaurant in no time and found Steve in a booth in the back. I slid into the seat across from him and quickly ordered when the waitress came over. I looked up at Steve, and he had this smirk on his face that I couldn't place. I scratched my jaw, feeling the itchiness of my facial hair coming in. Steve's eyes landed on the ring on my finger, and he furrowed his brow in confusion, and then it turned into an even bigger smirk.

"I thought TJ was joking," he commented.

I rubbed the back of my neck. "Uhh..."

"That explains you being late."

The color drained from my face, and I knew he could probably see the mortification from what he was implying. Thankfully the waitress came back with my beer, so I was able to take a sip of it without having to answer the question.

When I set it down, Steve gave me that stern fatherly look. "What?" I asked.

"Did you get a prenup?"

I sighed. Yeah, I was not going to bring that up with Fi at all. "Um..."

"Riley!" he scolded.

"I don't need one with her."

He stared me down and shook his head. "Okay, who is this woman that you up and married with no plans whatsoever?"

"Fiona Gallagher."

I swear Steve's eyes bulged out of his head. He took a huge sip of his own beer. "Does Cillian know about this?" he finally asked.

I nodded slowly. "Yeah, he was there. I got his blessing if that's what you're asking. Although, if Fi knew that, I think she would be pretty pissed about it."

"Damn it. I owe your mom money."

I raised an eyebrow. "Excuse me?"

Steve laughed. "Oh, we've had a bet going on about if you two would ever get together."

My mother had failed to mention that to me when I visited her a couple weeks ago. That was odd since she kept trying to talk me into letting Fi go. "Huh. Well, it's kind of complicated, so I would hold on to that money," I told him.

"How is it complicated? You look really happy."

I sighed. "Well, she was left at the altar, so *we* got married instead, and we're kind of trying to see if this will work between us."

Steve nodded. "Marriage is tough. If you really want to make it work, you'll find a way. Still pissed at you that you didn't get a prenup, but I know Fiona. She's good people."

I smiled. "She is."

"Oh man, she has you ensnared, doesn't she?" he asked, amused.

I smiled again. "Yeah, she does. But did we come here to talk about my weird marriage or to talk about contract stuff?"

He shook his head. "I DO NOT want details. Okay, let's talk about negotiations I want to put in front of the Bulldogs in the postseason."

"I want to stay in Philly."

"Okay, I figured. So here's what I'm—"

I cut him off, "No, Steve. I *have* to stay in Philly."

"Riley, I get it. We'll put numbers in front of them, and if they don't bite, we can consider our options. You could make a lot of money in a different city."

I shook my head. "I don't care if I have to take a pay cut. I literally do not give a shit about how many zeroes are on my check. I want to play hockey, but it *has* to be for the Bulldogs."

He frowned. I frustrated him all the time because I played hockey for love of the sport. But there was no way I was going to a different city when my marriage was still so fragile. I couldn't tear Fiona from her home or her friends.

"Riley, you're the weirdest client."

"I can't do that to her," I admitted.

"To who?"

"Fiona."

"Oh."

I nodded. "Do whatever you can, but I want to stay in Philly. I have to stay here for her, for my marriage."

His eyes widened, and he nodded in understanding. "Okay, I get it." He took a swig of his beer. "You really love her, don't ya?"

I nodded and twisted my ring around my finger. "She was the one that got away. I need to prove to her that this thing between us is real. I can't do that if I have to move to a different city come next fall."

"Okay. I'll get it done, but don't say I didn't warn you when it's not enough money."

"I don't care about that. I only care about her."

He shook his head. "Christ, kid, you're lovesick."

I gave him a dopey smile. I was, and I didn't fucking care.

CHAPTER TWENTY-ONE

FIONA

"Do you think you could talk to Dinah?" Riley asked me as he stood at the door about to leave for another game on the road after only being home for two days. This hockey wife thing was harder than I wanted to admit. Having him home for a few days for him to only be back on the road again did kinda suck.

I sighed and ran a hand through my hair. "I'll try. Is Noah really torn up about her breaking up with him?"

He grimaced. "She did it via text."

I cringed. "Oh, that's bad. I liked them together. I'll see what I can do."

Riley smiled at me and leaned down to give me a long, lingering kiss goodbye. I was starting to wonder why my heart fluttered whenever he kissed me or why it banged deep in my chest whenever he left me.

"Please don't hole yourself up here when I'm gone," he

told me sternly. His hands gripped my waist and pulled me flush against his chest.

"I have to work on edits!" I exclaimed.

He squinted his eyes at me. "I better not hear from Katie while I'm away again."

Damn her. I rolled my eyes at him and shoved him away. "Go on, get out of here."

"Not like these games matter now," he muttered.

Despite their best efforts, the team had found out that they were officially out of the playoffs. So even though they needed to finish out the season, there was no drive left in the boys.

I frowned at him. "Riley, I'm sorry."

"Not your fault, sweetheart. It's just hard to go and have to play more games when we know there's nothing at the end of the tunnel."

I kissed him quickly. "I know it sucks."

I felt bad for my husband. He worked so hard to be good at the sport he loved. He spent a lot of time studying stats and video, and the Bulldogs still weren't making the playoffs. Let's just say I spent a lot of time on my knees trying to cheer him up about it. I only think it partly worked, but at least my husband was sexually satisfied.

His thumb rubbed across my cheek. "I know, sweetheart. I better go."

I put my hands on his face, and he smiled big at the gesture. "I'll miss you," I told him sincerely. I tried not to think too much about what that meant. If I thought too much about that, the doubts would start to creep in again.

"I'll miss you too, sweetheart. So much," he whispered, and then he kissed me again, his tongue sliding across the seam of my lips.

"Baby," I protested and tried to push him away. "You have to go."

He groaned and rested his forehead against mine. "I know. I hate leaving you."

"I know, but you gotta go play hockey. Stop taking bad penalties and make sure you protect the slot in front of Metzy."

He laughed. "Okay, coach!"

"I'm your favorite coach."

"A sexy coach."

I pushed him away. "Oh my God! Leave now before I make you really late and Kat Metz calls me asking why you aren't on the jet again."

It might not have been the first time that Riley had been late getting to the jet and the GM's assistant had called me demanding where my horny husband was. I think the travel team called her because she was scary and kept all those hockey boys in line. I hadn't met the woman yet, but I had mad respect for her. She got shit done.

He gave me one last lingering kiss, and then he was out the door. Him leaving all the time was not getting any easier. I knew it was bad, but I was secretly glad the Bulldogs weren't making the playoffs because then I got to spend more time with my husband. I tried to push down the feelings of why that was.

I spent the next couple of days while Riley was on the road working on the edits for this new book. The first draft was painful, and I did have to rewrite a lot of it. Riley had given me a lot of the same notes as my editor, which was kind of surprising, but also really sweet that he cared enough that he read my book and wanted to help me make it better. I did hole myself up for a couple days, but only so I could hunker down and get work done.

I tried to talk to Dinah, but she hadn't been responding to anyone. We had gone to the last home game together and grabbed lunch beforehand. Noah had taken a bad hit in the game, and they made him sit out because of concussion stuff. Her reaction was weird about it, though. We had talked before the game, and she seemed really unsure about her feelings for him since he had told her he loved her and she hadn't said it back yet. I felt like she was ready to say it back, but Noah took that hit, and she freaked out. A few days later, when Riley told me she broke up with him, I felt awful for the young guy. I had been trying everything to talk with her. TJ had, too, since the three of them had been close before she and Noah started dating, but she had shut everyone out.

It was hard to watch our guys take the hard hits and wreck their bodies, but that was what they signed up for. I guess watching Riley do it all his life, I had grown accustomed to it. I really liked Dinah, and it was great to have a new writer friend in this city to bounce ideas off of. I didn't like how she hurt Noah and how she was shutting me out right now, though. I was going to have to try her again and coax what happened out of her. I didn't understand why she would break up with him because he got hurt during a game. He played hockey! It was kind of expected.

I groaned again at her dodging my calls and put my phone down, but then it flashed with my brother's name showing up on the screen. Finnegan never called me, so I assumed the worst.

"What's wrong?" I asked suddenly, my heart pounding in my head, thinking something had happened to one of our parents. I might not ever see eye-to-eye with my mother, but that didn't mean I didn't care about her. Or worry about her health.

Finnegan laughed on the other line. "Nothing's wrong."

"Oh. Well, then what do you want?" I asked.

"Nice to talk to you too, Fiona. No 'Hi, Finnegan, how are you? I haven't seen you since my bizarre-ass wedding. That was really fucking weird, huh?' RUDE!"

"Bite me."

Finnegan and I were like typical siblings in that we bickered constantly, and him being older, I was always his annoying little sister. We didn't always agree, and he was kind of a douche, but he was still my brother, so I guess I was supposed to love him or some shit.

"So, Mom's literally making me call you because she knows you won't answer."

I rolled my eyes. Last time I talked to mom, she hammered in the grandkids speech again. I ended up being a total brat and hung up on her. Since then, I had been screening her calls and texting her that I was super busy. Which wasn't exactly a lie, but she still called it my "little writing career" and didn't take my livelihood seriously. Now that I was married to Riley, I think she thought I was going to become a housewife and abandon my writing. No, I worked damn hard at this stuff, and there was a reason I was able to quit my job to do it full time. Although I had been debating if I should go back part-time, so I had a fall back since in the back of my mind, I was still worried this marriage with Riley wasn't going to work out.

"Sorry," I offered while making myself another cup of coffee. I was going to need more caffeine to deal with this. "What does she want?"

"Wants to know if you're gonna come visit once the season's over."

Riley did tend to go visit his mom during the off-season, but we hadn't talked about that at all. The last two days he had been home, we used our mouths a lot, but there were not a lot of words coming out of them.

"We haven't discussed it."

Finnegan sighed on the other line. "Are you doing this for real? This marriage with him?"

"Yeah, I guess we are."

"It's not like a—" he cut himself off and was quiet for a moment.

"Not like what?" I asked and took a sip of the coffee.

"A business arrangement?" Finnegan asked.

His question shocked me, but I guess I shouldn't have been surprised. My marriage to Riley had been a surprise. More surprising had been how eager we both were to get into bed together. We were enjoying ourselves for sure, and it wasn't exactly love, but at the same time, it wasn't exactly whatever the hell my brother was trying to insinuate.

"What?" I finally asked in disbelief.

"Fi, did he tell you?"

Panic wrapped tight around my chest, thinking only the worst thing possible. "Tell me what?"

"You know he loves you, right?"

"Of course. We're best friends."

I could almost see Finnegan face-palming over the miles we were apart. "No, dude. He really loves you."

"What are you talking about?"

"Why do you think he married you?"

"Because he said he was tired of the single-life, and he thought we could find happiness together," I explained, but when I said it out loud, it sounded really dumb.

My brother finally sighed into the phone. "Riley is full-fledged in love with you. That's why he offered to marry you when that douche-canoe stood you up. It's why he asked Dad for his blessing. It's why he convinced you that you two could have a shot together."

My mouth went dry. No. There was no way that Aaron Riley was in love with me like that. No freaking way. He asked my dad for his blessing to marry me? No way! Why would he do that? Because my dad knew getting his blessing didn't matter to me, but he wanted to be asked. He had been pissed when Eric never even told him he had an interest in marrying me.

"Fiona?" Finnegan's voice cut into my thoughts, but it sounded like he was on another planet.

"I have to go," I said suddenly and hung up.

My heart beat louder and louder in my chest, and my mind raced with all the thoughts in my head. Why would Riley up and marry me and convince me to stay? I thought of all the times his eyes slanted over me and the way he looked at me like I was the only woman in the world. Was that really lust the whole time? Or something more? I kept thinking back to our first night together, and how slow and gentle he had been with me on that first round of sex, how hurt he had been when I asked him for a divorce the next day. If he really felt that way, why hadn't he said anything?

I didn't want to think about this right now. I didn't want to think about how much I missed him when he was on the road and how much my heart melted when he told me how proud he was of me about getting my first book published. I especially didn't want to think about how I thought I was falling in love with him too and how much that scared me. Like really scared me because if he loved me, that meant he would eventually leave me like everyone else did. Like he already did once when he left for the NHL. He may have told me the ring on his finger was a promise that it wouldn't happen again, but I couldn't help the doubts from creeping in.

I went into the pantry and grabbed a bottle of whiskey. My hands flew back to my phone, ignoring the follow-up call from my brother, and tried Dinah once more. This time, she answered, and I berated her about breaking up with Noah. Then I promptly told her I was coming over and we were going to get drunk together. I was going to push my feelings to the side and pretend they didn't exist. If only to help my friend get back together with her super cute boyfriend who thought the world of her. I didn't want to think about the possibility that I had fallen in love with my best friend.

CHAPTER TWENTY-TWO

RILEY

*N*oah's eyes cut across to mine when we were getting off the jet. I saw he was on his phone and gritting his teeth. He sighed and then shoved his phone at me. I threw my hands up in a shrug, and he mouthed, "Your wife."

Oh no, what did she do?

"Heyyy..." Her words slurred into the phone.

I shot Noah an apologetic look. "Hey yourself. What are you doing?"

"Trying to fix everything," she sighed.

I raised my eyebrows at Noah, and he sighed. "Are you at Dinah's?" I asked.

"Yesss," came the slurred response. Oh geez, she was definitely drunk. I'd recognize drunk Fiona speech anywhere.

"Okay, sweetheart, I'm going to come get you and take you home. Okay?"

"Okay," she responded in a small voice before I heard the click.

I handed Noah back his phone. He cocked his head and pushed his long dark hair behind his ear. "Is everything okay with you and Fi?"

"I thought so..." I trailed off and then looked at my phone and saw a text from my brother-in-law.

FINNEGAN: *Sorry, man. Kind of let it slip to Fi that you are legit in love with her, and I think it freaked her out.*

"Shit!"

"Hey, man, everything okay?" Noah asked.

I sighed and ran a hand down my face. This wasn't exactly how I wanted her to find out about the "L" word. I wanted it to be this big grand gesture, and then maybe she would then tell me she felt it too. She had to feel it too, right? She nearly melted in my arms when I kissed her, and I knew when we were having sex that the look in her eyes wasn't just one of lust. Or was I just seeing what I wanted to see?

Fiona Gallagher was *it* for me. She was the only woman who would ever be for me and the reason why I drowned myself in casual hookups and relationships that never worked. None of those women could hold a candle to my best friend, the love of my life.

My chest tightened. That's why she was day drinking at Dinah's. She knew I was in love with her, and she didn't want to think about it. That kind of crushed me.

Noah clapped me on the back. "We're quite a pair, eh?" he asked.

I shook my head with a sarcastic laugh. "I think I need to collect my wife at your girlfriend's."

He hung his head. "I don't know if she's my girlfriend anymore."

I followed him to where our cars were parked. "I don't know about that one. I think you two can figure it out."

"She really hurt me."

"I know, bud."

"How can I forgive her?"

"Noah, you love her, right?"

He nodded. "More than anything."

"Then you two need to talk about it, tell her how it hurt you, and try to work through it. If you both really love each other, you can work it out."

I tried to believe my own advice to the kid. What the fuck did I know when it came to love? I hated watching Noah be so sad the last couple weeks, though. I also had a feeling that his girl still had some lingering issues over her late husband's death. I thought maybe that's why watching him get taken out of the game made her break up with him. She was just scared.

He squinted at me. "Yeah, I think you're right."

"Maybe not while she's drunk, though, huh?"

He nodded.

I had no idea what I was in for when I got to Dinah's. Fi getting drunk with Dinah made me nervous. If that's what she did when Finnegan told her I was in love with her, maybe our marriage was doomed to fail. Maybe we should have gotten a divorce the day after our wedding. Maybe it would have made this hurt less.

When we got over to Dinah's place, the two of them were quite the drunken pair. Fi was lying on Dinah's couch with the bottle of whiskey in her hands while Dinah was lying on her floor. Noah and I shared an annoyed look; maybe it was a bad idea to introduce the two of them. He helped Dinah into her bedroom, and I took that as my cue to get my wife out of there.

I held out a hand, and I was surprised when she actually took it and let me pull her to her feet. I took the bottle gingerly out of her hands and set it down on the coffee table, then put an arm around her shoulders.

She leaned into me. "Riley?" she asked.

"Come on, sweetheart, let's go home," I told her.

She slipped her hand in mine, and we walked together back to my SUV. She fell asleep on the ride back to the condo, and it took a bit of encouragement to get her to come upstairs with me. I ended up carrying her inside and to our bedroom.

I placed her gently on the bed when her small hands grabbed the lapels of my shirt. "Aaron? I'm sorry."

"For what?" I asked softly, nearly melting at her calling me by my first name. It was a small gesture, but it made my heart pound loud in my head. "Do you want to get out of your jeans?"

She flopped back on the bed and squirmed out of her jeans, kicking them onto the floor. "I'm sorry I'm a bad hockey wife," she moaned.

My heart softened at that. I sat on the bed next to her and stroked her hair. "You're not, I promise. Maybe we should talk about this later. You had a lot to drink today."

"Mmmhmm," she moaned softly and closed her eyes. I kissed her forehead and moved from the bed. I picked up her jeans off the floor and put them in the hamper before quietly closing the door behind me and going into the kitchen. I cracked a beer and gulped half of it down while standing at the sink. I didn't know what was going on in her head, but I knew it was nothing good. I also knew that I couldn't really focus on that right now.

Normally, I would have let myself be consumed by watching game tape to figure out how to prepare for our game tomorrow, but now our season was toast. We had to play a couple more weeks of regular season hockey for nothing. It kind of sucked, but there was nothing I could do about it now.

I finished my beer and decided it was time for me to go to bed too. I grabbed a glass of water from the kitchen and left it on the nightstand beside Fi. She was probably going to need that in the morning. She was on her back when I climbed into bed beside her and, being paranoid, I checked that she was still breathing and then promptly shifted her so she was on her side. She shifted and pulled my arm around her, holding her close. I knew she was asleep, but I nuzzled her hair and kissed her neck softly before clutching her to my chest and falling asleep.

When I woke for pre-game stuff, Fi was still dead to the world, but the glass of water on the nightstand was empty. I dressed for the game and refilled the glass, leaving a note to her that I would see her when I got home.

She stirred when I leaned down to kiss her goodbye. Her eyes fluttered open, but she still looked half asleep. "Hey, where are you going?" she asked.

"Shush, go back to sleep. I have to get to the arena," I told her. I sat on the bed next to her and pushed her hair out of her face.

"Don't be mad at me," she cried in this sad small voice, and it gutted me that I had to leave her right now. I thought she might still be drunk.

"Sweetheart, I'm not. We'll talk when I get home, okay?"

She kissed my big hand lying on her face, right on the

silver wedding band that I only took off when I was playing hockey.

"Aaron..."

"Shush, sweetheart. Go back to sleep," I urged and kissed her on the forehead.

"Aaron, I'm sorry, please don't leave me," she urged, and then she was crying.

I wiped the tears from her face and pulled her to my chest, not caring if her tears wet my suit. "Aw, sweetheart, don't cry. I'm here. I'm only leaving because I have a game to go to. Get some sleep, okay?"

"Baby, I'm so sorry," she said and pulled away from me.

I smiled at her and gently pushed her back down on the bed. I kissed her forehead again. "Sleep, sweetheart."

She yawned then but finally did go back to sleep, and I had a feeling she wouldn't remember the conversation we just had.

I pushed all the things out of my head about what her day drinking with Dinah meant and left for the arena. I was nervous, and I was scared, but not because of hockey. I did my normal pre-game rituals, but I was so on edge that I ended up taping and re-taping my stick way too many times. Like way more than normal. My usual visualization of getting the puck to the back of the net wasn't working either. I knew I wasn't the only one on edge when I locked eyes with Noah. I didn't even want to bring up whatever was happening with him and Dinah.

All my thoughts of anything other than the game melted away as soon as my skates hit the ice. I'm sure therapy really helped a lot of people, but for me, my therapy had always been this game. I took my place on the bench and watched the starting line take the first face-off, and of course, we lost the puck to New York. There was a tightness in my chest, and I suddenly had a really bad feeling about this game.

On the change-up, I hopped over the bench with my line and struggled to bat the puck away from our opponents. I made a big hit on one of the lumbering defenders, a six-foot-four massive Swede that I was sure actually hurt me more than it did him. I couldn't get the puck out from under his stick. When I did, I put too much pressure on my stick and flung the puck all the way down the ice. I hung my head at the icing call and skated down the other end to watch as Noah took the face-off. I think we were both off our game because the other team got possession and tried to one-time it into Metzy's net. Metzy—the fucking beauty—saved all our asses on that play.

I skated my ass off in the game, taking big hits and giving them back just as hard. It was my job to be that big tough guy on the ice who protected the net at all costs. Coach lit a fire under our asses after the second period, so we rushed the net hard and tied the game with a minute left in the third. It ended up not being enough, and we lost 4-3 in OT. It wasn't like this game mattered anyway.

After the game, Noah was getting hammered with questions by the media since he had gotten a goal and an assist in the game. Despite assisting him on the goal, I was able to slink away to the showers. I checked my phone after I got dressed and was a little disappointed that I hadn't heard from Fi.

Hallsy slapped me on the back. "Hey, man, you coming out for drinks tonight?"

I shook my head and started typing a message to Fi. "Nah," I answered.

"Oh," Hallsy said, dark eyes smiling. "You miss your wife; I get it. I miss Mia so much when we're on the road."

I nodded but was tight-lipped about the whole thing. Yeah, I had missed my wife, but I wasn't sure if she missed me. I also didn't like that this morning, she was so sad and crying. I think she had still been drunk, but I didn't know what to think. What was she sorry about? And why was she crying and begging me not to leave her? I had a whole day off tomorrow, no practice, no games. I wanted to spend it with her as much as possible. If she would let me.

CHAPTER TWENTY-THREE

FIONA

I woke groggily and in a haze with the familiar pounding of a hangover in my head. It felt like a giant took a sledgehammer to my brain. I didn't even want to open my crusty eyes, but when I wiped my hand across my face, I realized the problem was not just sleep. I had been crying.

What the fuck?

The last thing I remembered was freaking out when Finnegan told me that Riley married me because he loved me. Then I went to Dinah's with a bottle of whiskey to distract myself from the confusing feelings. And also to knock some sense into her so she would beg Noah to take her back. Since she broke up with him for no good reason, the kid had been a real shit to be around. I knew Riley tried to mentor the younger guy, which was why he had asked me if I could intervene. Well, I did, by avoiding the fact that my brother thought my husband was hopelessly in love with me. I vaguely remembered D trying to tell me the same thing last night after she had drunk texted Noah. *Oh, woof. I better call her later.*

I slid my eyes to the other side of the bed, and something wrenched inside my chest at the sight of it empty. I squinted up at the ceiling, trying to remember how I got home in the first place. Had D put me into an UBER last night? No, she was just as bad as I had been.

HOLY SHIT!

Noah and Riley had come over to her condo after they got off the team jet. Guilt, or maybe it was all the whiskey, bubbled up inside me as I remembered that Riley had a game today. I ran a hand across my face and groaned. I was the worst hockey wife.

I pulled my left hand back when it felt odd. My eyes widened, and I swore when I noticed my wedding ring was missing. Why was my wedding ring missing? I couldn't remember anything from last night.

The condo was quiet, but when I looked at my phone, I knew Riley had already left for the arena. He had left a note on the bedside table along with a glass of water, which I drank quickly. I didn't think there was any way I was going anywhere today. Especially not to the game if I couldn't find my wedding ring. What would Riley think if he saw me without it?

I got up out of bed and paced. Then I went to the kitchen to eat some toast because it was all I could stomach at the moment. Luckily, I was keeping the whiskey down, but all I was thinking about was how Riley would look at me when he came home and saw me not wearing my wedding ring. I didn't want that.

I finished my toast and started tearing apart our

bedroom, looking for that stupid ring. I looked under the bed, opened all the drawers in the dresser, checked the box in the walk-in closet where Riley kept his cufflinks, and finally went to the bathroom. Nowhere. My ring was nowhere to be found. I stormed around the living room, searching behind every cushion, and even checked the damn refrigerator. Drunk Fiona was known to put things in weird places. Still nothing.

I slumped on the couch in defeat. I pulled out my phone and dialed Dinah's number.

"You suck, you know that, right?" she said by way of greeting.

"Sorry, but it worked, didn't it?"

"I'm not sure. I was too drunk to talk to Noah last night. I think we're gonna talk when he gets home."

"That's good, though? You still want to be with him, right?"

She sighed. "More than anything. Anyway, do you feel like hot garbage too?"

I laughed. "Yup. And I have another problem."

"What's up?"

"I can't find my wedding ring."

She was silent for a minute. "Hang on. I'm going to go check if it's here."

I waited in silence on the line while she searched her condo. I sipped at my glass of water and tried to make my hangover disappear.

"Sorry, Fi, I can't find it, but I'll keep looking," Dinah said when she got back on the line.

"Fuck, okay. Thanks. I better go; I need to find it before Riley gets home."

"Good luck! It'll turn up."

I hoped she was right, but a part of me wasn't that optimistic.

I went back into the bedroom and got down on hands and knees, searching the carpet for that stupid silver ring. It wasn't even that nice a wedding band, but I loved the weird story behind my marriage. If Riley saw me not wearing it, he was going to think the worst. He was going to think that I didn't love him.

It was at that moment, crying on the floor of our bedroom, that I realized why I was so upset about losing my wedding ring. And why I decided to get drunk last night instead of dealing with my feelings.

I loved him too.

I loved Aaron Riley, my best and oldest friend, and the man who was always there for me when I needed him. Maybe that was the real reason the universe told Eric to leave me at the altar because he wasn't who I was supposed to be with.

I had always loved Riley in a way. In high school, we had been fooling around when his teammate Jackson had asked me out. Jackson was cute and sweet, so I had encouraged Riley to ask out Stacey Graves because I knew she had a thing for him. Jackson ended up being a douche, and I broke up with him a couple weeks later, but Riley and Stacey dated all senior year. She did not particularly like me. I think I made a mistake all those years ago, and now I knew why.

I'm not sure when Riley discovered he loved me. When Finnegan told me that was why he had saved my wedding day, it scared the shit out of me. Not because I didn't feel the same way, because I was pretty sure I did, but I was scared that if I allowed myself to love someone again, they would leave me again. Like Riley had when he left for the

NHL and like Eric had when I was supposed to marry him. Now Riley was probably mad at me for getting shit-faced with Dinah, and I had lost my wedding ring.

I was so afraid he was going to come home, see me without my ring, and think that I wanted a divorce, which I definitely did not want. Not anymore. I loved this man who protected and cared for me my whole life and would do anything I asked. I wanted to stay married to him and maybe later have babies with him.

Holy fuck, I wanted to have a baby with him. Not like this second, but one day. I wanted all of that with Riley. All those things that Eric decided I couldn't have because he didn't want them. Riley could give that to me, and I really wanted that. I wanted the happy life together that he had promised. I wanted our happily ever after.

I put my hands over my face and breathed heavily as tears fell down my face and my shoulders racked with my sobs. I gasped in shock suddenly when strong hands pulled my hands away from my face. Through tear-stained eyes, I stared back into Riley's worried blue eyes. He scanned me with an anguished look etched across his face. His thumb brushed across my cheek and wiped away a tear.

"Hey," he whispered softly. "What's with the tears? What's wrong?"

I shook my head, shaking tears onto the floor beneath me. "I can't find my wedding ring!" I blubbered.

His face softened, and he wiped more tears away from my face with his calloused fingers. "Why are you crying? It's just a ring."

"Aaron! It's my *wedding* ring!" I exclaimed. "I haven't taken it off since we got married! I--I felt like if I took it off, our marriage would be over."

His eyes got cloudy in confusion at my words. "Fi, why is it so important for you to find your ring?"

I pulled away from him with a hurt look on my face. "What do you mean why is it important? If I lose that, I lose you."

"Fi, what are you talking about?"

"Aaron, I love you. I love you so fucking much, and that's so scary to me to love someone so completely."

"What?"

"I don't want to lose you again."

He held my face in his hands, his blue eyes searching mine for answers. "Fi, when did you lose me before?"

"When I told you to ask out Stacey, and then you left for the NHL. Left me. Like everyone else does," I sobbed. Fuck, the tears were really coming now. I had a vague notion in the back of my memory of him kissing me goodbye this morning and this happening then, too. Fuck. "Like Eric did."

"Sweetheart, you didn't lose me, not then. Not now. I'm not going anywhere," he tried to reassure me. "I'm sorry if I made you feel like I abandoned you; that was never my intention. But to be fair, your ex didn't really want me around."

I slid my hands around his neck. "Aaron, I'm sorry I wasted so many years on a man who didn't appreciate me. I wasted so much time being afraid of my feelings for you."

He leaned into me and wrapped his arms around my waist. I didn't let him get another word in edgewise and instead pressed my lips to his. Kneeling on the floor in front of each other, he wrapped my hair around his hand and kissed me back. When he pulled away, he didn't look happy like I thought he would; he looked kind of annoyed. I shrank away from him and bit my lip.

"You so totally stole my thunder," he finally said.

"What?"

He laughed and ran a hand through his blond locks. "I came home right after the game, and I was going to take you out somewhere nice for dinner and do the whole grand gesture thing and tell you how much I love you. That it's the real reason why I married you."

"What?"

"I wanted to be your knight in shining armor. I thought if we stayed married, you would come to love me like I love you. Like I have always loved you."

I laughed. "Oh my God, we suck at communicating."

"Truly," he remarked. He fingered the ring on his own finger. "I only take my ring off when I have to play."

"C'mere," I urged and pulled his face back down to my lips, easing myself on my back on the carpeted floor. Riley hovered over me, his hands on the side of my head and an amused look on his face.

"Right here?" he asked. "You want to have sex on the floor? When we have a perfectly good bed two feet away?"

I already threw my shirt over my head and pulled his suit jacket off his broad shoulders. "Uh huh," I answered and unclasped my bra behind me. I grinned as the fire lit into his eyes at the sight of my naked chest beneath him.

"Seriously?" he asked again, but he undid his tie and rushed to get the buttons undone on his dress shirt. "Wait."

"What?"

"Why did you get drunk with Dinah yesterday? And why were you crying and apologizing to me this morning?"

"Fuck, baby, I'm sorry. I got drunk with Dinah because I was scared."

"Aw, Fiona. You're the love of my life; I would never leave you."

"The love of your life?" I asked with a raised eyebrow.

"Fiona, I've loved you since we were seventeen years old hooking up in your parents' basement."

"Really?" I asked, my voice hitching up an octave in surprise.

He nodded. "Okay, maybe before that, but that was when I knew."

"C'mere, big guy, and show me just how much you love me," I urged and started to peel my underwear off.

"Oh, fuck yes," he breathed as we shed the rest of our clothes, and he did what he was told.

"Hey, I'm still hungry," Riley mused later as we laid side-by-side naked and sweaty after having moved to the bed for a second love-making session. That phrase used to make me gag and roll my eyes, but the sex today had been slow and gentle. I usually liked it rough, but there was something nice about the way he cradled me softly and repeatedly told me how much he loved me. No wonder the sex was so good with him; it was because I was madly in love with this man. I regretted not realizing it earlier.

"Oh yeah, I guess I could eat," I replied and smiled at him sleepily.

He pulled me towards his side and wrapped his big arm around me. I sighed and snuggled into his chest. I didn't understand how it took me so long to realize that I was in love with this man.

"Never thought you'd ever be my wife," he said under his breath.

"Me neither, but I'm glad Eric never showed up. It was a blessing in disguise."

He stroked my hair gently. "Yeah, me too."

"I should have never told you to ask out Stacey Graves. I should have kept you all to myself."

He chuckled into my hair. "I wished you did too because that girl was a drama queen. Nothing like my calm and collected best friend."

I pulled away from him reluctantly and swung my legs over the bed. I surveyed the room; it was kind of a mess with clothes everywhere and all the drawers in the dresser opened wide. I was still kind of mad that I had lost my ring.

"Sweetheart," Riley stated flatly with annoyance in his voice. "What's this?"

I turned to look over at him and saw he was holding my ring in-between his fingers. "Oh my God! Where did you find it?"

"In the sheets!"

"What the hell!" I exclaimed. I had searched everywhere for that damn ring.

He grabbed my hand and slid the ring on my finger with the most intense look on his face. It almost made me want to jump his bones for a third time today. Almost.

I smiled sweetly at him, surveying the loving look he gave me in return. I never thought I would marry my best friend or fall in love with him, but here I was. Head over heels for Aaron Riley and mad it hadn't happened sooner. Fate must have been a prankster, that was for sure.

Riley held onto my hand and rubbed my ring finger. "Will you let me buy you a nicer ring?"

I recoiled and pulled my hand away, clutching the ring to my chest protectively. "No! It's bad enough I let you buy me those bookshelves."

"You were so happy about that. I want to make you

happy. And we bought them from IKEA, so they weren't *that* expensive."

"You do make me happy, but waving around your money is not something you need to do. I love my plain ring, and I love that we have an interesting story about our marriage."

Riley sat up in bed and leaned over to kiss me tenderly. "Me too. I know we kind of did things backward, but I wouldn't change anything."

"Me neither. So are we getting dinner or what? I'm hungry too."

He eyed me, still very much naked next to him, and he was certainly enjoying the view. "I think we better put some clothes on. Do you want to go out?"

I shook my head. "Nah, I'm still very hungover. Let's order takeout. Indian?"

"I'm game," he agreed with a smile. "I have tomorrow off, so I want to spend all of it with you."

A smile crept across my face. "Well, in that case, there is this cool used book store in West Chester..."

CHAPTER TWENTY-FOUR

RILEY

"*I* think I'm too big for this place," I commented to my wife as I ducked into the doorway and followed her up the steps of the Book Barn.

"Deal with it, baby!" Fi joked.

I smirked at her and watched her sweet ass from behind as I followed her further up the steps. I was not complaining if I got to check her out all day while she guided me along in the very old building. The place was legit a barn full of books, and it didn't appear to have any sort of organization to it, but if I knew Fi, she knew what she was looking for. She had that determined look on her face, a woman on a mission. I didn't care if she wanted us to drive all the way out to the Main Line to look at old dusty books on my day off; I would do anything she wanted, as long as I got to spend it doing it with her.

I was aware that I was whipped, and I didn't give a fuck.

I watched her fan herself and peer up to the next stairway. She gave me an apologetic look. "It's kind of hot in here."

I smirked. "I think it's just you."

She poked me in the stomach, and I jerked away. She knew I was ticklish there. "Har har har," she bit back sarcastically. She glanced at the sign in front of the next staircase and started up the wooden stairs. I ducked again and followed her up the steps, enjoying the nice view once again.

When we reached the top of the steps, she glared at me. "Stop staring at my ass so much. I feel like you're gonna burn a hole into it."

I held up my hands, but I couldn't help a laugh. She slapped my shoulder, but a smile spread across her face. She rolled her eyes and turned around to look at the shelf in front of us. I glanced at the titles on it, noticing some very old looking sci-fi books. "What are you looking for anyway?" I asked.

She shrugged. "Nothing in particular. Maybe I can find a special edition of Asimov or Le Guin. Or somebody I've never heard of."

I nodded but didn't say anything. I had absolutely zero idea what she was talking about, but that didn't matter.

She cocked her head at me. "You really don't mind doing this today? I know it's your day off."

I placed my hands on her shoulders and kissed her forehead. "I want to spend time with you, and if this is what you want to do, let's do this."

She gave me a funny look. "How the hell did I ever get you to marry me?"

I laughed. "I think it was my idea, remember?"

She leaned up and kissed me quickly on the lips. "Thank you for letting me do this."

"Of course."

She looked down at her shoes. "Eric would have been having a fit right now."

I narrowed my eyes.

She held up her hands in surrender. "Sorry, didn't mean to compare you two; it's nice to be with someone who actually shows an interest in the things I want to do."

I slid my hand in hers and grinned at the blush that crept up her neck and onto her cheeks. "You're cute when you blush. I'm glad I can still do that to you."

"Calm down; we're still newlyweds," she teased. "Can you grab that blue book there?" She pointed to the top of the shelf where she couldn't reach. Fi was tall, but I did have a good couple of inches on her.

I smiled and did as she asked and handed it to her. I watched her gingerly hold the book in her hands and carefully open the front cover.

"Whoa, I think this is a first edition," she commented more to herself than to me.

"Is that good?" I asked.

She nodded. "Yeah, very good."

"This is a cool building," I mentioned.

"I thought so too. I've been here once before, but I felt rushed."

"No rush, we have no obligations today. I will follow you around all day and watch you look at books."

Her eyes got all shiny, and she held the book to her chest. "Oh my God, if I wasn't already married to you... that was like the most romantic thing you could say to me."

"If you say so, sweetheart."

She nodded vigorously and leaned up to whisper in my ear, "You're so getting laid later."

"That's not why I did this, you know."

She smiled. "I know, but still."

Her gaze lingered on my belt buckle. I tilted her chin up with my hand. "Hey, my eyes are up here."

She swatted my hand away and started moving down towards the next aisle. We spent another hour in the Book Barn. It made me so happy to see the smile spread across her face as she explored old books in every nook and cranny of the place. I still couldn't believe what had happened the other night. Fiona Gallagher was my wife, and she actually loved me. I never thought this day would come.

She ended up buying a handful of books but absolutely refused to let me pay for them. I did kind of like that she would never give up being a feisty, independent woman; it made me love her even more. At the same time, she was my wife, and there was this patriarchal side of me that had a need to take care of her. To be the provider. I could hold back, though. I just wanted her to be happy.

We drove back to Philly, and she talked animatedly about all the books she had acquired today. It was so cute how excited she got about it. When we got home, she asked me to give her a couple hours so she could do some work, and I left her alone by heading to the gym. My body was aching from the hits I took in the game yesterday, but I knew I needed to shake it off and get serious.

I was halfway through my run when I saw a text come through from Benny.

BENNY: *Hey, man. What are you up to tonight?*

ME: *Hanging with my lady. Why?*

BENNY: *Stephanie broke up with me, so wanted to see if you wanted to get a drink tonight.*

ME: *Fuck...sorry!*

BENNY: *It's fine. I guess. But I have to find a new place to live.*

ME: *Fi's pretty cool about that sort of stuff; I think she would understand if you wanted to do something.*

BENNY: *Nah. it's all good. I'll see if TJ wants to hang. He's always down to drink.*

ME: *Truth. Don't let him drink you under the table - you're a lightweight.*

BENNY: *DICK!*

I laughed at him and locked my phone screen again. Nothing had come through from Fi, so I knew she was in the zone, and I really didn't want to bother her. I was finishing up with weight training when she finally texted me.

FI: *Did you get lost?*

ME: *Nope, still at the gym.*

FI: *why, tho?*

ME: *These muscles you love so much didn't appear out of nowhere.*

FI: *K!*

ME: *Don't K me woman! I'm almost done.*

FI: *What do you want for dinner?*

ME: *Not your cooking. Let's go out.*

I wiped down the free weights and headed back home. I had made a reservation this morning already because I had no idea how long Fi wanted to spend at the bookstore. The door to the office was still closed when I got home, so I hopped in the shower, not wanting to disturb Fi. I knew how she got when she was in the middle of her writing. I definitely knew that I shouldn't piss her off.

She was surveying the closet when I got out of the

shower and started getting dressed. She smiled up at me and gave me a quick kiss. "Good workout?" she asked.

"Mmmhmm," I answered noncommittally and rubbed my shoulder.

She eyed me cautiously. "Aaron..."

"Yeah, sweetheart?"

"Are you hurt?"

Of course she would notice that I was favoring one side and kept rubbing my shoulder. "Yeah, I'm hurt. Not injured, though," I assured her. "I got slammed into the boards hard last night. I'll live."

She didn't seem convinced, but she didn't push the topic and went to go get her own shower. I was cleaning up in the kitchen when she walked out in that sexy black dress she had worn to dinner in Vegas and black stiletto heels that I didn't even know she owned. I gulped and adjusted myself below the belt. Her red hair fell down her back, all silky and smooth, and I couldn't wait to run my fingers through it. That dress did wonders for her lean figure, and I didn't quite remember it having such a plunging neckline before. It was seriously making me consider skipping dinner altogether.

"You ready?" she asked.

I wiped my hands on a hand towel. "Yeah, let's go."

I grabbed my keys at the front door, and we left hand-in-hand. The restaurant was luckily walking distance from our condo, but I was wondering about the shoes she was wearing. She must have noticed the look I was giving her because she laughed and shook her head at me. "It's fine. Where are we going?"

"Sushi."

The smile lit up her whole face like I knew it would. "Ooh, my favorite!"

I squeezed her hand. "I know; that's why I picked it."

Her other hand, the one not interlaced with my hand, squeezed my bicep. "You really do know me so well."

"Well, we have been best friends since...well, birth."

She giggled but stopped when we arrived at the restaurant and saw her ex Eric and some leggy blonde walking out the door. Her grip on my arm tightened, and I squeezed her other hand reassuringly. I was hoping maybe the dumbass would not notice us and walk away so we could pretend we didn't see him either. The hockey gods weren't on my side because he glanced up and looked at her in surprise.

"Oh..." Eric trailed off when he saw the two of us. He pointedly looked at our interlaced hands. His date looked confused.

Fi was pissed, and I could tell because she was damn near crushing my hand by gripping it so tight. She gritted her teeth, so I decided to be the bigger man about it. "Eric, hey, long time no see."

"Riley, Fiona," he gritted out.

His date whipped her head back and forth, and when he said "Fiona," her mouth formed a little 'O.' She seemed to shrink back and swallow her question.

"Eric," Fi seethed.

"Hmm. I thought for sure you two would have been divorced by now," Eric snarled.

I was actually pretty proud of Fi for not punching the douche in the face, but she was probably going to tear off my arm at the rate she was gripping it.

The blonde looked at Eric. "Is this your ex who ran away with someone else on your wedding day?" she asked, confused.

Fi barked out the most sarcastic laugh I had ever heard. "Is that what he told you?"

"Fi," I warned.

The blonde looked even more confused. "Yes..."

I shook my head at her, hoping she would get the message to drop it so the two of them could go off on their merry way. Of course, Fi couldn't leave well enough alone. "I'm sorry, I didn't catch your name."

"Amelia," the blonde offered.

Fi nodded. "Amelia, sorry. No, actually Eric left me at the altar," she explained. She looked up at me and smiled. "But I found someone else to marry me instead. Probably the person I should have been with in the first place."

I beamed at that, and a warmth spread across my chest. But I also knew it was time to get the fuck out of there. "Nice seeing you, Eric, and meeting you, Amelia, but we have a reservation to get to."

Amelia waved to us, and I pulled Fi inside with me before we caused any more drama. I knew her ex still lived in the city, but I was hoping we would never run into him, like ever. Goddamnit, I really hoped the night wasn't ruined now.

CHAPTER TWENTY-FIVE

FIONA

*W*ho the fuck did he think he was? *I figured you would be divorced by now.* I was seething. I wanted to walk back there and punch the little turd right in the dick. Riley, my very patient husband, had been right to speed me along inside so I didn't do that.

I was happily married to Riley. Sure it had gotten off to a rocky start with me wanting to get a divorce and the two of us dancing around our feelings, but we were finally on the same page together, and I was ready to enjoy wedded bliss with my best friend. And then I had to run into that douche-canoe. So it really shouldn't have been a surprise that as soon as we got to our table, I chugged my whole glass of red wine.

"Easy there," Riley commented, but he poured me another glass anyway. I took a sip of my water instead. He reached across the table and grabbed my hand. "Hey...you're happy with me, right?"

I balked at that and furrowed my brow. "Of course I am! What kind of question is that?"

He sighed. "Then why is seeing your ex so upsetting to you?"

I took in a deep breath and drank some water to calm myself. "It's not seeing him that bothered me; it was more the line about us not being divorced yet. Who the hell does he think he is? Like he even knows our relationship. Fucking asshat."

Riley placed his hand over his mouth, and I knew him well enough by now to know that he was trying to hide a grin. "To be fair, you did ask for a divorce the next day."

"I'm sorry," I sighed.

"It's fine. We got through it, and now things are better."

"I'm sorry that I'm so mad about this, too. I..." I trailed off and glanced at him from across the table.

He looked so great in that smartly tailored suit. It made me want to rip it off of him. The way his eyes zeroed in on me and intently watched me while I spoke told me everything I ever needed to know about this man. This man loved me and would probably listen to me read the goddamn phonebook. That made me love him more and also made me a little bit horny.

"We're at a good place, and I want to enjoy that. He just really pissed me off," I explained.

The waiter came over to take our orders, so I never heard what he was going to say. He distracted me by clinking glasses with me, and all the drama from before melted away because all I was focused on was the man before me.

"This is a nice place," I commented.

He nodded. " I know you love your sushi, and Mia, Hallsy's girlfriend, recommended it."

"I like Mia; she's sweet."

"She's good people. Her and Hallsy, it's wild to me that they've been together since high school."

"Hmm."

He eyed me. "What?"

I shook my head. "Nothing."

"It's not nothing," he urged. "Spit it out."

I sighed. "Aaron, have you really been in love with me since high school?"

He smiled. "Definitely."

"What?" I shook my head. "No way."

He gave me a hard look. "What does that mean?"

"You were the star hockey player. You didn't belong with little old me, the nerd in the corner writing poetry."

"Very bad poetry," he joked.

I laughed. "You're not wrong about that one."

He caressed my hand and looked deep into my eyes. "Why do you say it like that? Say that we didn't belong together?"

I shrugged. "It was high school; we were from different cliques. I was pretty sure I was your dirty little secret."

He glared at me. "Because you asked me to keep it a secret. Do you know how many of my teammates I had to ward off with my stick to keep away from you? Is this why you pushed me to date Stacey?"

I bit my lip and drank more of my wine, so I didn't have to answer.

Luckily our food came, so we got preoccupied with that. I speared a California roll with my chopsticks and shoved it into my mouth. I could tell that Riley was still bothered by what I had told him, though.

I chewed slowly before saying, "Baby, it's in the past. That was high school. We're together now and happy, right?"

"Yeah," he agreed and then smiled at me. "Why did you bring it up again?"

"Oh!" I exclaimed. "I never imagined loving someone for that long. It's a long time. But you loved me all that time and never said a word. Did Finnegan know all this time?"

He shook his head. "Fuck no. I didn't reveal it until the day after our wedding when he asked me what the fuck I was thinking."

I snorted. "Sounds about right. It's been a weird time since then."

"I wouldn't trade it for the world, though."

I smiled at him. "Me either."

"So when did it become real for you? When did you figure out you felt the same way?"

I chewed some more of my food and thought about it for a moment. "I think it was slow at first. Like, when I first moved in with you, it was chaotic, but the next day when you were on the road, I hated being in your bed alone. We spent a couple days in Vegas together, and somehow I had gotten really used to you being there. When you weren't there, I realized how much I missed you. It kind of scared me. I don't think it really set in until yesterday when I couldn't find my wedding ring."

He nodded in understanding. "So when Finnegan let the cat out of the bag, were you just scared?"

"I was afraid that you would come to your senses. I mean, can you blame me? I dated someone else for half a decade, and they left me at the altar. I guess I have a lot of baggage about it."

"Listen to me," he urged and grabbed both my hands in

his. They looked so petite and small in his big manly hands. "That's not gonna happen with us. I love you with all my heart and have pretty much felt like that since I was seventeen years old. No woman has ever compared to Fiona Gallagher, and no woman will ever complete me like you do. I fucking love you."

"I love you too."

He pulled his hands away from me to take another drink. "Tell me where you are with your book so far?" he asked, abruptly changing the subject.

I made a face and downed the rest of my wine. "I think it's almost done. I just turned in the final edits."

His face lit up with a smile, his blue eyes beaming with pride. "Really? That's awesome!"

"I guess?"

He frowned. "It's not awesome?"

"I'm not sure yet. ARCs will go out, and then we'll see if we need to make any changes, and we'll get pass pages soon."

"What's an ARC?" he asked.

I laughed. Sometimes I forgot he wasn't as well versed in the publishing world. "Advanced Reader Copy. We send them out pre-publishing to get the word out, get reviews out prior to publication."

"I thought the changes you made were good. I think it will be good. I wish you would stop doubting yourself."

"Wait, what? Did you read the revised copy?"

He gave me a quizzical look. "Of course I did!"

I brought my hands to my chest and felt my heartbeat fluttering beneath them. My eyes got all misty, and I held everything in to keep from crying. "Aaron, that means the world to me, that you actually cared enough to read the second version. My parents don't give a shit about my writing career, but the fact that you do, it's..." I paused to wipe the tear that was now leaking out of my eye and hoped I didn't mess up my make-up. "It means a lot to me."

"I know, sweetheart. You've always been supportive of my hockey, even back when we were just friends. You work so hard at this, all hours of the night, and your brain's always racing. I want you to get the recognition you deserve."

"Goddamnit, did I build you in a factory?"

He laughed really hard at that. "What?"

"You're like the perfect man. You're so getting laid tonight."

"I thought we established this already?" he asked, and he was sporting that crooked, mischievous grin that I loved so much.

I nodded. "Uh huh, but like for sure. Why do you think I wore this dress?"

He eyed me from his position across the table, and I knew from his angle, he got a great view of my cleavage. "It's a nice dress. It's definitely working for me."

I smirked at him and quickly shoveled my last piece of sushi in my mouth. Riley stared back at me with an amused look on his face. I tried not to look him in the eye as I regretted the decision and had to slowly chew my way out of this piece. His shoulders shook, and his hand was over his mouth again. I gave him the finger while I chewed way too slow for my liking.

Finally, I swallowed the rest of my dinner and asked, "Hey, you want to get out of here?"

My husband grinned back at me. "Oh, most definitely."

CHAPTER TWENTY-SIX

RILEY

I was so glad we went to the sushi place that was walking distance from our condo because I felt a fire in my pants, and the only person who was going to put it out was the feisty redhead standing next to me. I had barely unlocked the door to our home before I shoved her up against the wall and kissed her hard on the mouth. My fingers threaded through her long, silky hair, and I moaned when she sighed into the kiss. My tongue slid inside her mouth slowly, and we touched each other cautiously. I pulled back to drink her all in, and she had an annoyed look on her face. That sexy black dress was one hundred percent doing it for me, and she so knew it.

I dipped my head to taste her neck while my hands roamed down her torso and pushed her tits into my hands. I smiled against her skin when I heard her moan some more.

"I think we need to get you out of this dress," I whispered huskily in her ear.

"Uh huh," she moaned, but I knew her brain was completely shut off right now. "Oh!" she exclaimed when I lifted her up by her hips and wrapped her legs around my waist. I smoothed my hands across her thighs and under her dress. I teased her by fingering the top string of her panties while I continued to kiss down her throat.

"Sweetheart, I need to be inside you," I moaned.

Her stiletto shoes dug into my ass, and I kind of didn't hate it. Kind of wanted her to keep them on while we fucked.

She pulled me back up to her face and kissed me, her hands gripping my hair between her fingers. "Then do it," she said angrily.

I moved her underwear to the side so I could have better access and dipped two fingers inside her. She was soaking wet and ready to go. She moaned, and I peeled the thin material down off her hips, untangling her legs from around my waist. The lacy pair of black panties fell to her ankles, and her hands made quick work of undoing my belt buckle and pulling my dick out of my boxers.

"Wait...condom," I reminded her.

She shook her head and guided me to her entrance. "I'm on the pill; it's fine."

I pushed her dress up but held her still. "You sure, sweetheart?"

She reached down and guided me inside her. I groaned in ecstasy at the feeling of being bare inside her. "Oh, fuck," I moaned and tipped my head back.

"Hell yeah!" she cheered and wrapped her legs back around me. "Aaron, fuck me raw against the wall."

I gripped her ass with a grin and pumped into her hard

and fast. She moaned and clawed at my neck. She squeezed her heels against my ass, and it turned me on even more. I gave it to her hard, going deeper and faster with each moan that escaped her lips. She gripped my hair as she came, moaning in my ear. I let myself go and joined her in ecstasy.

"Fiona," I breathed.

She smiled at me and kissed me slowly. "Was that your first time without a condom?"

I nodded.

She laughed. "Yes! I got to deflower you in two ways."

I tweaked her nose. "Brat."

She slid her legs from around my waist and dropped down to gather up her panties. I tucked myself back into my pants, my chest still heaving from the exertion. I spun her around and kissed her hard, my hand wrapping around her hair and holding her to me.

She pulled away to look down at my crotch again. "Oh, you ready for round two already?"

I gripped her neck loosely. "You know it, you vixen. Get your ass in our bedroom so I can watch you come again."

Her face flushed with desire, but she didn't move, so I lifted her up and carried her to our bedroom. I deposited her onto her feet in the room and watched as she kicked off her shoes and slowly pulled the zipper down on her dress. Fuck, that was so hot. I licked my lips when she stepped out of it to reveal the black lacy bra underneath. I gulped as I drank her sexy body all in.

I shrugged out of my suit jacket and loosened my tie, pulling it over my head. I smiled while I slowly undid every button on my shirt, and Fi watched me with hungry eyes. I pulled the shirt coattails out of my pants and dropped the shirt to the floor. Her hands were on my chest suddenly, running down it with her sharp nails, and she had this fiery look in her eyes that said she was completely turned on.

She kissed me feverishly, her hand gripping the back of my neck hard, and I was sure that if my cock wasn't already rock hard, it would have been from that. I leaned into the kiss but noticed her fingering the top of my pants and slowly undoing the zipper. My pants fell to my ankles with a thud, and I pulled away from her to kick them off. I slid the boxer briefs down my thighs next, releasing my pulsing cock, which was about to explode if I wasn't inside her again soon.

"Fiona," I warned as she got a sparkle in her eye and took my cock in her hand.

She knelt to her knees and licked me from root to tip. "What?" she asked all innocently before taking me in her mouth.

"Fuck..." I moaned and ran my hand through her hair while her head bobbed on my cock. She hummed in response, taking me as deep as she could and then pulling back to lick around the head. "Sweetheart..." I groaned when she was sucking me again. A little too good.

She glared up at me. "What? You don't want me to?"

"Get up here. I want you naked and in the bed," I growled at her.

Her eyes got wide, but I knew she liked the demanding nature of my request because she swiftly unhooked her bra. She bent over to climb onto the bed and looked over her shoulder at me with the sexiest fucking look she had ever given me. How did I get this sexy as fuck woman to marry me?

"Are you gonna join me or what?" she purred.

She leaned over the bed like we were ready to go at it doggy-style, which I was not opposed to, but the sex against the wall had been a little too fast, and I knew she usually liked a lot of foreplay before sex. And my wife would get everything she wanted from me.

I stood over her and flipped her onto her back on the bed before crawling in beside her. I stretched out next to her and stroked her face with my hand, bringing her face back to my lips.

"Fiona," I moaned against her chest when I felt her hand sneakily reach down to caress my hard cock.

"I like it when you say my full name," she admitted, but she didn't stop stroking me.

I moaned but buried it in my throat as I kissed her neck and trailed kisses down her chest to focus on her tits. I rolled one of her nipples with my hand and pulled the other one into my mouth, swirling my tongue around the bud and sucking on it hard. Her grip on my cock released since I was distracting her so much, and I danced my hand down between her legs and pumped two fingers inside her. I think I got even harder at how wet she was, especially since I was the one that helped get her that way again. It was such a turn on to be able to make my wife gasp at my touch. I didn't think I would ever get over it.

"Aaron," she moaned in such a soft whisper that I barely heard her. She didn't tell me to stop, so I continued to pump inside her while rotating which nipple to lick and suck on. I rubbed her clit and felt her body clench against my hand. Her small hand reached out to grip my bicep while she orgasmed for the second time. I smiled down at her and kissed her tenderly. I loved that I could do that to her; it was so hot watching her orgasm because of what my hands were doing to her. I really needed to have my cock inside her pronto, just to watch her orgasm all over again.

I pulled my hand away and dug into the bedside table

for a condom. Her hand stopped me. "Do we need it? I'm on the pill."

"Your call. I would love to not use it again, but if you want me to use it, I will."

"We're fine, but I think we need some lube."

"Noted," I answered. I set the condom back on the bedside table and reached for the bottle of lube in the drawer. I spread a liberal amount onto my cock and wiped my hand off on a tissue.

Her hand was on me again, stroking up and down my shaft so perfectly that I had a hard time focusing. I trusted that she was on the pill; she wouldn't lie to me. Plus, if she got pregnant, it wouldn't have been the worst thing to happen.

Before I could ask her what position she wanted to do, she pushed me onto my back and slid down on my cock. I laid back on the bed with a contented sigh and looked up at her as she rode me.

My hands roamed across her chest and then landed on her ass and squeezed it. She had a wicked look in her eyes. "Oh fuck, Fiona, you're so sexy," I groaned at her. She grinned and ground herself harder into me. I loved it when she rode my dick hard like this.

"Oh, yeah?" she asked and leaned down to kiss me, her long hair spreading across my face and down my chest like a curtain.

"Uh huh." I nodded and thrust up into her urgently. She might have thought she was in charge, but she wasn't. I gripped her hips and thrust fast up into her, satisfied with the sexy moan that escaped her lips. "I love that I can make you feel good."

She kissed me again slowly while we met each other's thrusts. "Me too."

My hand slid to the back of her neck and held her tight against my chest. "I love you."

"I love you too," she said, but then lost the sound of her voice to the moans of pleasure as she came for the third time tonight. I was so totally okay with that. Fiona Gallagher was my wife, and she loved me, and if we got to spend the rest of our lives fucking each other this good, I was going to be a very happy man. I thrust hard and fast inside her until I felt myself combust in ecstasy underneath her.

"Fuck," Fi breathed out and leaned her head against my chest. I smiled and kissed her temple.

She got off the bed to run to the bathroom, and when she came back, she laid on her back in the bed with a sigh. She closed her eyes and stuck her tongue out. "I think I'm dead."

I laughed and pulled her towards me. "That good, huh?"

She hit my chest. "Don't get cocky."

I rubbed my chest where she hit me, even though it didn't really hurt at all. "Too late on that one, sweetheart."

She glared at me, but her eyes were smiling. I tilted her face up to me and met her with a tender kiss. Her lips were swollen from all the kisses, but I didn't care about that; it made me love her even more. I stroked her hair, running my fingers through the copper strands. She purred into me and closed her eyes in post-sex bliss.

"So, I've been thinking," I began.

"Don't do that too hard; you might hurt yourself," she joked and poked me in the stomach.

"Shush, don't be mean."

"What are you thinking about?" she asked.

"We never went on a honeymoon."

She nodded. "Can confirm."

"We should."

"Um...you have a very strict schedule. Don't you travel again tomorrow?"

I sighed. "The next day. Fuck, I'm gonna miss you so much."

She laughed. "It's just a couple days. You were right, it's really hard you being away all the time, but I think I can manage it. It does force me to focus all my efforts on writing when you're gone, so when you get back, I'm all yours."

"Well, since we're not making the playoffs, once the season is over, we should go on our honeymoon."

She poked me square in the chest. "Okay, yeah, let's plan something. Where should we go?"

"You pick."

She rolled her eyes. "I want to go to Iceland, but that was where I was supposed to go with him. We should go somewhere else."

"I always wanted to go to Italy."

She smiled. "Us two pasty Irish kids in Italy?"

"Why not? What ya think?"

"Are we gonna drink lots of wine and not leave our hotel room?"

I winked at her. "If that's what you want to do, I'm game."

She twirled her fingers down my arm. "I could get behind that. However, are you planning on going back to St. Paul in the off-season?"

I shrugged. "Yeah, I usually go back. Why?"

"Oh, that's why my brother called me in the first place."

I narrowed my eyes at her. "Have you been avoiding your mother's calls again?"

She looked down at her nails that were apparently very

fascinating at the moment and pretended not to hear my question.

I nudged her shoulder. "Fi, come on. What gives?"

She sighed. "Ugh, you're the worst. Now that we're married, it's like I'm constantly getting harped on about giving her some grandkids. She already has a grandkid from Finnegan and Emily! Why do I have to give her one? Also, I'm twenty-seven years old; I would like to live my life a little bit."

I bit my lip, unsure how to broach the topic with her. When we first got married, it was chaotic and a mess. Now that we were sure this was what we wanted, I thought it was a good idea to talk about it. I would do whatever she wanted; if she wanted kids great, if she didn't, also great. Ultimately it was her body, so it was most definitely her choice. Although, the thought of having cute little redheaded babies with this woman? I was so on board.

I looked over and noticed her staring up at me questioningly. "Aaron, what's on your mind?"

I sighed and ran my hand down my face. "I know we tabled the kid talk, but should we talk about it?"

"I guess," she sighed. "Do you want kids?"

"It's your body," I told her.

Her face softened at that. "Goddamnit, Aaron, you would give me the whole world if I asked for it, wouldn't you?"

"Yes?"

She sighed again. "If you don't want kids, I'm cool with that."

"What if I do? I mean, I don't think I'm ready for that this second, but I don't hate the idea."

She narrowed her eyes at me and placed a hand on my

chest. "Baby, you won't be like him, you know that, right? You'd be a great father."

"You think so?"

She nodded. "You put up with my bullshit all the time."

I laughed and held her closer. "I don't know if that qualifies me as father material."

"Hmm, maybe not. I don't think I'm ready either; I want some time to have you all to myself."

I smirked at her and flexed my muscles. "Oh yeah, you want this hot bod all for yourself?"

She laughed at me but smiled. "Yes, exactly that."

"But the idea of having a kid with me...you would be on board with it?"

She nodded with a bright smile, that kind of surprised me. "Yeah, baby. We would have such cute little babies."

I leaned over and kissed her softly. "Babies plural?"

She pushed me away with a laugh. "Maybe...but not yet. Let's wait on that whole situation."

"Whatever you want, sweetheart," I told her and ran a hand through her copper-colored hair. "But..."

She eyed me suspiciously. "But what?"

I twirled her hair around my finger. "I can't wait to have cute redheaded little babies with you. Someday."

She put a hand over mine and gave me a sweet smile. "Someday," she agreed.

I beamed at her as I imagined the two of us having a child down the line. I wondered if they would have her feisty personality. I wondered about what it would be like putting those first skates on my baby.

"Aaron, what's with the face?" she asked, pulling me out of my daydream.

"I'm thinking about us having kids. That scares me but also excites me."

"Me too. I wasn't sure I actually wanted kids; I definitely didn't want them with Eric. Right now, I want to enjoy married life, but one day we'll have that."

"When we're ready," I agreed.

As I watched her bite her lip, I had a feeling "one day" might be a lot sooner than either of us were willing to admit. For now, I was going to enjoy our family just being the two of us.

I leaned over and slanted my mouth against hers again. I never thought Fiona Gallagher would become my wife, even in my wildest fantasies, but I was so happy it had come to this. One thing was for certain: she was never taking off that wedding ring. I was going to make sure of that for the rest of our lives.

EPILOGUE

RILEY

TWO MONTHS LATER

"Hey," I called into the office and walked in to see my wife hunched over the keyboard, typing away furiously. "You told me to come get you in an hour. We need to get ready."

She looked up at me with a pained look. "No!!!! I got to a really crucial part of this draft. Let me just finish this chapter."

I chuckled at that. Fi was working on her fourth book, a completely new thing from what she had written before. A romance! I had teased her about it a lot, but I had read some things over her shoulder, and holy fuck, my wife could write a sex scene. Considering the amount of...ahem, 'research' she needed to do for this book, I didn't care what she wrote about.

The last book in her sci-fi trilogy had done pretty well, even though some people really hated the ending. I forced her to not read the reviews and read them for her to tell her what constructive criticism to look out for in her next book. She got mad at me for doing it because she said that's what she had an agent for. I didn't mind doing it, though; I loved that I could support the woman I loved.

I texted Dinah that we were going to be late and went back into the bedroom to go fix my hair again. I had gotten lazy lately, and now my hair was getting a little longer than I normally liked. I wasn't sold on cutting it back to the short, cropped style I usually kept though, mostly because my wife liked to pull hair, and it was kind of a huge turn on. Not that I would ever admit it.

ME: *Ugh...I'm sure you understand. Fi's in a mid writing rage right now.*

DINAH: *HAHAHA! Omg, I so do. Don't worry about being late. I TOTALLY understand.*

"Did you tell on me?" Fi yelled from the office.

A few minutes later, Fi came into the room and reached up to push my hair out of my face. "So are you growing out your hair to get that hockey flow again?"

"I haven't decided."

"Hmm," was all the answer I got as she rummaged through the closet, looking for something to wear.

Things were going so well with Dinah and Noah that he was moving out of his condo with TJ and moving into Dinah's place next door. A lot of the guys had raised their eyebrows and thought it was too soon, but Noah had been in love with the woman for two years, so I didn't think it was soon enough for either of them. They were having a housewarming party to celebrate. Although, I felt like it was more a celebration that both Dinah's and Fi's books had been released last week.

It kind of worked out because after Benny and Stephanie broke up, he needed a place to stay. We had offered him the guest room, which he took us up on until the season officially ended. I think he thought he was cramping our style, though, because as soon as our season was officially over, he high-tailed it back to his abuelos' place in Boston. When Noah announced he was moving out, TJ offered Benny the now spare room, and he had moved in yesterday. TJ was off to play in the Worlds competition tomorrow, so Benny would get to settle in quietly for the next couple of weeks.

"What does 'hmm' mean?" I asked. I sat on the edge of our bed and didn't make it a secret that I was watching her change into a pair of skinny jeans and a low-cut blouse that showed off her assets.

"I kind of like it," is all she said. For a woman who wrote for a living, she sure didn't give me a lot of words to work with.

I ran a hand through my hair again. It was a bit too long for me, but if she liked it, I was thinking about keeping it.

I patted the box in the pocket of my jacket and contemplated giving it to her now. It felt like an anchor weighing me down, and I was still unsure if she would take what was inside or not. I glanced over at her brushing out her red hair and decided to wait until after the party.

I stood up from the bed and walked over to her, dropping a quick kiss on the top of her head. "Are you almost ready?"

She nodded. "Come on, let's go."

The drive was short, but I fidgeted the whole time,

wondering if Fi would actually take the engagement ring I bought her. We never were engaged, but that didn't mean she didn't deserve a nice ring. But she still wouldn't let me buy her a new wedding band, so maybe I could get away with this. If she noticed my anxiety, she didn't say anything about it, and as soon as we got to Dinah and Noah's, I was off the hook. I smiled and watched the two women hug each other tightly while I slunk away into the kitchen to find Noah and TJ.

"Hey, man!" Noah greeted me, and we fist pumped. TJ and I did the whole head nod thing.

"How was Italy?" TJ asked.

"You see much outside of the room?" Noah joked.

I slid my thumb across my bottom lip and gave them a knowing look. They both erupted into laughs, and I swore Fi heard because I felt her glare from across the room. I noticed TJ's gaze move across to the dining room, and I turned to see Benny failing really hard to talk to a tall, curvy woman with black hair. She had her arms crossed and a look on her face that said, "Don't fuck with me." She looked oddly familiar, but I couldn't place her. I winced when she threw her drink in his face.

Holy fuck, what did the big guy say to her?

"Sorry," TJ offered to Noah.

I cocked my head at both of them in confusion.

"You remember my sister, right?" TJ asked.

I nodded. Benny and Roxanne Desjardins' fights were the stuff of legends. She usually had bleached blond hair that fell to her waist, but now she was sporting black hair shorter than normal, so I hadn't recognized her at first. The darker hair made her look more like her twin. It suited her.

"I didn't recognize her without the blond hair. What's she doing in town?" I asked.

"Just moved here. Working for the Bulldogs," TJ explained.

"Huh," was all that came out of my mouth, and Noah raised his eyebrows playfully. TJ sighed and excused himself to go talk to his sister, who looked like she was about to storm out of here.

"They're so gonna bone this summer," Noah commented and handed me a beer.

"You think? Wait, isn't she gay?" I asked and furrowed my brow. I was pretty sure that TJ had mentioned she had a live-in girlfriend. I also thought that was one of the reasons she told Benny often to "dream on." She didn't like men, right?

"No, Rox is bisexual," Noah corrected me.

"Huh."

I looked across the room at my wife and his girlfriend still entrenched in conversation. I was glad those two had each other and had this almost unshakeable bond. Fi had that effect on people, even if she thought everyone abandoned her. I was still mad at myself that our bond was shaken when I left for the NHL and it made her feel like I had abandoned her.

She caught my gaze and excused herself from Dinah to come over to us in the kitchen. Noah leaned down slightly to greet her with a hug.

"Oh, Noah, I'm so happy for you," she blurted out as soon as he ended the hug. I put an arm around her waist and pulled her towards me with a smile. "I'm really glad you and D sorted everything out."

Noah smiled at her. "I think I have you and whiskey to thank for helping us figure it out."

"We're happy for you, man," I agreed and clapped him on the back.

Noah nodded, and I wanted to tease him about the tinge of red that crept up across his face, but then Dinah appeared beside him. Their height difference was kind of comical, but the way they looked at each other was how I thought Fi and I looked at each other. So blissfully in love. I wasn't lying when I said I was happy for them. Everyone deserved love, and I was glad that I had found it with my best and first friend.

We stayed at Dinah and Noah's for a while, talking with all my teammates and their significant others. I also got to meet a few of Dinah's work friends and some other publishing people who Fi also knew.

When we got back home, I was exhausted, and so was Fi, as indicated by the way she flopped on our bed with her shoes still on. Gross. Sometimes I thought she did things like that to annoy me. I pulled the boots off her feet and threw them onto the floor.

She smiled up at me in a way that made my insides warm. I felt the ring box in the pocket of my jacket burning a hole there.

"So what's the deal with Benny and TJ's sister Rox?" she asked suddenly.

I shook my head. "Those two do not get along."

She had a wicked smile on her face. "Maybe they need to bang it out and solve that."

I laughed. "I don't disagree with you, sweetheart, but I think she'd rather make-out with a skunk."

"Not with the way she was looking at him tonight."

"She looked like she wanted to punch him in the dick like she always does," I argued.

Fi raised an eyebrow. "No, she looked like she couldn't decide if she wanted to punch him or suck his dick. They're gonna fuck!"

I laughed. Her and D had definitely gotten into the sauce a little bit tonight. "God, I hope you're right because those two living together is gonna be a trip."

"You know they're gonna have a knockdown fight and fuck!"

I shook my head at her. "How drunk are you?"

She held her thumb and finger together but gave me a sly smile. "Just a bit."

I grinned at her and laughed.

Fi laughed with me. "Anyway, why are you still wearing your jacket?"

"What?" I asked.

"What's with you tonight? You look like you need to tell me something."

I wanted to sigh at her. I should have known keeping things from her was too much of a difficult task. She knew me a little too well.

I reached into my jacket pocket and placed the small black box into her hands. "Here. I wanted to give you something."

She looked confused and opened the box to see the ring inside. "Aaron, what the fuck is this?"

I smiled but ran a hand through my too-long hair. "Um...so we did all of this backward, and I never got you an engagement ring."

She stared down at the silver ring in the box with the petite diamond, vines wrapping around it, and little emerald accents. "Aaron, you...why...I really don't need this."

I took the ring out of the box and pulled her left hand into mine. I slid the new ring onto her finger where her wedding band was already secured. "I know, but I wanted you to have it. You wouldn't let me buy you a nicer wedding band, so let me give you the engagement ring I should have given you a long time ago."

Her eyes were getting misty, and I pulled her into my lap to kiss her gently. She curled her head into my neck. "Oh, Aaron. I really love it. Is that bad? I shouldn't be into fancy jewelry like this."

I smirked and kissed the top of her head. "I knew you would."

"You're perfect."

I smiled at her. "No, you're perfect."

"Ew. Are we one of those couples now?"

"Afraid so, sweetheart."

She beamed at me and then bit her lip. "So, I've been thinking."

"Yeah?"

"What if after I get this romance book published, we try."

I furrowed my brow at her. "Try what?"

"Aaron...for a baby," she explained slowly, enunciating all her words.

"Oh! Really?" I asked in surprise. I hadn't thought she would want to try so soon. I thought it would have been a couple years before we talked about kids again.

She nodded. "I think...I think I'm ready."

"Are you sure? So soon?"

She laughed. "Well, I'm going to be working on this book for a little bit. So once it's done, I think I'll be ready. Will you be?"

I held her face in my hands. "Fi, I think I was ready the day we got married."

She shook her head at me and scoffed. "Bullshit!"

I grinned at her and put my hand on her flat stomach.

"Okay, pub this romance book, and then we'll talk about making a baby again."

"A cute one!"

"We're gonna have the cutest baby. But when you're ready, sweetheart. Right now, I just want you all to myself."

She melted into me, and I kissed her gently, happy that finally, our marriage was no longer in the trial phase.

ACKNOWLEDGMENTS

When I published Take The Shot, I didn't think anyone would actually like the book! Or that I would have readers excited for Fiona and Riley's story. So this one goes out to all of you readers who have stuck by me while I have teased you about their story. You finally have it in your hands! And I hope you like it.

Huge thanks go out to my editor Charlie Knight for holding my hand a little bit with this book, and encouraging me to dig a little deeper. I appreciate your input and help so much! And I'm glad you got my Desjardins reference, because naming one of my hockey players Lindros would have been a bit too on the nose.

I dedicated this book to my Soul Sisters — Kia, Taryn, Tam, Mahogany, Grace, Dallas, Lisa, Valerie, Julie, Trisha, Michelle & Janet. Without your support, I'm not sure if this book would have come to fruition. Thanks for letting me annoy you in the group chat on a daily basis. Love you ladies!

He won't read this, but I have to thank my real life partner as well. He might not read my books, but he listens whenever I need to vent about book stuff and cooks me dinner. I literally do not deserve that dude! Seriously, if you thought Noah from the first book was too nice, sorry J was kinda the blueprint.

Finally, huge shout to all of the betas who helped me with this book. You are all amazing, and I am so grateful you helped out a little indie author like me.

Can't wait to bring you all more from the Philadelphia Bulldogs hockey team!

ALSO BY DANICA FLYNN

PHILADELPHIA BULLDOGS

Take The Shot

ABOUT THE AUTHOR

Danica Flynn is a marketer by day, and a writer by nights and weekends. AKA she doesn't sleep! She is a rabid hockey fan of both The Philadelphia Flyers and the Metropolitan Riveters. When not writing, she can be found hanging with her partner, playing video games, and reading a ton of books.